Dawnfire and Spellweave

Godhunter Saga: Book One

Torrin Taigh

Dawnfire and Spellweave

ISBN: 979-8-9931623-0-0 (trade paperback)

ISBN: 979-8-9931623-1-7 (EPUB)

ISBN: 979-8-9931623-2-4 (KPF)

Cover art by Jessica Smith | Unbound Designs.

In memory of Vicki Wilson, the first to read my stories and offer gentle encouragement.

For Devon, Aliyah, Joshua, Ariel, Arielle, Sander, Zach M., Sean, Nelly, Josh, Jojo, Nick, and a thousand others who made this book possible through their love and friendship.

For my endlessly supportive family, who called to check I was still eating when writing took over my life.

For Zach, Brad, Joe, Atlas, Matthew, Alex K., Alex R., Roger, Bradley, Max, Jake, Zak, and the others caught in their own form of divine bureaucracy.

For Andrew, Gary, Alex, Sierra, Garion, and the rest of my tabletop players through the years for encouraging me to keep telling stories.

For Mike. For Denny.

And for Kat, whose faith in me inspired Adinah and without whom her story would never have been told.

Go with the Dawn at your back and let no darkness take hold.

The Gods of Viremor

<u>Living Gods</u>:

Khavak'ahn, the Allfather:
God of Justice and Summer, all-male monastic order.
Radiant balanced set of scales which glow with light instead of holding weights.
The paladins of Khavak'ahn are known for their glowing red eyes and echoing, resonant voices when channeling His divine energy.

Rhuvena, Consort of Khavak'ahn:
Goddess of Healing and Hope, all-female monastic order.
A flowering vine entwined around an open hand with a single droplet of light hovering over the palm.
Rhuvena's healers, all women, are able to heal wounds without leaving so much as a scar.

Ptyraxa, the Morning Lord:
God of Dawn, the Sun, Rebirth, and Spring.
A rising sun with three unfolding petals at the base.
Ptyraxa's temple focuses on driving away monsters, preserving peace, and bringing Light to those lost in and to darkness.

Khoravae, the Tomb Keeper:
God of Death and Memories.
A downward-facing crescent cradling a skull, surrounded by a circle of small stars.
His clerics and paladins keep to themselves, primarily taking up arms when funeral grounds and libraries are threatened. They have limited healing abilities.

Xernaea, Lady of Magic:
Goddess of Magic, Arcane Wisdom, and Secrets.
An eye with a swirling spiral pupil set within a geometric arcane circle, a crescent key beneath it.
Xernaea is mostly unconcerned with the actions of mortals, and She allows arcanists to use magic as they please with very limited stipulations.

Zhauremis, the Trickster:
God of Deception, Lies, and Illusions.
A mirrored mask with a serpent biting its own tail behind it with an upside-down triangle below.
A sower of discord, He was primarily responsible for the Cataclysm. He sees thieves and charlatans as His to protect.

Velirune, the Silent One:
Goddess of the Moon, Forgotten Places, and Winter.
A hollow crescent moon eclipsing a black circle.
Another goddess who keeps to Herself, She focuses on decay and the physical wasting away of places and persons after abandonment or death.

Talyros, the Silver-Tongued:
God of Music, Poetry, and Autumn.
A silver quill crossed with a harp string, framed by a falling leaf and a crescent smile.
A sharp-witted god who sometimes finds Himself working near Zhauremis' and Xernaea's followers more than He'd probably like to.

Kaevryn, the Unknowable:
God of Chaos, Time, Dreams, and Fate.
A broken hourglass spilling stars into a spiral vortex with a veiled eye above.
Kaevryn is unfathomable in scope.

The Dead Gods:

Elyvarra, the Verdant Embrace:
Goddess of Earth, Harvest, and Fertility.
A twisting vine encircling a ripe apple, with roots dangling below.
Slain by Rhuvena.

Shaelmyra, the Tempest Queen:
Goddess of Storms, Sea, and Fury.
A jagged lightning bolt piercing a crashing wave. *Slain by Zhauremis and Velirune.*

Nyserath, the Veiled Star:
Goddess of Dreams, Prophecy, and the Night Sky.
A crescent moon cradling a seven-pointed star, draped in a sheer veil.
Slain by Velirune.

Nekirha, the Crimson Bloom:
Goddess of Passion, Pain, and Rebirth.
A blooming rose impaled by a thorny dagger. *Slain by Zhauremis and Ptyraxa.*

Arivelle, the Golden Accord:
Goddess of Trade, Oaths, and Diplomacy.
A golden scroll crossed with a merchant's scale. *Slain by Khavak'ahn and Zhauremis.*

Varkhal, the Iron Wyrm:
God of War, Conquest, and Discipline.
A dragon's head with a spiked crown, jaws gripping a sword. *Slain by Khavak'ahn, Zhauremis, and Ptyraxa.*

Eiranthus, the Flamebearer:
God of Inspiration, Invention, and Sacred Fire.
A stylized flame rising from an open palm. *Slain by Talyros and Zhauremis.*

Molien, the Serene Current:
God of Peace, Rivers, and Healing Waters.
A gently curving river winding through a circle of reeds. *Slain by Rhuvena and Shaelmyra.*

Zeryn, the Hollow Laugh:
God of Madness, Revelry, and Forbidden Lore.
A broken mask with one eye open, grinning. *Slain by Zhauremis, Velirune, and Khavak'ahn.*

Chapter 1

Adinah

Adinah woke with a gasp.

The symbol of Ptyraxa seared against her breastbone, heat blooming sharp as a brand. Her hand flew to the amulet, clutching the sunburst crest through her tunic as if she could smother the burn. She sat upright so fast the book balanced across her lap tumbled to the floor with a heavy thud.

The library was quiet around her. Morningstrike Hall's library kept its silence even at midday–the shelves stood like solemn sentinels, sunlight flickering against their books' gilded spines. She dragged in a shuddering breath, then another, willing her pulse to steady. She was safe, safe in Taranok. She had been here for three weeks. No shadows stalked her but the ones cast by parchment and candlelight, and yet her stomach twisted, threatening to empty itself on the polished floor.

The dream still clung to her like ash on skin. She remembered the ruin, its sky gone red and bleeding fire, the foreign temple shattered into jagged cliffs that loomed like the bones of a slain god. She remembered the sunken chamber of black stone, how it recoiled from her, revealing the Dawnfire Heart beating within. It was not like the heart of man, nor the relic cloaked in gentle radiance as the hymns promised, but a molten thing: a raw, unnatural, caged crystal pulsing like some colossal beast's organ. Its call still throbbed faintly in her veins.

She shut her eyes, but behind her lids the vision burned on. Ash fell thick as snow, her god's voice threading through it all like a command pulled taut by desperation. The Dawnfire Heart--she must find it. She must.

But why like this?

Her holy texts spoke of Dawn as renewal and gentle warmth, not the horror of a world ending in blood and fire. Her throat burned as if the smoke of the dream still lingered there. She bowed her head, pressing the amulet harder to her skin until the heat dulled. Even when the visions

1

contradicted everything she had been taught, she could not doubt. She would not doubt. Ptyraxa's will was not always hers to understand.

Still, bile rose as the memory sharpened; His voice was not the gentle light of dawn this time, but edged with nearly frantic urgency. The dreams were worsening, too. Each night was more vivid and insistent. She dreaded sleep, yet her god did not allow her peace in wakefulness. The call only grew stronger.

Her hands trembled. She curled them into fists against her knees, grounding herself in the stillness of the library and the faint scent of vellum and candlewax. With a sigh, she picked the book back up and turned her limited attention to reading.

"And so it was that in the waning years of creation, when the Morning Lord's radiance first clashed against the shrouding dark, a beacon was placed upon the land: the Dawnfire Heart—"

She struggled to read as raised voices threatened to pull her focus. Two men were arguing a few yards away in a different aisle, and it took everything in her to keep looking at the book. She stayed, scowling at the tome, until she heard High Archivist Orlan's adenoidal shrieking.

"Of course the Dawnfire Heart is an allegory!" Adinah's head snapped up. She leaned as far as she could in her seat without tumbling, but she couldn't quite see the argument.

"Oh, come off it, Archivist!" countered a smooth voice laced with condescension. "It was absolutely real!" Even from here, she could hear Orlan scoff. While she hoped this wasn't Ptyraxa's sign, she tucked the book under her arm and quietly moved closer to the debate, staring at shelves to pretend she wasn't eavesdropping.

Orlan was quick to set his position. "The Heart is just a metaphor," he insisted in a patronizing voice. "It's all a parable about the importance of divine inspiration and kindling the faith of Ptyraxa's champions, not a literal object."

"It absolutely was—maybe is—an incredibly powerful magical object. I'll grant you it's not some impossible relic to wake the dead, but there's too many similar stories for it to be entirely fictional." She quietly shifted to the end of the aisle of shelves, still pretending to search for some hidden title, so she could look at who had Orlan in a tizzy. *Might have to get him an ale for that alone*, she thought.

Looking at the man heckling Orlan, she wondered if it would be possible to find a more stereotypical scholar. He was tall, carrying himself with the vain grace of an academic. His stance betrayed the cocky confidence of one who'd never lifted a sword or toiled in a field.

2

His chestnut hair was pushed back but disheveled, as if he ran his hand through it absentmindedly. His features were handsome, with sharp cheekbones and a strong jaw softened by wry amusement. His deep blue robes were slightly weathered, though the golden embroidered sigils along the edge remained immaculate.

Her brow raised in interest. *A mage*, she realized. *Strange to see one here*. She leaned toward the shelf a bit as if trying to decipher a faint bit of text, attempting to remain partially obscured.

"No historical records confirm its existence!" argued Orlan, face flushing with frustration. "It's all been in flowery poetry and conflicting legends."

"Those 'legends' are far too widespread and similar to be fiction."

"If the Heart was real, why did Ptyraxa allow it to disappear? Why does no temple hold any record of its whereabouts? A great many 'artifacts' exist solely in the minds of desperate seekers and the most blindly faithful zealots."

"You archivists dismiss things far too quickly when they don't fit neatly into your well-worn scrolls and narrow understanding of things." The mage crossed his arms, drawing himself to full height.

Orlan squinted at him, sneering. "And you arcanists love to claim every lost fable as 'misunderstood magic,' as if that validates your own scholarly failings."

The mage threw up his hands and stalked off in Adinah's direction. He jumped slightly as he passed, clearly startled to notice another person eavesdropping. The sudden rush of embarrassment sent warmth to her cheeks and the book falling to the floor as her hand flew to her sword. He raised his hands defensively.

"Goodness," he laughed, a little breathless. "Sorry to give you a fright. I'll try to avoid doing that again, lest I end up on your sword." He bent to retrieve the book, eyes locked on the cover as he returned it. His lips curled into a mischievous grin.

"Ah," he said, "A fellow pursuer of knowledge! Perhaps you can help me finish up my disagreement. Tell me—do you think the Dawnfire Heart is real, or is it just another starry-eyed dream peddled by poets?"

Orlan looked at her apologetically as he approached. "I fear you are seeking answers from one with sense, Ezra," he said smugly. "You will find my argument prevails."

Judging by Orlan's gloating, she knew he was infuriatingly certain of his incorrect position. Nevertheless, the mage was looking at her, wry grin firmly in place, hazel eyes sparkling. She held his gaze a moment longer than she meant to before looking to the High Archivist.

"Well," she cleared her throat, "I think it's pretty clear from various

3

histories that it exists. Even the halls of Morningstrike carry texts dedicated entirely to the relic." She practically felt the corner of Ezra's mouth twitch upward as Orlan's demeanor soured.

"Additionally," she continued, "the Heart is divine in nature, far more powerful than a simple enchanted object, making you both incorrect."

And unfortunately for me, she thought, *its location remains a mystery.* She looked to Orlan, seeing the betrayal behind his mask of indifference, but was increasingly aware of Ezra's studious gaze on her. Orlan frowned as he scoffed and sulked away to a different part of the library.

"Now that his nonsense is out of the way," said Ezra, "allow me to introduce myself properly. I'm Ezra Moldravius of Surland, a mage of great renown, connoisseur of arcane mysteries, and a rather accomplished debater. I fear the latter is wasted on Orlan."

Her stomach dropped. She'd heard of Ezra around Morningstrike. He was a brilliant wizard with a tendency to wax poetic. Though the archivists regarded him as a nice enough fellow, they said he was vexing to be around long term.

He gave a self-effacing chuckle, gesturing toward her book. "And you, it seems, are a seeker of lost truths," he continued. "A fascinating subject, the Dawnfire Heart. Might I ask–are you reading out of idle curiosity, or do you have a vested interest?" He leveled her with a knowing look as if he could already tell she was not the type to read for leisure.

"And my name is Adinah Thorne, Dawnshield of Ptyraxa, thanks for asking," she said, an edge creeping into her voice.

His face flushed and he pushed a hand through his hair. "And there I go, immediately fumbling an introduction. I assure you, I intended no offense. I just wanted to make small talk with my savior in the battle of wits."

"Pity you joined unarmed," she quipped with a smirk. "What is it to you why I read anything?"

"None of my business, I'm aware. Still, I'm pleasantly surprised to find a Ptyraxite paladin, especially in Morningstrike, who believes the Heart to be anything other than a myth. I was just curious."

"Careful with that curiosity, Ezra," she warned. "It could get you into trouble someday."

Ezra held up his hands defensively. "Yes, yes, I get it. Ptyraxite paladins are indeed as the stories say–sharp of wit, sharp of sword, and hot of temper."

She let out a defeated sigh. "I have a vested interest," she admitted. "I'm trying to locate it and bring it to a temple so it can be guarded."

"And I assume cloistered away from any arcanist scholars?"

"Orlan was right. You mages will do anything to avoid admitting that some magic is not yours to handle."

"Then I see you have only encountered pitiful excuses for arcanists. No wonder you hold us in such low regard."

"Not low," she corrected. "We are bound by our deities, locked into strict moral codes. Arcanists are unpredictable, stripped of assurance of morality, as Xernaea is more lenient with your usage."

Ezra rolled his eyes. "Oh, ye silly faithful, tying divinity to morality." His face turned stony, eyes darkening. "Some of the greatest monsters in this world are the most faithful." The shift of his tone made her uneasy, like he'd spoken a chill into the air.

"Now that we're even in this verbal sparring match," she conceded, "what are you doing in Morningstrike?"

His smirk returned. "Learning I might have judged a certain paladin too harshly. Hopefully that's not the only thing I'll be learning; I came here to look through the libraries. I wanted to find some new knowledge to expand my abilities, or maybe learn of a valuable relic."

Her interest grew with her suspicion. *A hunger for knowledge*, she thought, *but only the kind that brings him power. Typical.* She could see through his charms. She'd known hundreds, maybe a thousand, of wizards across Viremor just like him. They wandered, craving the next shred of power, influence, and fortune. They chased power as if it could slow the cold hands of Khoravae.

"If you've found enough to have opinions on the Heart," she said, "perhaps you've come across information I need."

"Maybe. I have a few theories."

"Theories are better than anything I have." She motioned to a small reading nook in the corner. "I'd love to hear what you've found so far."

His demeanor lightened as he crossed to one of the chairs, dropping into the seat and making himself comfortable. His infuriating, cocky grace carried over into the way he reclined to one side and crossed his ankles as if he belonged there. Adinah sat on the front of her seat, straight backed, her book balanced in her lap. The posture of a soldier.

"Since we've been in agreement so far," he started, "I wonder if you also assume the Heart is held in some distant ruins by a lost Ptyraxite order?"

She shook her head decisively. "Absolutely not. The shattered temple it's in is far from Ptyraxa's light."

He raised a brow, eyeing her inquisitively. "That's a bold statement. I haven't seen anything about stone, other than the Heart itself being crystalline." A heavy silence fell between them and she felt her heart beginning to race. Nerves twisted her stomach and she wondered if she looked as sick as she felt.

"You've seen it," he said. It wasn't a question. His gaze held hers and her breath caught. She wanted to lie, even felt that she should lie, rather than risk him racing her to the Heart. Possibly winning. To lose would be to fail Ptyraxa and to fail those she'd sworn to protect if he used it for ill.

"I've seen it, yes." The words came out before she could control them. "It was only in a vision, and it didn't look like I expected, but I've seen it."

Oh, Morning Lord, she prayed, *please don't let this be a mistake*. The ensuing silence drove the air from the room. Ezra sank back in his seat, lost in thought, the first two fingers of one hand pressed against his lips. His other hand fidgeted with the ends of the fabric tied at his waist, thumb rubbing against a near threadbare edge.

"I suppose this means that you have some hint of where it is?"

She sighed. "No clue where it is, other than the vague memory of some kind of shattered ruin among cliffs." The longer she was awake, the fainter the dream became.

"I really need to find it," she said quietly, "so I'm here to study."

"You mentioned ruins. Do you think they would hold other relics or enchanted objects of worth?"

She sighed inwardly. "Possibly, though it would be nothing I could guarantee." *Or would*, she thought.

"Well of course not. If you knew what was there, you'd already be in possession of the Heart."

"Exactly," she said, nodding as she stood. "Now, if you'll excuse me–"

"What would it take for me to accompany you?" he interrupted. Her mouth opened and closed a few times, but words failed her.

He scowled. "Come on," he pleaded. "I'm not the worst for company, and you might find a mage is useful on the road. Xernaea's magic would surely be of some help."

"And what do you charge for your usefulness?" she asked, dumbfounded she was even entertaining the idea.

"A share of any items, an artifact or two. Maybe a share of any wealth. Any of that would be worth the trip."

She sat back down. "I have only one objective," she replied. "I'm only pursuing the Heart for Ptyraxa, so finishing my task is my reward."

He scoffed. "So noble. Truly." He changed the subject. "What does Ptyraxa want the Heart for, anyway? And shouldn't He be able to get it Himself?" She fought to remember, but the dream was fuzzy now.

"I'm not certain of the details," she admitted, "but I think I'm only returning it. I don't understand why Ptyraxa can't retrieve it Himself, but it's not my place to question."

He hummed, scratching at his face. "Sounds like we need more information before we set out."

"That we do," she agreed.

"In the interest of finishing this century," he said, voice dripping with condescension, "perhaps you should let me do the research." She bristled, though the idea of taking a break appealed to her. An extra set of eyes would make it quicker work, too, and give her a chance to peruse maps.

I should see this as an unexpected blessing and a chance for rest. Ezra reached out and took the book, the movement so smooth she almost didn't register it.

"If I'm taking over for now," he continued, "I suppose I should get started."

The corner of her mouth turned up in relief. "I appreciate—"

"Besides," he cut her off, "You look like shit. Find a bedroll and get an hour or so of sleep, gods preserve you." Her expression soured as she rose and stormed out of the study.

He was right, of course, but it didn't mean she enjoyed hearing it. Dark bags hung under her eyes, making them seem darker than they were. Her scowls seemed more exasperated than threatening, and her hair grew increasingly disheveled as the days passed.

Since her arrival at Morninstrike Hall, her purposeful stride and intense gaze had created a subtle ripple of unease among the priests and scholars, who instinctively gave her a wide berth. Young apprentices ducked into side corridors and alcoves when she approached, eyes glued to the floor as they half-whispered polite greetings, fear evident in their shaky hands.

The very traits that Ptyraxa chose me for end up turning away His clergy, she thought ruefully. *It's a bit of a surprise that a paladin of the Morning Lord is more like the scorching rays of summer than the caress of daybreak.*

Weariness set in as she navigated the temple halls. She found her temporary lodgings, a room barely larger than a closet, intended for passing paladins and clerics. She found it comforting, like the weight of a warm wool blanket on a cold night. She often found herself on the road with no roof, sometimes with no bedroll, so a room like this felt luxurious. She barely made it through the door and into bed before falling asleep still in her day clothes. As the depths of sleep claimed her, she was pleasantly surprised as no ash-covered ruins rose to meet her.

For the first time in a long while, Adinah slept uninterrupted and unburdened, drifting into a deep and dreamless sleep.

Chapter 2

Ezra

Ezra's love of books and study could not keep his mind from periodically drifting to painful memories: the crackling of arcane energy, cascading black hair, and eyes of shimmering starlight. The tattoo on the back of his hand throbbed, causing him to curse under his breath.

One would think I'd be safe from these thoughts in another god's temple. Looking around, he watched various clerics milling about the library, looking up in admiration and rapture at shafts of light filtering through stained glass. He both envied and pitied them and their relationship with Ptyraxa, knowing they would never know His power the way he'd known Xernaea's.

My goddess, he thought, *without whom I never would have tasted divinity.* His mixed emotions gave way to grief, his throat growing tight. He dabbed at his eyes with his robe sleeves, hoping to keep his tearful moment hidden. The tattoo ached again, starting to burn, as the dark sea of melancholy rose inside him. He took a few steadying breaths, pushing the tide down.

Determined to keep that paladin from finding the answer before he did, he steeled himself, focusing on the pages before him.

"What is known is this: the Dawnfire Heart does not burn with heat, but with purpose.

The last known keeper of the Dawnfire Heart was High Paladin Elidane Starcrest, whose name is all but lost to time. When the wars of that age drew to their bitter end, she vanished, and the relic with her."

His mind wandered, haunted by Xernaea's vast, astral whispers. The tension in his muscles ratcheted up, making him grind his teeth. The tattoo burned more intensely, as if responding to his agitation. He estimated he'd spent nearly two hours researching, accumulating a tall stack of books and stray parchment on a table beside him.

Despite the tower of tomes, he hadn't made much progress. The name Elidane had come up repeatedly, but she died centuries ago, her body never recovered or properly laid to rest. While certainly noteworthy, it didn't tell him anything about who she was or if she had the Heart with her when she passed. Normally, even that shard of information would be a handy place to start, but he was in a rush.

That paladin, he thought, *so smug and self-righteous*. She was interesting, certainly, as were all folk on grand quests for artifacts and relics. Morningstrike echoed with the whispers of Adinah's reputation: a fearsome, devout warrior who climbed the ranks quickly and never questioned the demands of her service.

A chance for her to be like the old Inquisitors, destroying all things arcane, he thought. She'd be just as likely to betray him on their journey as she'd be to help him.

Our journey? He caught himself. *There doesn't really need to be an 'our' at all. I never said I wouldn't go on my own journey. I owe her god nothing, and owe her even less.*

He could picture her face clearly if she discovered his betrayal. Her eyes would burn with divine fury–a terrifying ability of paladins–as she raised her sword. Would she pursue him? What price would he pay if captured? Not that he would be captured. One did not draw so close to and fall so far from divinity without being forced to evade enemies. She'd become just another person left in his wake to curse his name.

His mouth twisted into a wry grin as he plotted. He had Elidane's name; he just needed a direction to go. There were far too many books in the vast library to go through them all. Paladin Thorne would return by then. He simply needed another thread of information to work with before he could depart.

Thankfully, he had an idea of where to find the thread, though he was unsure how eagerly they'd give it to him. He rose, arranging the books into a tidy stack on the table. After all, it would be improper to seek out the help of an archivist after leaving the library a mess.

The library was not merely vast. It was overwhelming, in and of itself a labyrinthine cathedral of knowledge. Tinted glass vaulted high overhead in sweeping arcs, each panel catching the daylight and scattering it across the floors in fractured bands of gold. Pillars soared like trees in midsummer, carved with winding motifs of vines and sunbursts. Between them, alcoves opened into rows upon rows of shelves that seemed endless, gilt script gleaming on the age-darkened spines of ancient tomes.

At each of the four great entrances stood a wooden circulation desk manned by solemn clerics clad in robes that caught the shifting light as if half-lit by dawn. Behind the eastern desk, secluded and set apart, the private studies of the archivists waited: narrow doorways tucked into a mural of the rising sun, each chamber a sanctuary for the most devoted. Within, their windows allowed in the blinding morning light so no one who studied there could forget whose sight they labored under. The silence felt larger here outside the offices. It was a living hush, like a breath held in reverence.

Ezra took a moment to steady himself before stepping into one of the many offices. The scent of incense and old parchment hung thick in the air, a mixture of the sacred and the studious. High Archivist Orlan sat in his usual place at the back of the room, looming over a large hardwood desk and poring over a tome. His sharp focus and furrowed brow suggested he had not let Ezra's earlier argument slip from memory.

"High Archivist," Ezra began smoothly, inclining his head with practiced humility as he crossed to the desk. "I must offer my sincerest apologies for my—let's call it overzealous enthusiasm—earlier. A man of your wisdom deserves far more deference than I displayed, and for that I am truly remorseful."

Orlan did not look up immediately, but Ezra caught the faintest twitch of amusement at his mouth. "You are certainly practiced in the art of apology."

"I have, on occasion, been known to talk myself into situations that require it," Ezra admitted, clasping his hands in a show of contrition. "But my reverence for the knowledge you guard is sincere. So, if you'll permit me, I was hoping to ask another question."

Orlan exhaled sharply, closing his book with the measured weight of someone making a point. "I suspect that even if I did not permit it, you would find a way."

Ezra smiled. "You wound me, High Archivist, but you are not incorrect." He stepped closer. "I wish to know about Elidane Starcrest." That earned a more significant reaction. Orlan's brow furrowed further, his fingers steepling atop his book.

"A name rarely spoken these days. What interest do you have in a paladin long since passed?"

Ezra paused, debating his answer before opting for something close to truth. "Curiosity. Respect for a legend, and for one whose path I may be walking in some small way."

Orlan studied him suspiciously for a moment before sighing. "She perished in the Dusklight Glade, by all accounts. There are several ruins there. Which are associated with her, none can say with certainty. The followers of Ptyraxa whisper that only the most faithful of the Morning Lord may find them. A place of great holiness, they claim. Some even say

High Paladin Starcrest still watches over the ruin."

Ezra lost himself in thought, his fingers fidgeting with the edges of the scarf at his waist. *I have faith,* he reasoned. *Not strictly in the virtues of Ptyraxa, perhaps, but certainly in His existence and the gods in general.* He shuddered inwardly. Thinking of the gods always brought back the memory of Her, the feeling of Her hand tracing the sigil tattooed on the back of his...

Stop it, he scolded himself. *Now is not the time.* He looked at Orlan, expression soft with gratitude.

"My thanks, High Archivist. As ever, your wisdom is a light in the dark."

Orlan huffed. "Save your flattery for those who enjoy it, Ezra Moldravius. Do not let your curiosity lead you where you are not meant to tread."

Ezra smiled, offering a final bow before turning to leave. *Not meant to tread? Perhaps.* But then, he had never been one for heeding warnings.

The Dusklight Glade wasn't terribly far, only about four days' travel on foot to the nearest town in the region. He'd traveled further than that before stopping here in Taranok. He left north out of the library toward the study room offered to him as temporary quarters. It wasn't glamorous, certainly not his preference, but he wanted to make the money in his purse last as long as possible, plentiful though it was. With autumn's bite beginning to take hold of Viremor, he wanted money for a proper inn whenever conditions grew too uncomfortable to sleep outside.

Passing an archway, he spied a large room with several wooden tables. He hesitated, seeing a young woman inside, carefully laying out food. The flickering light from nearby lanterns cast soft shadows across her features as she arranged the serving bowls. It was a humble meal for clerics and paladins after evening prayers, but to Ezra, it might as well have been a king's treasury. He stopped in the archway, catching her attention as she reached for another piece of bread. His eyes twinkled with mischief, a practiced smile curling his lips.

"Ah, the noble task of nourishing the righteous," he said smoothly, stepping closer. "Tell me, my lady–do Ptyraxa and His faithful truly require so much of your generosity? Surely a humble traveler like myself could partake in a small portion to fuel his own prayers." She glanced up, blushing. She was clearly not accustomed to being approached in such a manner.

Her fingers fumbled with the bread as she straightened. "I... I'm just–this is for the worshippers. They have their rituals, and–" Ezra tilted his head, smile never wavering as he stepped closer, his voice low and coaxing.

11

"Of course. I wouldn't dream of disturbing their sacred rituals." He gestured to the food. "But surely they could share a sliver of that cheese? Perhaps a few slices of bread? After all, my feet are weary, and I find that a small gift freely given is as much a blessing as any prayer."

She slowly placed the bread on a serving tray before fidgeting nervously, never taking her eyes from him. After a moment, her gaze flickered between Ezra and the food, her cheeks flushing. Naivety gleamed in her eyes, but so did kindness.

"I'm not sure. It's not for me to decide. The food's meant for the others, and—"

Ezra took another step closer, voice low as if sharing a secret. "You see," he said conspiratorially, "I've heard whispers of your generosity. A woman with such a heart can surely see the wisdom of sharing with a stranger in need. Why, I might even say you'd be earning favor from Ptyraxa Himself." He smiled softly, eyes alight with the charm that had won over countless hearts before hers. He nearly felt bad for what he was doing. Nearly.

"Just a little?" she asked, her soft voice uncertain.

"Just enough to take the edge off," he replied with a wink. "A few slices of this, a bit of bread, maybe some dried fruit to sweeten the evening?" Her hesitation faltered, and with a shy smile she nodded, preparing a small bundle of food for him.

"Just a little. But please, don't tell anyone," she whispered, as if it was a grand betrayal to the temple.

He gave a low chuckle. "My lips are sealed, I assure you." He gave a small bow. "You've done a good deed tonight, my lady. May your kindness return to you tenfold."

She beamed at him, more confident now as she returned to her task. He turned on his heel, food tucked away neatly. When he reached his room, he grabbed his few belongings and set the area back in order.

After a final check through his equipment, he quietly slipped back out into the hall, navigating between the sea of the faithful dutifully walking to evening prayers. With all the stealth he could manage, he left the temple's southernmost entrance. As he walked through the quiet courtyard, through the main gates, and onto the road toward the Dusklight Glade, the only sound was the rustle of leaves. In bright hues of gold, red, and orange, it was as if the ground surrounding the temple was bathed in a lightless sunrise.

Chapter 3

Adinah

A deep unease pulled Adinah from sleep. The room beyond the comfort of her blanket held only a whisper of warmth, and the weight of exhaustion still pressed against her limbs, but something felt off.

She sat up, brushing her curls from her face as her eyes adjusted to the candlelight. The only sounds in the temple this late were the scratch of quills against parchment and the murmur of quiet voices echoing off the vaulted ceiling. A few archivists and paladins still moved about, keeping watch over the hall's dwindling candles.

She pushed herself to her feet, rolling the stiffness from her shoulders. Something unsettling tugged at the edge of her thoughts. She hoped Ezra was still awake somewhere, nose buried in some ancient text, having discovered a new direction for their search. Assuming he wasn't engaged in conversation with an unfortunate soul unprepared for his particular brand of charm, that is.

Charm. Not sure you can really call it that, she mused. *Charm implies one might want to talk to him.* She combed her fingers through her mess of curls and stepped into the hall. One of the newly recruited paladins, Vylander, walked the halls on watch. His strides were confident, but when he locked eyes with Adinah, his step faltered a bit. She struggled not to roll her eyes.

"Excuse me," she said, just loudly enough for him to hear. "Have you seen the wizard wandering around? Ezra?" Vylander stopped, casting her a quizzical look.

"A wizard, not a cleric?" She nodded.

"I'm sorry, Paladin Thorne," he said softly. "I know of no wizard visitor. I know we had a visitor in a spare study recently, but the room has been returned to its original use."

She grew pale, feeling as if the world was suddenly very far away. A cold weight settled in her stomach for a moment before determination seized her, bringing movement back to her body as she started sprinting toward the library.

"Light guide you, Vylander," she called over her shoulder. She didn't hesitate to see if he replied as she ran.

Without the waves of worshippers milling the halls, she quickly came across High Archivist Orlan's personal chamber doors. Her knocks were firm, loud, and insistent. Normally she'd have no business knocking like this in a temple, but she was desperate. The door flung open wide, revealing a sour-faced Orlan in aging mismatched fabric pants and a robe, clearly the first two things he could grab.

"Thorne," he spat. "I should have known it would be you. You're the only one with the audacity–"

"Is Ezra still here?" she interrupted.

He raised a brow. "Him? Really?" he asked incredulously. "No. He left earlier in the afternoon from what I've heard."

Her stomach dropped. "Alone?"

"Judging by his reputation, I believe that's how he prefers it."

"Did he talk to you before he left? I fear he is in possession of information which could lead to an artifact of Ptyraxa. I can't risk it falling into the hands of anyone, especially an arcanist with no good sense."

He rubbed his eyes with one hand. "He just asked about High Paladin Starcrest, that's it. I told him she perished in the Dusklight Glade, and that was the extent of the conversation. I expected him to want more, honestly, but he went back to study for a while. A few hours later someone noticed he was gone, but I don't know if he spoke with anyone else."

A knot of tension set in her shoulders. "Then I suppose I'm off at once. I appreciate your hospitality as usual, High Archivist." She gave a small bow.

"If he is after an artifact or holy site, should I send you with additional paladins or clerics? We can spare plenty," Orlan offered.

"No need," she said, shaking her head gently. "I can handle the likes of Ezra on my own, assuming he hasn't already become food for wolves. The only thing I could ask for would be some supplies for the road."

He sighed. "You should know by now there's really no need to ask. Take what you need from the kitchens." He thought for a moment, shifting his weight a bit. "Take a horse, too. Assuming the boy isn't dead yet, he's got far better chances if you can get to him before the dangers of the road do. The ones in the stable should be plenty rested and watered." She gave a small grin, nodding. "You're too kind, but it is a kindness I will take this time." She bowed again. "Light keep you and guide you, High Archivist."

His expression warmed a bit. "Go with the Dawn at your back, and let no darkness take hold," he whispered, a quiet benediction. She smiled,

14

genuinely, before turning toward her own room.

She'd laid out her armor carefully to keep it from getting damaged, so finding and putting it on was simple, even at this late hour. As she put on each piece, from her breastplate to her greaves, she sent up silent prayers to Ptyraxa. She turned putting her armor on into a sacred ritual, as if the peace of this act would help shake off the violence she'd committed while wearing it. *Even when the violence is justified*, she thought, pulling on her crimson tabard, *the weight of duty weighs heavy on us all.*

She was self-conscious of the clanking of her armor as she walked the halls, making her final preparations. Those on watch snapped to attention before she'd even rounded the corner to see them. She waved a dismissive hand to each of them, not taking the time to explain her sudden departure. *Sure to start plenty of rumors,* she realized. *Might be nice for the gossips to have something new to talk about.*

"Time is short." The voice of Ptyraxa crept into her mind as if bubbling up from the depths of the sea. She stumbled a bit when she heard it, but it only served to confirm what she already knew: Ptyraxa needed her to maintain single-minded focus and channel her ferocity into her duty. There was no time for distraction or pleasantries.

She made quick work of gathering supplies and a small meal from the kitchens before heading out to the stables. Despite being devoid of people, one horse was saddled, already awake and freshly watered. Clearly, someone had just readied him for the journey.

"Tirin," she said softly, reading the name on the door of his stall. She reached up, offering him a hand to sniff. He was a massive warhorse, with a snowy white coat and grey spots dappled across his back half, his mane and tail the color of smoke. The horse leaned to press his nose against her hand in greeting before leaning a bit more to ask for a scratch, which she happily gave him. She led him out of the stable, attached her leather saddlebags, wound his lead rope, and led him to the main road.

Just before she left the hallowed temple grounds, she stopped at a small locked charity box, sliding in one gold coin. With a groan, she climbed into the saddle and commanded Tirin forward down the dark southern road toward the Dusklight Glade.

Chapter 4

Ezra

Sleep had come easily that night, despite the unfamiliar weight of the road settling into Ezra's bones. The air was crisp with the dying warmth of autumn, the distant scent of woodsmoke and damp leaves threading through his tent. He had spent the evening in relative comfort, almost forgetting he was sleeping alone in the wilds.

The rustling at the entrance of his tent did not wake him, nor the faint shift of fabric, nor the muted scuff of boots against the dirt. What finally dragged him into consciousness was the sensation of cold steel pressing against his neck.

His eyes snapped open.

"Evening, stranger," a low voice rasped. "I'd advise against any sudden movements."

Ezra exhaled sharply, feeling the steel bite just enough to warn him. His hands remained where they were, open, fingers spread in a universal sign of peace. Looking up, he saw three figures crouched in the entrance of his tent. Two men and one woman stood in the tent, all clad in patchwork leathers, their weapons aged. He reckoned they were probably still sharp where it counted.

"Ah," he murmured, voice still thick with sleep. "This is quite the rude awakening."

Their leader, a broad-shouldered man with a jagged scar cutting through his brow, grinned down at him. "Not half as rude as it'll be if you don't hand over anything valuable. No tricks or magic, or that pretty head of yours might find itself rolling in the dirt."

Ezra arched a brow, his usual smirk forming even as the blade stayed at his throat. "A shame, truly. I was hoping for a warmer welcome. Perhaps a conversation over tea instead? I assure you, my company is quite–" The woman cut him off with a swift kick to the ribs. He grunted, curling around the impact, but forced an easy laugh through gritted teeth.

16

"Ah, I see," he chuckled. "Not tea drinkers, then."

The woman scoffed. "He's got a sharp tongue for someone in such a poor position."

"Comes with the territory," Ezra quipped, carefully shifting more upright, even with the knife still pressed to his neck. "I don't have much, but what I do have, I might be persuaded to part with, if I find your terms reasonable."

The leader snorted. "You don't get to make the terms, mage."

Before he could answer, a cry outside pierced the air. The bandits turned at the sound. The sharp clang of steel rang through the trees, followed by the unmistakable clash of battle. Ezra's brows lifted.

"It appears you've miscalculated," he mused. The woman cursed and grabbed the collar of his shirt, yanking him forward. The thunder of hoofbeats split the night. Just as he was yanked out of the tent and into the dim firelight, a streak of silver and gold tore through the camp.

A warrior rode in on horseback, navigating over bodies at the edge of his camp, a blur of motion barreling through the chaos. Their armor caught the light like a gleaming beacon in the dark, and their sword, already slick with blood, caught the flickering embers of the dying fire. With a single fluid motion, they were off the horse, boots hitting the ground hard.

"Unhand him," ordered a woman's familiar voice, cold as steel. Ezra could see the woman's eyes burning with a golden radiance. *Paladin Thorne,* he realized, suddenly unsure if he really wanted to be saved at all. The woman holding him hesitated for a second.

It was a second too long. Adinah moved.

Stepping forward in a flash of steel, her sword cut the space between them in an arc of silver, forcing the woman to release him and leap back. The second bandit beside her barely had time to react before Adinah was upon him, blade meeting steel with a sharp ring.

Ezra wasted no time. The instant the grip on his collar loosened, he wrenched free, rolling sideways as the third bandit lunged for him. With a flick of his wrist and a whispered incantation, a burst of force slammed into the bandit's chest, sending him sprawling with a strangled curse. Now freed, Ezra straightened, adjusting his clothes. He barely had time to recover before the woman was coming at him again, her dagger flashing in the dim firelight. He twisted just in time, the blade skimming past his ribs.

Damn, he cursed, *she's fast.* Too fast to conjure anything time-consuming, anyway. He needed something immediate. His hand rose. A sharp crack of blue arcane energy erupted from his fingertips, striking her in the shoulder. She hissed in pain but didn't fall. Ezra swore, shifting his weight as she lunged again, pressing the advantage.

In his peripheral vision, he could see Adinah locked in her own battle.

She moved with power and grace, her sword an extension of her will. With a decisive strike, she forced the leader back, his own blade ringing under the force of her attack. She barely spared Ezra a glance, but her voice was steel.

"Get your bearings!" she called.

Ezra gritted his teeth. "I'm quite aware of my bearings, thank you."

"Then use them." She caught the leader's next strike on her sword, her boots planted firm to hold her place, and shoved him backward. The moment he stumbled, she lunged, carving a ruthless arc across his midsection. He reeled, staggering back with blood soaking into his leathers.

The woman recovered first, eyes blazing, pivoting from Ezra and turning to Adinah. Ezra saw the flash of steel and the trajectory of the knife first.

No.

His reaction was pure instinct, just an outstretched hand and a single, forceful push of magic. The dagger stopped, suspended mid-air. The woman's eyes went wide. Ezra's fingers curled into a fist and the knife snapped backward. She jerked violently, barely dodging her own weapon as it embedded itself into a tree behind her.

Before she could recover, Adinah was there. With a swift step and a brutal strike, her blade sank deep. The woman gasped–a sharp, broken sound–before crumpling. Ezra turned to see the last bandit fleeing.

"Coward," Adinah muttered, already moving to follow. Ezra stopped her.

"Wait," he exhaled, extending his fingers. The ground beneath the bandit shuddered with a pulse of arcane energy, subtle but effective. His foot caught on nothing, his body lurching forward as though his leg had been pulled from under him. He hit the dirt hard.

Adinah stared. "Did you just trip him?"

"Yes. Ingenious, isn't it?" Ezra dusted off his sleeves as she exhaled through her nose. In frustration or amusement, he couldn't be sure. Adinah closed the distance to the bandit before he could get to his feet again.

The bandit yielded, and Adinah made quick work of tying him up with a length of rope from Ezra's pack. They bound him to a tree and stripped him of weapons, though he glared daggers at them both. She took a quick look over the scene of the battle before turning her attention to him, and he realized he was absentmindedly rubbing at his ribs.

"Are you hurt?" she asked.

"Nothing dire, just some light bruising. A minor offense to my dignity."

She huffed. "Are you saying you had dignity to offend?" He smirked, but noticed something about her stance had shifted. She wasn't looking at him or their prisoner. Her posture was rigid, gaze sharp as it flicked to the treeline. The moment stretched as a whisper of unease settled in his gut.

There was a snap and a hiss of air. She moved, but not fast enough. The arrow stuck in her shoulder, the shaft sticking out between her armor and pauldron. She inhaled sharply, the impact knocking her off balance. Ezra's stomach lurched, his pulse roaring in his ears. His hands moved in a flash. With a flick of his wrist, power surged, the tattoo on the back of his hand burning and glowing bright blue as a wave of force slammed into the archer. It sent the bastard flying back into the trees. They didn't get back up.

He turned back to see Adinah barely standing. "Paladin–" The word left him sharper than he meant.

"I'm fine," she gritted out. She wasn't. The arrow was still buried deep in her shoulder. Panic clawed at his insides, his hands already reaching for her before he caught himself.

"We need to keep you from bleeding out." She didn't argue. She wavered, then sank to a knee, breath ragged. Ezra dropped beside her, hands steady even as his heart raced. Clever words failed him.

He helped her carefully work off her armor, taking care of buckles and leather bindings she couldn't reach. Pauldrons and breastplate free, the fine chainmail glinted in the firelight, links damp with sweat and speckled with blood. She hissed as he broke part of the arrow shaft to pull the mail off.

"Damn it," he muttered under his breath. "This will hurt." He knew enough to handle field injuries–he'd patched up his fair share of wounds in his travels–but this was different. Adinah scoffed, rolling her eyes despite the tension in her jaw.

"Not my first arrow wound, thank you."

He gave her a sharp look. "Forgive me if I don't find that reassuring." With a final tug, the mail slipped free, clinking softly as he let it fall. The thick, quilted fabric of the gambeson had absorbed most of the blood, the wound seeping through in dark patches. It clung stubbornly to her, unyielding as he tried to work the sleeve down her arm.

She tensed beneath his hands, a sharp breath escaping her. He hesitated before gripping it more firmly and easing it away from the wound. It pulled back slowly, revealing bare skin beneath–her shoulder, her collarbone, the curve of her upper chest exposed to the cool night air. His face flushed.

She smirked despite the pain. "If you wanted me out of my armor, Ezra, you could've just asked." He jerked back, ears burning as he wrenched his focus to the wound. Just the wound.

"Next time, I'll send flowers first," he said, regaining composure. He exhaled and reached for his knife. "Hold still. The arrow still needs to come out."

"No need for your half-baked surgery attempts," she chuckled, recoiling a bit. She placed a shaking hand over what remained of the arrow in her shoulder.

She exhaled, closing her eyes. To his surprise, golden light flickered at her fingertips. The air around them grew warm, divine magic rolling through the air like the first rays of morning. He'd heard of paladins' healing, but had never seen it in person before.

Slowly, the bleeding stemmed, flesh knitting itself together. The arrow, still slightly buried, trembled and pushed itself out, falling with a soft clatter. Though the wound was closed, a dark bruise bloomed across her skin. He let out a breath he hadn't realized he was holding.

She sighed, slumping. "Done." He wasn't convinced. He looked her over, studying the way her hands trembled and exhaustion set behind her eyes.

"You're not 'done'," he said. "Not entirely."

She smirked. "I said I healed it, not that I was at full strength."

He exhaled through his nose, rocking back on his heels. "Of course not, too easy." She stretched experimentally before wincing. Ezra scrubbed a hand through his hair, forcing himself to steady. She couldn't handle another fight.

"You need to rest," he insisted, even as she was putting her armor back on.

"Not here." She was pushing herself up.

He caught her arm. "Just let me help." She hesitated, then nodded once. He took it as a victory. She swatted away his offer of help as she put her armor back on, but once she was ready, he wrapped an arm around her waist, helping her get to her feet, then–eventually–back onto her horse.

He packed quickly, shoving things haphazardly into bags and loading them onto the saddle. His tent was a crumpled mess and his bag bulged at odd angles, but it would have to do. She reached down, inclining her head as if to beckon him.

"Tirin will be fine. He might not be as fast as he normally would be, but you're welcome to get up here so we can get somewhere–oh, how did you phrase it before? 'In this century?'" His ears went red, but he took her arm and got into the saddle behind her.

"Hey!" cried the bandit, still bound on the other side of the campsite. "Are you going to just leave me here?" Ezra glared at him. Lifting his hand, he cast another spell, putting the man to sleep.

"Let's go," he whispered to Adinah, placing his hands on her waist as

20

she set Tirin back toward the path. She looked back over her shoulder.

"Ptyraxa's light protect you, and may His light guide your fallen comrades toward a new dawn," she prayed softly. Even Ezra knew the silence that followed was a melancholy and holy one, so he let it hang thick in the air around them.

Chapter 5

Adinah

The road stretched ahead, swallowed in shadows, with only the moonlight and stars to guide them. Tirin's hooves clopped steadily against the dirt, the only real sound besides the occasional whisper of autumn leaves. Ezra rode behind her, arms loose around her waist. He was barely holding on, yet somehow perfectly at ease with the motion.

Adinah glanced down at her shoulder where she could still feel the dull ache of her injury. She'd used Ptyraxa's power to knit the flesh back together, but it hadn't completely restored her strength. When they came upon a rocky outcropping with a small grove of trees curling against the hillside, she pulled back on the reins.

"We'll stop up here," she murmured, voice just above a whisper. He shifted slightly behind her.

"An excellent choice, though I almost expected you'd try to push us until dawn." He was teasing, but she caught the faint note of concern beneath it. She didn't want his pity. She'd gotten more than enough pity for one lifetime after her first missions.

Making camp was quick work, made easier by his helping set up her tent and handle Tirin. They made a modest meal of the food in their packs, settling down by the fire to eat and relax. For a while, neither of them spoke.

Then, quietly, she said, "Thank you."

He turned his head slightly. "For what? My unparalleled charm? My devastating good looks?"

She huffed. "For not running off again. Plenty would have taken that arrow strike as an opportunity to flee. You could have left me for dead back there."

He chuckled. "I really should be apologizing here. As badly as I messed up our first interaction, I messed this up even more. My leaving was not intended to be a personal slight." A heavy beat of silence sat

22

between them.

"I suppose," he continued, "I should also thank you for not doing to me what you did to those bandits." She heard him shudder a bit. "I know the fate that usually befalls those who flee from paladins, and I am grateful I did not meet my end."

"Your actions didn't necessitate divine judgement. Just my personal frustration."

He shifted to one side to look at her more directly. "Unlike the bandits. Like the one we left tied up?"

"I didn't pass any divine judgement on the bound one."

"Didn't you?" His expression was intent. "You–well, we–left him bound in the wilds. If something finds him first, his fate is out of our hands. That's still a death sentence, just a delayed one."

"He had a chance," she said evenly. "A chance to escape and turn away from banditry. If I had taken him to authorities, he'd be executed or left to rot in a cell. This way, he chooses his own path."

He made a thoughtful sound. "And you think that's the moral choice?"

She exhaled sharply. "I think it was the right one. I neutralized the threats to an innocent person. He yielded, so killing him would be improper. Letting him go and carrying him with us weren't options, either. I made the right choice."

"For him? Or for you?"

She shot him a lethal glare. "You think too much."

He smiled faintly, something searching in his gaze. "And you don't think enough."

She huffed, turning to her tent, pausing only to ask over her shoulder, "Which town are you heading to in the Dusklight Glade?" When he didn't reply, she turned on her heel to face him. Ezra sat by the fire, looking like a child caught stealing sweets.

"Ezra," she started again, edge creeping into her voice. "Please tell me you had a destination in mind." He pushed himself to his feet and raised his hands defensively, his face flushing a particularly deep scarlet.

"I know what this sounds like–"

She sighed, leveling him with a steely gaze. "I don't know if you've ever looked at a map, but this is an entire region you've taken on searching." She took two confident strides forward before he twitched his fingers, knocking her to the ground as a wave of force slammed against her breastplate.

"Listen," he said, his voice more desperate than angry. "I know running off without a more... definite plan was a poor decision. I'm keenly aware of that. I am also aware that being sorry doesn't change that we're both wandering to the Dusklight Glade without a precise destination." His voice went low, a dangerous edge creeping in.

"I can't necessarily fix our situation," he admitted, "but we have two options here: we can go back to Morningstrike and spend weeks reading dusty books–which I wouldn't necessarily mind–or we can go on from here and find whatever we find."

Adinah glared at him, getting up slowly, keeping her hands open and visible. He had a point, even if the options were less than ideal. She knew the rising tensions wouldn't get her answers, either, and she didn't want to spend her little energy on a fight in the middle of the Yllandra Trail.

"Ezra," she said finally, working to soften her voice, "You're right. Neither option is desirable. I am shorter on time than I'd like, so I don't think Morningstrike is an option. We need answers, and we'll need to find them on the road. Chembrus is about two days away by horse. If we get there, we can at least come up with a better plan without the stress of the road."

He seemed to think about this suggestion for a long moment before nodding. "I'm glad we could come to an understanding." His expression softened, almost as sheepish as surprised. He clearly hadn't expected to reason with her. She nodded once, walking back to her tent.

"One last thing," she said before closing the tent flap.

"Yes?" he asked, half in his own tent.

"Don't hit me with a spell like that again, or I will ride off and leave you to the road and the bandits." She ducked in, curling up on her bedroll before he could reply, nearly forcing herself to sleep.

24

Chapter 6

Adinah

They ate breakfast and broke camp quickly in relative quiet. Ezra seemed cautious, as if he was trying to avoid setting off her temper or remind her of his recent missteps. Adinah was content to let the quiet hang between them through the morning, broken only by the briefest small talk, even as they continued on the road south toward Chembrus.

They rode until early afternoon, when the strain of riding caused tension to settle into her shoulders and back. *As good a time as any to rest*, she reasoned, pulling Tirin to the roadside. She unburdened him, setting him to graze in the shady clearing near a ravine. She took the time to gently scratch and rub his sides where the bags and saddles chafed, whispering little reassurances that he was, in fact, the best warhorse. Behind her, Ezra laughed softly, sinking down to sit in the grass.

"You know," he started, "you are so gentle with that horse I can almost forget you shoved your sword through someone not even a day ago."

She rolled her eyes. "Well, Tirin didn't try to rob and stab one of us, so I feel like he's deserving of some kindness."

"I understand that," he acknowledged, "but you are exceptionally kind to him." She scowled. "Ah, yes, go on. Keep scowling. It's very intimidating. I'm trembling, truly. But it doesn't cover up how kind you are to Tirin."

She gestured to the grazing horse. "Tirin, and the other horses kept by temples and paladins, make our work possible. We can travel quickly to provide assistance to families and even entire villages. We can transport goods to areas ravaged by war and disaster. No matter the deity, holy warriors would be far less capable without our mounts."

Ezra reclined back comfortably on his elbows. "I thought I had the reputation of talking too much?" he asked with a particularly smug grin.

Her face flushed. "I was just making polite conversation, which *you* started–"

"You just don't like people pointing out your soft spots." She went quiet, fidgeting with a blade of grass.

It was a long moment before she broke the silence. "You think too much." The accusation lacked the edge she expected to hear in it. She stood and stretched, suddenly eager to get back on the road. As she offered Ezra a hand up, her stomach twisted with the feeling of being watched.

As he stood, they heard a distant sound, low and guttural. Ezra's expression shifted from its previous wry amusement to wary calculation. The sound came again, closer this time. A rustling came from the underbrush in the ravine, then another. Whatever it was, there was more than one. Her hand was on her sword hilt before she had time to think. They turned to face the ravine, putting themselves in front of Tirin.

"Ezra."

"I hear it." His fingers flexed in preparation, the tattoo on his hand faintly gleaming.

The creatures burst forth.

They were twisted things, like wolves gone wrong. Their shapes carried the echo of canines, but every detail rang with corruption. Patchy, mange-ridden fur barely clung to their gaunt frames, stretched too tight across bones that jutted at obscene angles. Their eyes shone with a feverish, unnatural light. They carried no color, only a predatory gleam like moonlight warped through broken glass. Their jaws gaped open too wide, hinges unbound by nature, crammed with serrated teeth like shards of shattered bone.

Their limbs were oddly long, bent wrongly as though sculpted by careless hands and forced to bear weight they were never meant to. Claws curled like hooked sickles, gouging the dirt as they moved with a loping, spasmodic gait. A stench of rot rolled off them, a sour, distorted wrongness that made the skin crawl.

Ezra inhaled sharply. "Those are not wolves," he said, voice dark. Before she could reply, the creatures lunged.

Adinah moved on instinct, stepping forward to meet the first with a swift, brutal swing. Her blade connected, biting deep into its malformed shoulder. It shrieked—a piercing, broken keen like iron grinding on glass— and twisted around her strike, joints bending backwards as it snapped its slavering jaws at her in a frenzy.

Beside her, Ezra was already casting, a flick of his wrist sending a bolt of energy searing through another beast's flank. It yelped, stumbling, but did not falter; its flesh writhed around the wound, clinging stubbornly to the abomination. Behind her, Tirin reared back, hooves lashing out. One beast crumpled with a crunch of bone, but two more surged in, their claws scoring furrows in the road as they drove the group toward the far edge.

The pack pressed them with a mindless, ravenous persistence, shrieking and snapping, the sound of their pursuit echoing through the wood like an unholy chorus.

Adinah barely had time to register the moment the tide shifted against them.

One of the creatures broke past her guard, claws raking across her armor. She staggered, hissing through clenched teeth as she drove her blade upward in retaliation. The thing fell, but another took its place. Ezra muttered something sharp in a language she didn't recognize, voice laced with urgency. Magic gathered around him, the tattoo on his hand burning brightly. He reached out, grabbing her and pulling her to stand behind him.

"We need to end this," he said. "Now." She didn't argue; they were being overwhelmed.

Ezra raised his hand, the air around them crackling. The veins in his arm pulsed with blue light, tracing jagged lines up to his neck and across his face. His hazel eyes were swallowed by an eerie, glowing blue. The sheer force of magic he summoned made the very air vibrate, setting her teeth on edge.

He spoke and the world exploded with light and force.

It was not fire, ice, or lightning, but something far greater and deeper. Pure arcane energy surged outward in an unrelenting wave, tearing through the creatures like they were nothing more than mist before a storm. The ground quaked beneath them, the pressure immense. For a brief moment, she thought she saw something else in the light: lines of intricate, ancient symbols, shifting and pulsing with an unnatural rhythm. The tattoo on his hand was no longer just glowing. It was brilliant and bright, as if the light of all the stars was shining out from his skin. His expression twisted, pain and concentration warring on his face. The energy didn't stop.

Something was wrong. The vision of him wavered at the edges, as if he was no longer entirely physical. He was unraveling. Adinah didn't think. She moved.

She grasped his arm, fingers pressing against the burning tattoo. The moment she made contact, a violent jolt ran through her. It was like being struck by lightning and submerged in freezing water all at once. The force of it sent her gasping, but she held firm. In desperation, she did the only thing she could think of–she prayed.

"Ptyraxa," she called, unsure if her voice even made a sound, "help him. Please."

Warmth answered. A golden glow spread from her fingertips, seeping into Ezra's skin, clashing with the violent blue. The two energies met, warred, then twisted together in a strange, volatile harmony. Some of it turned back, flowing into her.

Adinah inhaled sharply as her vision swam. It was like nothing she had ever felt before. Pure arcane energy, the very foundation of Xernaea's magic, unfurled before and within her, pressing against the edges of her mind. It felt endless. It burned and pulsed, seeking, searching, and wanting. She felt her heart hammer against her ribs, felt her limbs tremble with raw power that was not hers to use. For the first time, she understood what Ezra felt.

The power ebbed.

The light dimmed, the arcane pressure lifting. Ezra staggered backward, eyes wide and unfocused, barely catching himself before collapsing entirely. The tattoo on the back of his hand was still glowing, but the veins of energy had receded. His breath came in ragged gasps, sweat dripping from his brow. Adinah barely kept her balance, her own body screaming in protest. Her head throbbed. Her hands still tingled with residual magic.

They stood in silence, the only sounds their heavy breathing and the distant crackle of dissipating energy. The creatures were gone: obliterated entirely, their remains nothing more than scattered wisps of dark magic dissipating into the air.

Ezra's voice was hoarse when he finally spoke. "What did you do?"

Adinah swallowed, steadying herself. "I stopped you from destroying yourself." He blinked at her, clearly still dazed. His gaze flickered to her hand. She still felt herself trembling, hand tingling with the faint, fading glow of the arcane.

His lips parted, then closed, then parted again. "That was–" He shook his head. "You felt it, didn't you?" She hesitated. Lying was pointless.

"Yes." A slow breath.

He dragged a hand through his hair, still looking at her like he wasn't sure if she was real. "That was your first taste of magic, then. Xernaea's magic, at least." She clenched her jaw, still feeling the echo of it in her bones. It had been intoxicating. Terrifying. Beautiful.

She forced herself to focus. "Did you feel it?"

He held her gaze and her stomach twisted. "Ptyraxa?" he asked. "Yeah. Wow. I didn't think it would feel that different." His eyes still seemed unfocused, causing a knot of worry to tighten in her chest.

"Ezra, you need to rest."

He let out a breathless chuckle. "That, at least, I won't argue with. Looks like we both need to take it easy." She sighed, looking around. It seemed like Tirin had fled back the way they'd come, which Adinah couldn't blame him for. She'd seen immense power in battle, but Ezra's display was probably the most intense she'd witnessed.

So intense that he'd nearly come apart. She was previously unaware that was a danger facing wizards. They usually handled much more magical energy at once than most paladins, so she'd never entertained the idea that they could be overcome. Shaking herself, she whistled for Tirin. He came trotting over, slowing down nervously as he got close.

"I understand, sweetheart," she cooed as he approached. "That was even scary for me. But we need to get back on the road, okay? Rest is over." She went to gather his saddle and the bags. "You'll just have one rider this time, so it should feel like a break."

"What do you mean, 'one rider?'" asked Ezra. "Are you really going to leave me behind?"

"Gods, no," she answered, putting Tirin's equipment and load back on. "But you're in no shape to walk." Ezra's silence was deafening. If he wasn't fighting her on it, he was completely spent.

She exhaled and winced, pressing a hand to her side where claws had raked against her armor. The armor was fine, just dented, but she could tell there was an injury underneath. She could barely recall it even happening. *I'll take a better look tonight*, she promised herself.

She looked Ezra over again, this time getting a better view of how he was faring. He was still on the ground, unsteady, his breath uneven and shoulders tense. Sweat dampened his brow despite the chill, and his fingers trembled slightly as he looked at the back of his hand where the tattoo still glowed faintly against his skin.

"You're definitely riding this time," she said firmly.

Ezra blinked at her as if coming out of a daze. "I beg your pardon?"

"You're exhausted from… whatever that was. You're riding."

"Adinah," he said, standing, "really, I assure you–" She closed the distance between them, eyes sharp, so close she could nearly feel his breath.

"Ezra. Get on the damned horse." For once, he had the good sense not to argue further. With a weary sigh, he hauled himself into the saddle, gripping the pommel with a bit more effort than usual. Adinah took Tirin's reins in hand and started forward at a steady pace. The warmth of the battle still clung to her skin, but the road ahead was long, and they had to keep moving.

As they walked, she reached into the pack at Tirin's side and pulled out her tabard, the simple crimson cloth embroidered with Ptyraxa's emblem. She hadn't worn it in a while, preferring to travel without drawing too much attention. After today, however, she decided it was necessary. She pulled it over her head, letting it settle over her armor, the sunburst on the front gleaming faintly in the fading light of the late afternoon.

Ezra, watching from atop Tirin, arched a brow. "Is this a ceremonial occasion? Should I be preparing a grand speech?"

"It will deter anyone looking for trouble," she answered simply. "There are plenty who would target a lone traveler or a pair. Fewer who would challenge a paladin."

He hummed in consideration. "Practical and intimidating. Quite fitting for you." She scowled up at him. "Ah, yes, there it is again. That signature move of yours: the scowl. Monsters of Viremor, be wary, for the most fearsome creature walks at my side."

They lapsed into a comfortable silence, the steady rhythm of Tirin's hooves filling the space between them. After a time, Ezra spoke again, voice quieter than before.

"That power of yours," he mused, "it felt warm. I didn't expect that."

Adinah glanced up at him. "Ptyraxa's power?"

He nodded. "Yes. I've never quite felt divine magic like that before. It wasn't just light or force. It was comforting, like dawn breaking after a long, cold night. Then again, I suppose that's fitting for the Morning Lord."

She considered his words. "You're right. Ptyraxa is renewal and hope. His magic feels like what He is."

Ezra was quiet for a long moment, watching the horizon. "Xernaea's magic isn't like that."

Adinah hesitated, then asked, "What does it feel like? Under normal circumstances."

He exhaled, leaning forward slightly in the saddle. "Her arcane power is pure, unshaped potential waiting to be wielded. It's like fire: alive, shifting, always crackling at the edges of your thoughts. There's an exhilaration to it, an unrelenting pulse."

She let the quiet stretch again, watching as the shadows lengthened through the hours. The first hints of Chembrus were coming into view on the horizon as they stopped for the evening, pulling off near a small gathering of trees. She helped Ezra down from the saddle. He sat by one of the larger trees, leaning back against the wide trunk while Adinah meticulously went through setting up their campsite. After, she walked over to Ezra, crouching in front of him.

"Good news, Ezra," she said, "I just need to start the fire and we'll be set for the evening." Ezra locked eyes with her, giving her a wry smile before barely flicking his fingers. His face drained of color as a fire formed in the middle of camp behind her. Adinah's smile fell.

"You were saying?" chuckled Ezra quietly. He glanced around the camp, eyeing the one tent in the clearing. "Are you really going to make me set up my own tent?"

She shook her head. "Of course not. You'll be sleeping in my tent, and I'll sleep in front of it. You're still spent, so I want to be sure you're not

30

clearly visible."

Now it was his turn to be frustrated. "But I have a tent of my own so you can be just as comfortable and out of the wind." She stared at him before making a dramatic flop onto the bedroll by the fire, clearly choosing to ignore his protests.

"Now you have to sleep in the tent," she argued, "since this one's taken." Ezra sighed dramatically, but finally moved to the tent, though he kept the flap open. He settled in quickly, sitting on his bedroll and absently rubbing his hand where the tattoo still glowed faintly.

I wonder if the fire made it worse. She tried to pull her mind away from the idea. *If it made it worse, it's his fault for doing it.* She shifted, getting ready to take off her armor, when a deep ache shot through her side, making her swear. Now that the adrenaline of the day had completely worn off, a deep throb radiated from where the creature's claws had struck her. She glanced back to Ezra, who had just finished tugging his cloak around himself in preparation for sleep.

"I need your help with something," she said, trying not to alarm him.

He cracked one eye open, peering at her in obvious reluctance. "Does it involve immediate danger or me exerting myself?"

She rolled her eyes. "No."

"Then I suppose I have no excuse, do I?" With a quiet groan, he crawled out of the tent, pushing his weariness aside. "What is it?"

Adinah hesitated. She wasn't fond of asking for help with injuries, but she knew she couldn't get a proper look on her own. Without a word, she pulled her tabard off and began fussing with the various buckles and laces and belts of her armor.

"I just got a little tap from that thing earlier. It's mostly on my side, but I can't get a good look at my back."

He looked confused. "You never said you were hurt."

She gave an exasperated sigh. "I'm not that hurt, just some bruising. Probably."

"Why not use Ptyraxa's power to fix it?" he asked. She supposed she could understand the confusion.

"I can't expect Ptyraxa to heal every papercut I get, or every scraped knee," she explained. "Even if I could, major healing is seldom as precise and perfect as people might assume, aside from what the priestesses of Rhuvena do. I keep myself from dying and the minor things are left up to nature and time."

He appeared to ponder it for a minute before giving a quick nod. "Ah, got it. Divine power for life or limb, tinctures and poultices and potions for everything else." She laughed weakly. She turned a bit to give him a better view of her back and side and lifted the bottom of her shirt.

Based on what she could see, she knew the injury would leave a terrible bruise. The skin was mottled with deep purple and angry red, the shape of claw marks just barely visible where the blow had struck hardest, starting at the middle of her ribs and sweeping toward her back. Ezra swore under his breath the moment he saw it. To her surprise, there was no teasing remark or dramatic exclamation, just quiet concern. He shifted closer, brows drawn as he reached out.

"May I?" She nodded, and his fingers were careful as they brushed along the edge of the bruise, barely skimming her skin. He groaned disapprovingly. "Nothing broken. That's fortunate. But you'll be feeling this for a while."

She exhaled. "I know." His fingers stilled for a moment. Then, slowly, she felt his gaze drift past the bruise.

Adinah knew the moment he saw them: the old scars, thin lines that crossed her abdomen and wrapped around her back. Most were faded, some barely visible unless the firelight caught them just right. Each marked an old battle, a wound taken and survived. None were particularly gruesome, but together they told a bloody story. Ezra's hand hovered on them, hesitant. His voice was quieter when he finally spoke.

"What happened to you?" Adinah didn't answer immediately. She wasn't sure how to. Her fingers tightened slightly where she rested them on her knee, her posture carefully neutral.

"There were battles," she said at last. "Some worse than others." Ezra was quiet, studying the scars with a gaze that was no longer just assessing. It was understanding. Realization.

"Adinah…" His voice was softer, no humor to be found in it. He shook his head slightly. "How many times have you come close to joining Khoravae?"

"Enough." She smirked, but it didn't quite reach her eyes. A shadow flickered across his face, but he didn't press. Instead, he let out a slow breath, withdrawing his hand and settling back.

"You're relentless, you know."

"That's one word for it."

He scoffed lightly, but there was no real amusement in it. "You shouldn't have had to endure all of that alone."

She shrugged. "I wasn't alone." She'd had Ptyraxa and the other paladins. There'd been others on the battlefield. Ezra looked as though he wanted to say something more, but in the end, he nodded. A quiet moment settled between them, the fire crackling softly as the night deepened around them. After a while, he exhaled and rubbed at his temple.

"I'd offer to heal it, but I'm afraid that is outside of my abilities. Even if I had the ability, I suspect you'd refuse out of some misguided

32

stubbornness."

"You suspect correctly."

"Of course." He shook his head with a weary smile as he leaned over to dig through his bag, retrieving a tin and handing it to her. "Then at least allow me the satisfaction of knowing you'll use this and get some rest. I can help you put it on, if you like." She felt her ears get hot. She tugged her shirt back down and took the bottle from him, letting out a shaky breath.

"I will. Thank you. I can do it myself, though." She promised herself she'd use it eventually, maybe even after he went to sleep. He didn't look convinced at her assurances, but he seemed too tired to argue. He crawled back into his tent, lying back down on the bedroll and shifting to get comfortable.

"Wake me if you need anything."

She huffed. "Go to sleep, Ezra." His chuckle was quiet as he closed his eyes. Within moments, his breathing evened out, the weight of exhaustion finally seeming to drag him under. Adinah sat by the fire a while longer, her gaze lingering on the embers as they pulsed like dying stars. Then, finally, she laid down as well, staring up at the sky.

She had endured worse. She always would. It's been a very long time, though, since anyone has actually looked at the scars, rather than just seeing them. It was a strange feeling, a warm twisting from the pit of her stomach up through her chest.

Best not to think about it, she decided, allowing the crackling fire and the rustling leaves to lull her to sleep.

Chapter 7

Ezra

Ezra woke to the scent of something sizzling over a fire and the distant hum of morning birdsong. He blinked against the early light filtering through the branches above, taking in the muted orange glow of embers and the sight of Adinah crouched beside them. Her curly hair, still tousled from sleep, framed her face as she carefully turned over what looked to be strips of meat on a flat stone near the coals.

"Ah," Ezra murmured, pushing himself up to sit. His limbs felt weighted, exhaustion still clinging to him from the day before. "Have I slept past dawn? A rare occurrence."

Adinah glanced at him, her face unreadable. "I'm sure it's not truly rare," she said as she nudged the meat with the tip of her knife, "but I'm sure you needed it in this case. Breakfast will be light. I didn't have much to work with, but I found some eggs in a hollow and caught a few snakes."

Ezra paused mid-stretch. "Snakes?"

"They cook quickly." She pulled a strip from the stone and tore off a piece, chewing with an air of disinterest. "Rations are running low. We need to reach Chembrus by nightfall. No stopping."

Ezra hummed, rubbing the sleep from his eyes. A twinge of guilt pulled at him; he still had some of the food the serving girl had given him untouched in his pack. It felt wrong to keep it to himself while she hunted and scraped together what she could. With a quiet sigh, he reached for his bag and withdrew the remaining bread and dried fruit, setting them beside the fire.

Adinah raised an eyebrow. "Where did you—"

"A gift," he said, breaking the bread and handing her half. "It seems only fair to add to our meager breakfast. Consider it my penance." She gave him a look, one that he suspected was meant to be skeptical but softened at the edges.

"Penance," she repeated, tearing off a piece of bread. "Odd concept, coming from you."

He chuckled, something thoughtful in the sound. "Believe me, I'm aware."

They ate in silence, the morning air brisk against their skin as the fire crackled between them. Once finished, Adinah stood and pulled on her dented armor piece by piece, securing the straps with practiced ease. She broke down the camp, packing things carefully back into their bags. Turning to Tirin, she readied and saddled the warhorse with deft hands and tied on the bags before motioning for Ezra to climb up behind her.

He hesitated. "Are we certain about this arrangement?"

She shot him a look. "You're still exhausted. I'm not letting you collapse in the middle of the road."

He sighed, climbing into the saddle behind her. "You wound me with your concern."

"Good. Be glad that's the only way I'm wounding you." With a nudge to Tirin's sides, they set off, the rhythmic gait of his strides steadying as they rejoined the road. The morning passed in relative quiet, broken only by the rustling of wind through trees. After a time, Ezra leaned slightly forward, resting a careful hand on the back of the saddle.

"May I ask about them?"

Adinah tilted her head slightly. "Ask about what?"

"The scars."

She was quiet for a long moment before answering. "Which ones?" He could tell she wasn't stalling for once, simply asking for clarification. Ezra exhaled, glancing down at where her armor covered what he'd glimpsed the night before.

"The ones on your abdomen. I assume they came from battle." She nodded. He paused, giving her space to decide whether to elaborate.

"We were clearing a ghoul nest from an old shrine," she said after a moment. "They had been picking off travelers, dragging them back there to feed. It wasn't a small nest, either; a dozen of us went in with just swords, shields, and prayers."

He could picture it as she spoke: armored figures stepping into the crumbling remnants of a once-sacred space, the oppressive stench of undeath thick in the air. He had read of such battles, but hearing her tell it, steady and sure, made it feel real in a way books never could.

"The fight was brutal," she continued. "Ghouls are fast and they don't tire. We cut through them as best we could, but there were too many." Her voice remained even, but he could hear the weight behind it. "I took a few hits to the side when I pulled another paladin out of harm's way. Being young and dumb, I didn't wear as much armor then. We won in the end, of course. Cleansed the shrine, burned the bodies."

Ezra noted the way her jaw tensed. "But?"

"We lost someone," she said quietly. "One of ours. He was younger than me, had just taken up the Oath. He thought he could hold the line alone. By the time we reached him, it was too late."

Ezra's grip on the saddle tightened slightly. "A friend?"

"A brother-in-arms. Good-hearted, reckless. Deserved better." She exhaled, steady but measured. "I became a paladin to save people. I didn't save him." There was no blame in her voice, no self-pity, only the quiet weight of loss.

"Who was he?"

She paused. "What do you mean?"

"Your friend, the other paladin. Who was he?"

She took a deep, slightly shaky breath. "Eryn Vale. Good man." The ensuing silence suggested she was done with the topic.

Still, he pressed. "You are good to remember him. He was lucky to serve with you." She only let out a soft hum of acknowledgement.

Ezra found himself studying her more closely. She'd turned her head slightly to talk to him, so he was better able to see the set of her jaw, the way her lips pressed together, the way her curly hair bounced slightly as Tirin walked. He had noticed these things before, he realized, but now they held his attention in a different way. The way the armor caught the light, how it cast a soft glow on her tawny skin. The depth of expression in her eyes, even when she tried to mask it.

He steadied himself, forcing his gaze away. It had been too long since he had brought someone to bed. That must have been the reason for this awareness. He let out a slow breath, shifting his thoughts elsewhere.

Xernaea. A pang of longing struck him, sharp and familiar, as magic buzzed at his fingertips.

"You were never meant to be mine forever," came the voice from his memory. Her voice had been gentle that day, tinged with something like sorrow. *"You were always good. I had hoped you would be great."* He thought of Her, the memory of Her presence, the way Her power had once felt warm in his veins. Guilt soon followed. He frowned, unsettled.

The road stretched on long into the afternoon, dust rising in soft plumes beneath Tirin's steady pace. Ezra's hands lightly rested on the back of the saddle and he watched the landscape shift from wild, untamed brush into the cultivated outskirts of Chembrus. The ride had been uneventful; comfortably so, if he dared to admit it.

By the time they crested the last hill and saw the town sprawled below them, the sun had long since set, leaving the sky awash in deep blues and purples. Lanterns flickered along the main road, casting warm pools of light onto the dirt streets. A sense of weariness settled in Ezra's bones at the sight.

"Well," he exhaled, "we're back in civilization." Adinah made a small sound of agreement, guiding Tirin down the road into the heart of town. It was quiet at this hour, the day's labor concluded, and those not already in their homes had sought refuge in the few visible taverns. They rode past darkened storefronts and shuttered houses before stopping in front of a modest inn, its sign swaying gently in the evening breeze.

"The Tired Fox," he read aloud, dismounting. "Fitting." Adinah swung down from the saddle, patting Tirin's side before leading him toward the small stable attached to the inn.

"I'll see to him."

"And I'll secure us a room," he replied. Inside, the inn was warm, the air thick with the scent of burning wood and the remnants of hearty meals. A handful of patrons sat scattered at tables, low murmurs of conversation filling the space. The innkeeper–Thorman, by the nameplate on the counter– a stout man with greying hair, looked up from wiping down the counter as Ezra approached.

"Looking for a room?"

"For two, if you have it."

Thorman grimaced. "Only got one left, I'm afraid. Small place, fills up quick. Only one bed in there, too."

Ezra considered this, then shrugged. "We'll take it." Adinah entered just as he slid a few gold coins onto the counter.

She stopped short, eyes narrowing. "That much?"

Ezra arched a brow. "Hardly a dent in my reserves."

Adinah gave him a long look, as though reevaluating him entirely. "How much gold do you have?"

"Enough," he smirked. Her lips pressed together, but she didn't argue. Instead, she took the offered key, glancing toward the staircase.

"We should turn in." She hesitated, then added, "You can take the bed. The floor's better for my back anyway." Ezra sighed dramatically. He knew there was no point in arguing about sleeping arrangements, but he at least wanted to celebrate not dying on the road with her.

"Not even a toast to our successful journey?"

She frowned. "We still have work to do."

"Yes, but surely even you can see the merits of a quiet moment of indulgence." He softened his tone, adopting something more persuasive. "One glass of wine, a bite to eat, and then I shall trouble you no further."

Adinah stared at him for a long moment before exhaling in exasperation. "Fine. One glass, a small bite. Then straight to bed."

They sat near the fireplace, the glow casting flickering light against the wooden walls. Ezra retrieved a plate of warm bread and a modest selection

37

of cheese, sitting it on the small table between them. Making a second trip to the bar, he procured a decent bottle, filling two glasses with a deep red wine before raising his own.

"To the road behind and the road ahead," he said, raising his glass.

Adinah clinked her glass against his with little ceremony and took a measured sip. She did not seem particularly moved by it, but she did not complain either. Instead, she reached for a piece of bread, tearing off a bite and chewing thoughtfully.

"Better than hardtack," she admitted begrudgingly. He laughed softly as she quickly ate her portion of the cheese and bread.

She'd probably rather have hardtack than admit to enjoying something as simple as bread, cheese, and wine. She certainly was an odd creature, so committed to austerity that it made her dry humor almost jarring by comparison. True to her word, she drank the single glass, then rose.

"Goodnight, Ezra." She hesitated before reaching for the last piece of bread, breaking it in half, and passing part of it to him. It was a simple, almost absent gesture, but he accepted it with a small smile.

"Goodnight, Adinah."

She disappeared upstairs, absently nibbling on the bread as she went, while he moved to the bar to nurse another drink. One became two, then three. The warmth of the wine softened the edges of his exhaustion, dulling the ache in his limbs. It had been too long since he'd allowed himself this kind of leisure. Suddenly, a woman slid onto the stool beside him, her presence easy and confident. She was curvaceous and beautiful, dark-eyed with a teasing smile as she swirled her own drink in her hand.

"Haven't seen you around here before."

"Passing through," Ezra replied, offering his most charming smile.

"Shame. I do enjoy good company." Her fingers traced the rim of her glass. "And you seem like a man in need of some."

There was no mistaking her intent. She leaned in slightly, the scent of something floral clinging to her. He had thought about this—about taking someone to bed again, about losing himself in the warmth and simplicity of another's touch. He should want this, but as he met her gaze and her fingers brushed his sleeve, he felt only the hollow weight of expectation, not desire.

He wasn't interested.

Strangely, his thoughts drifted elsewhere: to the woman who had left the bar earlier, who had turned down a second drink in favor of rest, who had stubbornly insisted on sleeping on the floor. He imagined her upstairs, curled in her makeshift bed, armor neatly set aside, her sword within reach.

He frowned, the realization settling uneasily in his chest. He missed her presence. Not in the way he missed Caedmon–no, this was different. Simpler, yet no less perplexing.

The woman ran a finger along his sleeve. "What do you say?"

Ezra exhaled, setting his glass down. "I say I must regretfully decline."

She gave him a slow, assessing look before laughing softly. "Your loss."

He nodded, reaching for his coin purse and paying their tab before making his way upstairs. The alcohol made the steps feel heavier beneath his boots, his mind pleasantly hazy but not so far gone that he wasn't aware of his surroundings. Their room was at the end of a short hall. Testing the knob, Ezra was grateful to find it unlocked.

Their room was small but comfortable. Adinah lay curled on the floor, her bedroll tucked around her, breathing slow and even. For a moment, he simply stood there, taking in the sight. She looked peaceful, almost younger, somehow, in sleep. The stubborn set of her brow had eased, the sharp edges of her expression softened. Something in him twisted at the sight.

He hesitated before stepping forward, kneeling beside her. Carefully, gently, he gathered her into his arms. She didn't stir, lost to whatever realm her dreams carried her to. He settled her onto the bed, tucking the blankets around her, lingering just long enough to brush a stray curl from her face.

Foolish, he thought. *Sentimental nonsense, brought on by wine and exhaustion.*

Shaking off the strange weight in his chest, he retreated to the floor, settling into the space she had claimed before. The blankets were thin, the boards hard against his back, and his thoughts came muddled and tangled with images of a woman who, against all reason, had begun to occupy his mind more than he cared to admit. With a long sigh, he drifted to sleep.

Chapter 8

Ezra

The dream was always the same.

A swirl of stars, shifting in a cosmic dance, their brilliance pulsing in time with his heartbeat. Power flooded through him, too much and never enough, a song he once knew by heart now turned discordant and cruel. Then came the fracture: light shattering into darkness, the warmth of Xernaea's presence ripped away as if the universe itself had turned against him. He reached out, desperate and pleading, but She was already gone, and in Her absence there was only the howling void.

The surge of magic within him twisted, corrupted and uncontrolled. Fire roared up his arms, spiraling into destruction. He screamed, but the sound was drowned beneath the crash of something immense and final. Arcane energy curled away from him, recoiling like a wounded beast, and then he was falling–

Ezra woke with a gasp, heart hammering, lungs aching as if he'd truly been plummeting through empty space. A hand on his shoulder startled him further, grounding him in the present. He blinked rapidly, trying to focus on the face before him.

Adinah.

She was kneeling beside the bedroll, silhouetted by the morning sun streaming through the window behind her. For a moment, his sleep-addled mind saw a halo of light, as if she were some celestial thing made of warmth and golden edges. He swallowed hard and turned his head away.

"Just a nightmare," he said, voice rough from sleep. Her eyes remained steady on him, assessing.

"That wasn't just any nightmare."

Ezra forced a lopsided smile. "You must be very familiar with my sleeping habits, then."

She didn't return his attempt at levity. "What I'm very familiar with is

40

having nightmares," she said, crossing her arms. "If we're going to travel together, I need to trust you. And that means knowing you'll tell me when something is wrong."

His fingers curled against the blanket, then slowly relaxed. "It's nothing to worry about," he said after a pause. "Just memories. A difficult time in my life that I must relive every now and then."

She studied him a moment before exhaling sharply through her nose. "Fine," she said, standing. "Get up. We need food before we start asking around."

"Asking around?" He realized she was already dressed, even her armor and tabard.

"About the ruins. You know, the whole story with Elidane? The reason we wandered this way?" She worked to tidy the room.

Ezra dragged himself out of bed with a groan, only to regret it as a dull ache settled behind his eyes. By the time they reached the main floor of the inn, he was keenly aware of his mild hangover, though he did his best to ignore it. He ordered breakfast–bread, cheese, and a few eggs–while Adinah stepped outside to care for Tirin. When she returned, they ate quickly and set out into Chembrus.

The town was small but busy, with merchants setting up their stalls and farmers moving about their daily work. Their first stop was a general shrine, a modest building that served as the spiritual center for the town. Small statues of the gods stood sentinel on either side of the walkway to the entrance, the offering plates at their feet littered with trinkets, coins, and flowers. Inside, a priestess in simple robes greeted them with a warm, if tired, smile.

"Travelers? And seeking knowledge, no less? A rare kind of visitor," she said, folding her hands before her. "How may the gods guide you?"

"We're looking for information about Elidane Starcrest, High Paladin of Ptyraxa," Ezra said. "Any records, any myths–whatever you have." The priestess hummed in thought, moving toward a small wooden cabinet lined with brittle parchment and bound tomes.

"Elidane is a name seldom spoken in these parts. Most who remember it think of a fringe group of Ptyraxites, long faded. There are vague stories, whispers of a time when a radiant fire lit the path of the devoted. But if you are seeking ruins, that is another matter." Adinah exchanged a glance with Ezra before stepping forward.

"What can you tell us about them?" she asked.

"Not much, I'm afraid. This town was built upon the bones of many before it. Some old foundations still lie in the hills and valleys beyond Chembrus, but I have nothing concrete to offer you. Only the lingering faith of those who once prayed here." She pulled a delicate scrap of parchment from a nearby pile, holding it out. "This is the only record I have of an old symbol linked to that name. It is similar to that of Ptyraxa, so I'm not certain it would be of any use."

Ezra accepted it, his brow furrowing as he studied the faded ink. He frowned. Time and wear had rendered the shape almost entirely unrecognizable, much less as one of Ptyraxa. His eyes flicked over to Adinah who seemed equally unimpressed. In an effort to remain polite, he offered the priestess a warm smile and slight bow.

"Thank you," he said, tucking the parchment safely away in his satchel before bidding her farewell. They needed more.

A hours-long visit to the town's aging, and particularly chatty, historian proved similarly fruitless, though the elderly man did point them toward an old stoneworker named Garrun who had spent years cataloging carvings in the region. When they found the craftsman, he was working on a modest restoration project, chiseling away at an old monument.

"Looking for ruins, are you?" the stoneworker mused, brushing dust from his hands. "Plenty of them scattered across the Glade, but most are just old watchtowers or abandoned waypoints."

"We're searching for something tied to High Paladin Elidane Starcrest, a champion of Ptyraxa," Adinah said. "Does that name mean anything to you?"

The man frowned. "Not much. But–hold on." He set down his chisel and rummaged through a collection of sketches and old notes. Eventually, he pulled out a worn parchment. "Found this rubbing off an old relief years ago. Never could make much of it. Unsure if it means anything to you."

Ezra took the parchment, eyes scanning the image. At first glance, it seemed to depict a withered tree standing against a rising sun, but something about the shape nagged at him. He turned it slightly, and realization struck like a spell finding purchase.

It wasn't a tree. It was a flame: a stylized, ancient depiction of a sunburst wreathed in fire, worn with time and weather until its true shape had become obscured. He glanced at Adinah, hearing her breath catch. Her expression was unreadable, but he could see a sharp glint of realization in her eyes.

"This carving. Where did you find it?" she asked, voice carefully even.

The stoneworker shrugged. "A couple days' ride southeast of here near some old ruins. Didn't think much of it at the time."

Adinah nodded. "That's our lead," she sighed, seemingly weary of interaction.

They thanked the craftsman and made their way back to The Tired Fox. By the time they returned, the smell of warm spices, baked apples, and fresh bread filled the inn. The steady crackle of a hearth fire blended with the comforting clatter of kitchen work. A pot of hearty soup simmered nearby while a spit turned slowly over the fire, roasting a thick cut of meat, its juices hissing as they dripped onto the embers below. The scent wrapped around them like a promise of warmth and comfort after a long day's search.

Thorman sat a fresh tray of apple tarts onto the counter, their golden crusts glistening in the afternoon light. Ezra caught the way Adinah's eyes lingered on them, the brief flicker of interest that crossed her face before she schooled her expression into something more neutral.

"I could get us some," he offered lightly. "It's no trouble, and it's close to dinner anyway."

She shook her head, almost too quickly. "I'm fine." He made a mental note.

It's just an apple tart, he thought. *No reason she shouldn't have one. Or even a tray of them.* He wondered why she seemed so set on denying herself simple joys.

"Go sit down," he said, inclining his head towards the scattered tables. "You paladins may be able to travel for days on the blessings of your gods alone, but I am only a man." She rolled her eyes, but didn't argue. She took a spot along the back wall near the fireplace, back straight. He sighed as he turned to the innkeeper, ordering them each a drink and a bit of food before tossing a few coins on the counter.

The man passed him two mugs of warm cider and plates of bread, vegetables, and meat. Proper meals. Ezra carried them to Adinah, placing them down carefully before taking his seat. She eyed the mug warily.

"It's just cider," he said, voice sounding a bit injured. *Am I really such a scoundrel that she can't trust a mug of drink?* It felt awkward to let silence hang between them, especially if he was going to keep accidentally looking at her.

Maybe I am that big of a scoundrel.

He swirled his mug in his hand, watching the liquid move against the ceramic. He spent a moment grasping at conversation topics before finally settling on what he knew best.

"Magic isn't just power," he started quietly, tracing a finger along the rim. "It's art. It's intention. The power of Xernaea is, in itself, alive in its own way. If you don't treat it with care, it will recoil from you."

Adinah leaned back slightly, her eyes on him rather than her plate. "You must treat it well," she mused. "It responds so quickly and well to you."

His breath left him in a sharp exhale, a wry smile ghosting his lips. "Yes, but you should have seen me a few years ago." She gave him a quizzical look. "I used to be much more adept. I've just made some mistakes." She nodded apprehensively, cutting another bite of food. Ezra was grateful she didn't press the issue.

"I don't think magic, at least the kind from Ptyraxa, is art. Not entirely. To me, it's… well, my divine magic is a means to an end. A tool to survive. We are only given so much power to draw from, so I must decide carefully about how to use it. Maybe that makes me pragmatic, or maybe I'm just narrow-minded."

"Not narrow-minded. Just different." Ezra studied her, taking in the thoughtful set of her jaw, the flicker of something behind her eyes. He took a bite of his own meal, savoring the warmth of it before continuing. "So, what would you do with it, if you could wield it without limit? No constraints. No risk."

She was silent for a long moment, gaze dropping to her hands. "I don't know," she admitted. "I've spent so long thinking about what I must do with what I have, I've never let myself consider what I would do if there were no weight attached to it."

He hummed, stabbing a piece of roasted vegetable with his fork. "Regret is often tied to such things. The choices we made because we felt we had no others."

"Is that what you regret? That you did something because you felt you had no choice?"

He hesitated for a heartbeat, then another. "No." His voice was quieter now. "I regret that I did have a choice, and I made the wrong one." She didn't press him, but she was listening. He could feel it in the way she held herself, attentive and braced, as though she expected something more. And maybe, he considered, she deserved more than vague confessions and half-truths. He set the mug down and leaned forward, resting his elbows on the table.

44

Chapter 9

Ezra

"I thought I could fix everything," he continued, "if I just had enough power. I convinced myself it was noble. Necessary, even. But really, it was selfish. I wanted to prove I was worthy of something–or someone–who never asked that of me." He let out a dry chuckle. "I justified every step deeper into ruin. Told myself I was walking a path of sacrifice to help others, when really, I was chasing a mirage of my own making. By the time I realized it, the damage was already done."

A muscle in Adinah's jaw twitched. She looked away, fingers curling against her thigh. "I, too, regret not stopping something I should have. And I can't undo it." The words felt like stone, heavy and immovable.

Ezra tilted his head. "Then why not tell me what it was?"

"Because you can't fix it either."

"I'm aware," he said evenly. "That doesn't mean I can't listen."

She let out a slow breath, then, after a long pause, said, "There was a village. Years ago, this was. I was young, and I thought I knew what I was doing. I thought I could protect them." Her throat worked around the words. "I was wrong." Ezra waited.

"A warband came through," she continued. "Slaughtered half the town before I could even reach them. I–" She swallowed hard. "I hesitated. And in that hesitation, people died. People who shouldn't have. And the ones who survived, they didn't thank me for saving them. They looked at me like I was no better than the ones who'd done it. Like I should have been able to do more. And they were right."

He frowned, setting his fork down. "Do you truly believe you were to blame for that?"

She hesitated. "Does it matter? I can't change it."

"No. But it matters if you let it define you." She let out another sharp exhale, something like frustration flickering behind her eyes.

"Are you speaking from experience?"

"I'm speaking as someone who knows how easily regret turns into self-destruction." He watched her carefully. "You carry this like a debt that can never be repaid. Debts like that have a way of turning into shackles. If you don't let yourself move forward, then those people–the ones you wanted to protect–what did their loss mean?"

Her fingers tightened into a fist. "I'm moving forward."

He huffed softly. "Are you?" She opened her mouth, then closed it again, jaw tight. The silence stretched. Then, with deliberate slowness, Ezra pushed back his chair and stood. "Come with me."

She narrowed her eyes. "Why?"

"You need to do something other than sit here and let your thoughts eat you alive. Come on." He gestured toward the door. "A bit of swordwork might do you some good."

"Oh, and you're going to spar with me, are you?"

"Hardly," he smirked. "But I am going to watch you put that brooding energy to better use."

She snorted but stood, following him outside. The air was crisp, the sky painted in hues of deep blue and fading gold. Ezra stepped aside, gesturing toward the open space of a clearing near the stable.

"Go on."

Adinah rolled her eyes but drew her sword, beginning a slow, methodical series of movements. He watched her relax into it, her eyes glazed over with a far away look. Her form was practiced, precise–but then, her shoulder faltered. Just a fraction. Just enough.

He frowned. "You're still injured."

"I'm fine."

"You're stubborn."

"That too."

He crossed his arms. "We should stay another day, at least. Maybe two."

"We should keep moving. We're so much closer!"

"Your shoulder disagrees. Besides, the ruins will still be there and ruined in a day or two."

She turned to face him fully. "Ezra, I appreciate the concern, but we don't have time to waste."

He exhaled through his nose. He knew she wouldn't concede, not openly. And he also knew she needed the rest more than she'd admit. *She only had half a night in the bed, anyway, after a night of sleeping outdoors while I had the warmth of my tent. Just one more night.* Instead of arguing further, he sighed and pinched the bridge of his nose.

"Fine. You win. But–" He glanced away, just briefly, adding with a careful measure of feigned reluctance, "I could use another day myself."

Adinah blinked, the sharpness in her gaze shifting into something closer to surprise. "You?"

He nodded solemnly. "Yes. Dreadful, I know. But magic takes its toll, and I'd rather not push myself back to exhaustion." She considered him, suspicion flickering just behind her eyes.

But then, slowly, she relented. "One more day, then. But that's it."

"Naturally." He smiled, just slightly. "I'd hate to be accused of slowing you down."

She huffed, sheathing her sword. "You already are."

"And yet, you're still here."

She leveled him with a burning look. "Somehow, yes, I am still here."

He flashed her a smile. "Ah, well," he said, determined to change topics, "since we're staying another night, let's go back up and get things sorted." She eyed him suspiciously but followed him back into The Tired Fox. He went up to the innkeeper again, inclining his head toward the stairs as he slid payment for another two nights across the counter.

"Two more nights," he said so quietly only he and the innkeeper could hear, "assuming you haven't already resold it." The old man flashed a crooked smile and tilted his head toward the stairs as he pocketed the gold. Ezra and Adinah headed up the stairs, and he felt her eyes burning into his back as he led the way. Once in the room, she shed most of her armor, leaving her mail shirt and gambeson. She caught him eyeing it and shook her head.

"Don't start," she warned.

He sighed theatrically. "Really? No proper relaxation?"

"This is relaxed," she countered, flopping down to sit on the bed as she stretched, rolling her shoulders back. It occurred to him that she rolled them so often, there shouldn't be any room for tension left in them.

"Well, we'll see about that." He made sure his bedroll was laid out– because of course he planned to take the floor again–and that his bags were secured before walking back to the door.

"Where are you going?"

His hand was already on the knob as he cast a playful smile over his shoulder at her. "To relax. You're welcome to join me, if you like."

She made a face as if she'd just tasted something sour. "Like you did last night? What are you celebrating tonight?"

"Yes, another few drinks. As for celebrating? Rest. And not dying. Both very beloved pastimes of mine." He heard her slide off the bed as he stepped out of the room.

"I'm just going to make sure you don't get into trouble," she said, as if rationalizing it to herself rather than to him.

Back downstairs, the tables were beginning to fill up, the sound of

47

laughter and conversation bouncing off the wooden walls. Adinah seemed more nervous in the crowd now, as if she was no longer used to being seen without the rest of her armor. They made their way to two of the few seats left at the bar, the innkeeper practically running to keep the patrons fed and drunk.

"Just for tonight," he said, leaning down to talk into her ear, "let's indulge–drinks, revelry, the whole experience."

Her nose wrinkled slightly. "I'm not really a drinker."

Ezra smirked. "Trust me, we'll go drink for drink. After all, your constitution as a paladin is so much better than mine. You've spent your life enduring hardship in the wild. I, on the other hand, spent mine in libraries. Surely you're not worried about being bested by a mere wizard?"

Adinah rolled her eyes. "That's ridiculous."

"Very," he agreed. "Now come on."

She was hesitant, but soon, the first drink was in her hands. And then another. By the time they'd had two, she stopped commenting on the taste. By the third, she was laughing more freely, her shoulders no longer stiff with awareness.

Ezra found himself watching her. The way her curls fell into her face when she laughed, the way she pushed them away with a hand but they tumbled right back down. The light in her eyes when she let herself smile without thinking. She had a habit of glancing down at her cup before taking a sip, her lips parting slightly before the rim met them. And then there was the way she leaned forward when speaking: earnest, engaged, and unguarded in a way he hadn't quite seen before.

He blinked and looked away, a strange warmth coiling in his chest. It wasn't–well, it wasn't anything. Just an appreciation of beauty, of familiarity, and of comfort. He glanced around at other patrons. There were plenty of beautiful women in the room, some even throwing glances his way. But none of them held his attention.

None of them were her.

He swallowed, forcing himself to focus on his drink, but even the ale couldn't drown the feeling tightening in his ribs. A realization hovered just at the edges of his thoughts, unspoken and uncertain. He wasn't ready to name it yet. Not now. Still, his gaze drifted back to her, drawn like a moth to light.

48

Chapter 10

Adinah

The first drink warmed her from the inside out, its heat settling in her belly and spreading in slow, lazy waves. The second smoothed the edges of her thoughts, made her laugh just a little easier, and let the world blur into something softer. By the time she finished the third, her limbs felt loose, her tongue quick and clever, and she was comfortably sunk into the easy revelry of the inn. Not beyond reason, certainly not to the point of losing herself, but she was delightfully unburdened.

Adinah was telling a particularly harrowing tale of facing down a troll outside of Ravander's Pass, its fetid breath thick with the stench of rot and its claws the size of shortswords. She made a grand motion, mimicking the arc of her blade through the air, and the gathered patrons gasped, then roared with laughter when she described the way the beast had tripped over its own foot in an almost comedic display.

The tavern was alive with mirth, a chorus of chuckles and sloshing drinks, but amidst it all, she felt the weight of a gaze.

Her eyes flicked over the crowd, and there he was: Ezra, nearly right beside her, watching her intently. His drink sat forgotten in his hands, and though the expression on his face was carefully schooled, there was something in his eyes she couldn't quite place. *Curious.* She finished her story to the sound of clapping and cheers, then, emboldened by the drink and the heady warmth of the room, lifted a hand in invitation.

"Ezra, let's go sit over by the fire again. It's getting a bit cold with the door opening so often." He hesitated only a moment before rising with her, crossing the now-thinning crowd to settle into the seat opposite hers at the small table near the fire. The flames cast long shadows across his face, highlighting the sharp planes of his cheekbones, the curve of his mouth. He studied her, the corners of his lips twitching up with the threat of a smile.

"You're quite the storyteller," he mused, taking a sip of his drink.

She smirked. "You don't do too bad yourself. Though I notice yours tend to be a bit more… scholarly."

"Ah," he sighed theatrically, "and yours tend to be more about flinging yourself into mortal peril without a second thought."

Adinah chuckled, tilting her head as she regarded him. "You say that like you don't do the same. Who was it that nearly unraveled their own existence trying to pull off some grand evocation?"

Ezra pressed a hand to his chest as if wounded. "It's not like that was planned! Besides, it saved both of us, so I really consider it to be for the best."

She snorted. "Somehow, I don't think 'sling spells and hope for the best' is what the arcane had in mind. Maybe I should be the one to save us both."

His eyes gleamed with amusement. "If you keep throwing yourself in harm's way for me, I may have to start thinking you like me." The words were light, teasing, but something in her stomach twisted all the same. Her cheeks warmed—not from the fire or the alcohol, but from a far more disconcerting realization.

Do I like him?

She'd never truly considered it before, but now that the thought had lodged itself in her mind, it was impossible to ignore. He was handsome, undeniably so. He was sharp-featured and keen-eyed with a voice that curled around words like poetry. A bit of arrogance, of course, but it was tempered with warmth. He'd been a reliable companion on the road so far, keeping the trip light and enjoyable despite the weight of her mission.

She scoffed, shoving the thought away. It was just the drink making her thoughts wander. Nothing more. *A good indication that I've been ignoring certain needs a bit too long.*

Ezra ordered and downed his fourth drink, officially overtaking her in their "drink for drink" competition. He exhaled, slow and considering, nearly swaying in his seat. Then, slowly, he leaned forward just slightly, his voice a murmur only the two of them could hear.

"You know, Adinah, I've seen you looking at me more than once. Makes me wonder if I should just kiss you already."

Her breath hitched. He was close enough already that she could feel the heat of him, even from across the table, and smell the scent of wine lingering on his breath. She didn't move—didn't dare to—even as he moved closer to her, close enough that his lips ghosted just shy of hers as he leaned in.

"Tell me to stop," he murmured, voice quiet but heady with desire.

Her thoughts went hazy and a gnawing voice at the back of her mind suggested it wasn't just from the alcohol. For a moment, the temptation to close the distance gripped her, a pull low in her belly that had nothing to do with drink and everything to do with the way he looked at her like she was something to be discovered and unraveled. She shoved the feeling away, steeling herself as she leaned back.

"You're far too drunk," she said, voice steadier than she felt. "Let's get you into bed." He let out a long, plaintive sigh before leaning back, devilish grin still firmly in place. He stood, offering her his arm before they left for their room.

He didn't resist as she helped him up the stairs, though he was heavier than he looked. She managed to get him into the door of the room, rolling him onto the bed with a huff.

"Sleep," she ordered, reaching for her bedroll.

Ezra groaned, turning on his side. "You should take the bed."

She arched a brow. "You're very drunk, Ezra. Your hangover tomorrow will already be something out of the hells. You might as well enjoy the bed."

"If I'm sleeping on the bed, so are you."

She blinked. "Excuse me?"

He cracked one eye open. "Either you take the bed and I sleep on the floor, or we're both sleeping in the bed. Your choice. But you are sleeping in the bed."

She frowned, realizing that in his current state, there was no arguing with him. In a moment of either brilliance or sheer stupidity, she unrolled another bedroll onto the floor.

"Fine. If we can't agree, neither of us get the bed." Ezra gave her a sour expression before rolling off the bed, clearly willing to sacrifice comfort to win an argument. Each of them, equally stubborn, curled up on their respective bedrolls and let the stupor of wine pull them down into sleep.

In the morning, she woke groggy and aching, the floor doing little to spare her from the consequences of the previous night's indulgence. They trudged downstairs for breakfast where Thorman greeted them with a wry smile.

"Slept well, did you?" he asked, eyes twinkling with something unsaid.

Adinah blinked. "Uh–yes?"

The innkeeper chuckled. "You make a good pair."

Her stomach twisted. "Oh–we're not–" She gestured vaguely between herself and Ezra. "We're just traveling together. Not a couple. No attraction or anything."

She thought she saw Ezra's smile falter for just a fraction of a second before he started looking at a few pastries on the counter, his expression smoothing over. The innkeeper nodded, but the look on his face suggested he didn't believe a word of it.

She and Ezra grabbed a few of the remaining pastries on the counter and a bowl of oatmeal each. He slid a few silver across the counter, but the coins were immediately passed back.

"No, sir, I can't take this," the old man said, sliding the coins back to Ezra. "You've been very generous, but you've already overpaid." Adinah was, admittedly, shocked. Ezra didn't seem the kind to overpay. She wondered at first if it was a mistake, but he just waved a dismissive hand.

"Your room has kept us from needing to camp outside of town," he said, flashing a particularly disarming smile. "And it can't be easy running a business like this. You've kept us fed and, at least in my case, plenty drunk when the time called for it. You deserve to pocket any extra, and I have plenty to spare."

The old man looked at Ezra for a long moment, clearly debating whether to take him up on the offer, before finally nodding. "Still, the breakfast is free this morning."

Ezra hesitated before pushing the silver back across the counter. "Then take this to take care of our horse," he said, clearly not giving in. "The white one, grey spots. Tirin. Absolute sweetheart."

The innkeeper took the silver, pocketing it. "I'll go out and give him some extra food. Some nice oats and some vegetables." Adinah couldn't help but smile slightly. She always appreciated gestures of kindness to horses and those who worked to support a paladin's cause. A flutter in her chest arose when he'd called Tirin a sweetheart, but she pushed the feeling down. *That's nothing special. That's the bare minimum.*

"Excuse me," Adinah said to the innkeeper as he went back to work, "just one more thing."

"Yes?" He seemed almost irritated at this point, clearly something better to do on his mind.

"I need a place to find a map of the region. Something a bit more detailed than the usual map for travelers and traders."

The old man raised an inquisitive brow. "Well, then, there's a shop around the corner that can take care of you. Luther's store. He tends to carry maps from more specialty cartographers in the region."

She nodded. "Perfect. I'll visit him then. I sincerely appreciate it." She gave a short nod. "May dawn's light keep you." The innkeeper nodded back before, rather pointedly, turning back to his work as if to discourage further discussion.

Luther's shop was easy to find, his stock unremarkable other than the map collection. Behind the counter were some of the most ornate maps Adinah had ever seen. Some were grouped in fully bound volumes while others were individually folded. Luther recommended a particular map, spreading it out on the table in front of them. It wasn't as extravagant as many of the others, but it did include markings of various ruins and fallen temples. Adinah was quick to pay and thank him, practically dragging Ezra behind her toward the stoneworker.

They found Garrun where they'd left him the day before: bent over his workbench, sleeves rolled high, grey-streaked arms coated in limestone dust. At their approach, he set aside his hammer and leaned back, rubbing grit from his beard.

"Did your companion forget something?" he asked.

Tilting her head, she asked, "Pardon?"

Garrun rocked back on his heels, hands on his hips. "I figured if one of the Ptyraxites came back, it was because one of you lost something. I didn't notice anything, but I haven't been looking."

Her pulse quickened, but she forced herself to remain still, schooling her expression into something impassive. Garrun was watching her with narrowed eyes, clearly unimpressed with the idea of repeating himself.

"'One of?' You met another Ptyraxite?" she asked, her tone light and measured. "When?"

The man huffed, arms crossing over his chest. "Earlier this morning. Before sunrise. That's why I figured you two were working together." Adinah exchanged a glance with Ezra. He, too, looked tense now, his fingers twitching near the edge of his robes. There weren't many devoted to Ptyraxa operating in this region, at least none that she knew of. The idea that another was sniffing around and asking the same questions didn't sit well with her either.

"Did they give a name?" she pressed, offering the stonemason an easy smile, as if this were nothing more than idle curiosity.

He shook his head. "Didn't say, and I didn't ask. Seemed like the righteous sort. You know: clean-cut, serious, the kind that's got an opinion about everything." He gave her a pointed once-over. "Bit like you, actually."

Adinah wasn't sure whether to take that as a compliment or as an insult, but she let it pass. "What did they ask you?"

"Same as you, mostly," he said, rubbing a hand over his beard. "About the stonework in the old temple ruins southeast of town. How long it's been there, if anything odd's been going on. Told him the same thing I told you. It's just old with that weird symbol I showed you yesterday. It's not right, if you ask me."

Ezra leaned in slightly, curiosity flashing in his eyes. "And did he seem concerned by that?"

The stoneworker shrugged. "Didn't say much after that. Just nodded, thanked me, and left. Headed back toward town, far as I could tell."

She considered this, turning it over in her mind like a whetstone against steel. Whoever this was, he'd gotten an early start, far earlier than she and Ezra had. That meant he was either local and already in place, or he had something pressing him to move quickly. Neither of the options gave her much comfort.

"And the ruins?" she asked. "Where exactly are they?" She offered Garrun her map. With a piece of charcoal, he marked a rough spot southeast of town.

"About three days' foot travel that way. Not much left standing, but it won't look much different from any of the other ruins out there. Just a few piles of old stone."

She nodded and tucked the map away. "Thanks for your time."

He grunted. "Just don't come asking a third time. Got work to do."

They left him to his chiseling, stepping back onto the narrow, sun-dappled street. It was nearly noon now and the town had come alive, the smells of lunchtime wafting through the air with the sound of carts rolling over dirt and uneven cobblestones. Merchants called out their wares, and laughter rang from somewhere near the well. Despite the cheerful energy of the town, a thread of unease wound itself through her spine, settling deep.

"Thoughts?" Ezra asked, his voice lower now, quiet enough that only she would hear.

She hesitated, then exhaled slowly. "Someone else is looking."

"Maybe Ptyraxa sent them as well," Ezra offered.

That hit a nerve. She had been chosen for this. Hadn't she? The dreams had guided her here. Well, they'd guided her to the beginning of the search. The urgency had filled her bones, but now she hadn't had the dream in a few days.

Is that why another has come? A flicker of panic sparked in her chest. *Have I failed already? Has Ptyraxa withdrawn His favor?*

Ezra must have seen something in her face. "Adinah? You look off." He sounded distant, his voice trailing off as a ringing filled her ears. She swallowed hard, trying to steady herself. She thought he might still be speaking, but the dread rose in her, driving the air out of her lungs. Looking at the ground, she focused on taking one step at a time, determined to make it back to The Tired Fox even with the leaden anxiety making her limbs heavy.

By the time they reached the inn, her mind was a storm of uncertainty. She didn't hear the patrons inside, just pushed past them to and up the stairs. Right as she crossed the threshold, she pushed the door to close behind her. A thud and a swear briefly cut through her racing thoughts before the tide of desperation brought her to her knees, as if dragging her where even Ptyraxa's light could not reach.

She heard Ezra enter behind her, but she was already on her knees, digging through her bags until she pulled out a worn holy text. She clasped it tightly in both hands and bent her head, lips moving frantically in prayer.

"Adinah?" he tried. She heard him step a bit closer. Even though she was aware of him, she couldn't bring herself to move. She didn't respond. Her whispered pleas grew more fervent, her voice barely above a breath as she clutched the worn holy text against her chest.

"Ptyraxa, Morning Lord, guide me," she prayed, voice shaking. "Where have I faltered? Have I strayed from Your light? Have I misunderstood Your will?" Her grip on the book tightened as she bowed her head further.

"I have tried to follow where You led me. I have obeyed, I have listened, I have searched. But now another comes, walking the same path, and You are silent." Her breath hitched. "Have You withdrawn from me? Have I failed?" The words spilled from her lips like a tide she could not stop.

"Please, Morning Lord, let me hear You again. Let me feel Your presence, feel Your light. Show me that I am still Yours."

Ezra took another step closer. "Adinah, you're scaring me." She couldn't bring herself to reply. He reached for her, gripping her shoulders, and pulled her to her feet. She stiffened, but he turned her to face him, his gaze searching hers.

"What in the hells is going on?" he asked, his voice raw and sharp. For a moment, she only stared at him, chest rising and falling rapidly. His presence was solid and steady, and she latched onto it.

"The dream," she said at last, the words barely a whisper. "It guided me to start this journey, but now it's gone. It's been gone. What if Ptyraxa has turned His back on me?"

Ezra frowned. She could feel her expression shifting. It wasn't grief or fear. She was beyond that. The room felt like it was spinning. He exhaled, releasing her, and after a moment he stepped out of the room without a word. She barely noticed his absence, lost in her own racing thoughts. When he returned a few minutes later, he carried a bottle of wine, two glasses, and a small plate of spiced apple hand pies, their golden crusts glistening with honey. He set them down carefully and sat on the floor, pouring them both a drink. She sank down to sit with him. Her body was rigid, but everything inside her felt fragile, like the most delicate glass that would shatter if touched. The air was thick between them with unspoken words, but he didn't let the silence linger long.

"Alright," he said, his voice quieter now, gentle but insistent. "Tell me more."

She hesitated, eyeing him warily. His presence was steady, his expression gentle and almost pleading, so she spoke.

Chapter 11

Ezra

She picked up a glass, looking into the liquid as she swirled it, the wine catching the light filtering in from the window. He could tell the words were heavy on her tongue. He sipped his own drink with patience before, finally, she exhaled, setting her glass back down.

"For weeks," she began, voice quieter than usual, "I had a dream." Ezra arched a brow but didn't interrupt.

"A shattered temple with flaming skies," she continued, "the chaos stretching on forever. And I heard His voice–Ptyraxa's–telling me of the Dawnfire Heart. Showing it to me." She spoke slowly, deliberately, as if each word carried weight. "It was always the same. The same ruin, the same words, always with the insistence that I rush to find it, that time was of the essence."

"That's why you were studying so much," he said, setting his own glass aside. "You were rushing. Now you think you're racing someone to it."

She nodded. "And now the dream is gone. It has been for the past few nights. Suddenly another paladin is here, which can't be a coincidence. What if I was too slow? What if Ptyraxa has turned to him instead?" She picked up her glass, knuckles white from her tight grip on the stem. "What if I've failed?"

Ezra tilted his head, studying her, taking a long sip before continuing. The wine was incredibly strong, numbing his tongue, and almost sickeningly sweet.

"Why not accept their help, then? If another of Ptyraxa's chosen seeks it, wouldn't that be a boon?"

Adinah scoffed softly, shaking her head. "You don't understand. I'm already a Dawnshield."

His brow furrowed. "I assume that's… impressive?"

"It is," she confirmed, taking another measured sip. "Few of Ptyraxa's paladins reach it. But a holy mission directly *from* Ptyraxa?" She inhaled deeply. "Completing such a task would elevate me to High Paladin."

"Ah," he mused, nodding. "Ambition."

She scowled. "It isn't ambition. It's duty." He gestured for her to continue.

"Elidane was the last to ascend to High Paladin," she said, leaning back against the wooden frame of the bed. "Her mission was the cleansing of the Cursed Mirror of Othren. It was an artifact that twisted the souls of those who gazed into it, binding them in torment." Adinah traced the rim of her glass. "She retrieved it from the ruins of Nelthaar, carried it through the Ashen Wastes, and cleansed it with the first light of dawn. The Dawnfire Heart."

Ezra considered that. "A fine tale."

"A true one."

"Even better." He smiled faintly. She drained the last of her glass, settling a bit and leaning back against the side of the bed.

"So you see why it matters, why it can't be someone else." She hesitated, then muttered, "Though maybe He disagrees."

Ezra's lips quirked. "Frustration with one's deity? A daring sentiment." She rolled her eyes. "You wouldn't understand the pressure."

Ezra stiffened. "Wouldn't I?" His usual flow of words faltered. He scoffed, shaking his head. "Oh, Adinah. You think you alone know what it means to strive for the favor of a god? To push yourself further and further, convinced that if you could just do more, be more, they would see you? Approve of you? Listen to you?" The darkness of anger and hurt rose in him, setting him on edge. He took a steadying breath.

"Once, I sought knowledge so profound, so divine, that it would elevate me beyond mere mortal limits. I chased secrets of ascension, of divinity itself, convinced that if I could prove my worth, I might…" He trailed off, then gave a humorless chuckle. "Well, let's just say that path was not as noble as yours."

Adinah stared at him, her anger cooling. She swallowed hard.

"I didn't mean–"

"No," he interrupted, "You didn't." A long silence stretched between them, the room settling into a heavy stillness. He signed and, with an exaggerated gesture, motioned toward the plate between them. "You've not touched the hand pies."

She looked at them, then away. "I feel like I haven't earned them. Nothing worth celebrating."

Ezra blinked. Then he scoffed, as if she'd deeply offended him. With great theatricality, he leaned forward.

"Paladin Thorne, you have quite literally fought, bled, and endured for this cause. You have faced dangers that would send lesser souls fleeing. You have shouldered the weight of divine expectation with unwavering resolve. And now, now, because your god has chosen to be cryptic–oh, how surprising–you deny yourself the simple pleasure of a pastry?"

She cracked a smile. Barely, but it was there.

"Ptyraxa would be a fool to set you aside," he continued. "And I am quite convinced He is not a fool."

A quiet laugh escaped her, breathy and unguarded. She filled each of their glasses. Raising hers, she smirked.

"To doing the best we can with what we have. Damn what they think." Ezra lifted his own in return, but as she drank, his gaze lingered on her, realizing as she easily downed the glass that she had crossed into inebriation. They would definitely need another night here. He made a mental note to ask about paying for the full week. *If we leave earlier, he can just call the extra money pure profit.*

He watched as she put down her glass and reached for a hand pie at last, her fingers brushing over the flaky crust as if testing the weight of it. She hesitated a moment longer before taking a careful bite. At first, she remained unreadable, chewing methodically, her gaze fixed somewhere on the plate between them. But then her brows lifted just slightly, and the corner of her mouth turned up–not quite a smile, but close. He didn't need need to draw attention to it, but he couldn't resist.

"Ah ha! You see?" He gestured toward her with his glass, his triumph bubbling up through the haze of the wine. "A well-earned indulgence if ever there was one." She huffed, the sound edged with amusement as she took another bite. This time, the effect was unmistakable; the tension in her shoulders eased and her eyelids fluttered just so, as if savoring something more than the taste.

Ezra was fascinated. Not merely by her enjoyment, though that was its own small victory, but by the way she allowed herself this moment. For all her doubts, for all her weighty burdens, she was here, taking pleasure in something as simple as a pastry. Somehow, impossibly, that enough to make his chest tighten. He cleared his throat, tilting his head as he studied her. The afternoon light streamed in from the window, painting her face in gold and shadow.

"And when you do become a High Paladin, what then?" She chewed thoughtfully, washed down the bite with another sip of wine–straight from the bottle this time–and sighed.

"I suppose I'll do what's expected. Carry Ptyraxa's will into the world. Perform miracles, if I can." Her voice was quiet, a little rough at the edges, but steady. "Maybe I'll become a hero in my own right."

The way she said it wasn't self-important or self-deprecating. It was simply fact, as if it had always been the natural course, whether she doubted her worth or not. The certainty she carried even in moments of doubt never failed to inspire him. She seemed to catch herself mid-thought, then blinked at him, brow furrowing slightly.

"Wait. You said 'when.'"

Ezra tilted his head, wry smile teasing his lips. "Did I?"

"You did." She narrowed her eyes, watching him now with something close to suspicion, though softened by the wine's haze. "You really believe I'll become a High Paladin?"

"Yes." His answer came without hesitation. He finished his glass before setting it down, fingers tracing the rim absently. "And I believe we should keep pursuing the Heart. You will find it first."

Adinah let out a breath, her gaze dropping to the floor. Her fingers traced the stitching in the bedroll. The wine had begun to settle into her movements, softening them, making her slower and looser. He watched as she blinked heavily and, without much preamble, stretched out onto the bedroll. Ezra observed her quietly, his own thoughts slowing to match the drift of the golden light filtering through the window. She lay on her back, staring up at the wooden beams above, her expression unreadable in the warm glow.

Hope and sorrow warred on her face. The weight of her faith, her doubts, the desperate need to believe in something–it was all there, written in the creases of her brow and the way her lips parted just slightly, as if holding back words she wasn't yet ready to speak. She had carried this hope for so long, even when it seemed impossible and even when it seemed like it had been taken from her. Now, in the quiet lull of the afternoon, in the warmth of the wine and the safety of the moment, she seemed to finally let herself feel it.

He swallowed hard, a knot forming deep in his stomach. It wasn't fear or apprehension, but something he wasn't ready to name. Instead, he leaned back, watching the sunlight shift across the room as he let the silence stretch on.

Chapter 12

Ezra

Ezra stirred as consciousness returned to him in sluggish waves, the weight of sleep still heavy in his limbs. The room was awash in the hazy glow of evening, the little bit of light filtering through the window much softer now, touched with the hues of the setting sun. He had dozed off sitting up, an offence his back certainly would be reluctant to forgive him for. Across from him, Adinah remained curled on her bedroll, her breaths slow and even. For a brief, unguarded moment, he simply watched her, taking in the rise and fall of her chest and the way a stray lock of hair curled against her temple.

With a reluctant sigh, he stretched and shifted. She stirred at the movement, blinking groggily before rubbing a hand over her face.

"We dozed off," she murmured, her voice thick with sleep.

"So it would seem." He sat up properly, rolling his shoulders. The remnants of the wine nap still clung to him, but clarity was returning. "Judging by the light, I'd say we've just missed the busiest stretch of dinner."

Adinah groaned softly, rubbing her temples. "A tactical error."

"Indeed." He smirked, pushing himself up to his feet and offering her a hand. She took it, her grip firm despite the grogginess, and together they made their way downstairs.

The common room of the inn was comfortably full, the scent of roasted meat and fresh bread thick in the air. The lingering warmth of the day still clung to the wooden walls, and the murmur of conversation filled the space in a low, steady hum. They found an open table near the hearth and settled in. Dinner was uncomplicated: roast fowl, root vegetables, and a thick slice of bread with fresh butter. It was simple fare, but satisfying after an afternoon of wine, stress, and restless thoughts.

When the innkeeper came by to collect their plates, Ezra reached for his pouch and, without hesitation, slid a generous stack of coins across the table.

"For the rest of the week," he said, "and a bit extra for the trouble." The innkeeper's brows lifted in mild surprise, but he accepted the payment with a grateful nod.

Adinah cast Ezra a sidelong glance as the man walked away. "Generous of you," she said.

"I find it prudent to secure a comfortable home base," he replied, swirling the last of his drink. "And, well, we could use some small luxuries."

Adinah huffed a quiet chuckle but said nothing more. Instead, she leaned forward, resting her arms on the table.

"We should talk plans, if we're serious about finding the Heart. If we leave tomorrow, we need to be sure we're ready."

Ezra took a measured sip before setting his glass aside. "I understand you'd prefer to leave sooner rather than later, but you must understand the necessity of preparation."

She nodded. "Five days' worth of supplies each should do. Enough for the journey and any unforeseen delays."

"Rations, waterskins, torches," he mused, counting off on his fingers. "A spare bedroll, in case one of ours meets an unfortunate end. A few potions, if we can find them at a reasonable price."

Her brow furrowed slightly. "And perhaps something to deal with wounds beyond what magic can mend. Salves, bandages—"

"Always wise," he agreed. "I can handle procuring anything of an arcane nature. I assume you'll manage anything more militant?"

"Checking my armor and sword for any necessary repairs, yes." She stretched. "Though, if we want to leave tomorrow, we need to start early. I won't set out unprepared."

He gave a theatrical sigh. "There goes my hope of a lazy morning."

She smirked. "Perish the thought."

They lingered a while longer, refining their plans. When the conversation finally wound down, the common room had begun to empty, the evening stretching toward night. The warmth of the hearth was pleasant, and despite the earlier nap, the weight of the long day was still clinging to their bones.

Adinah pushed back from the table. "We should turn in. Early start and all."

He exhaled through his nose, a ghost of amusement on his lips. "Yes, yes, duty calls."

They made their way upstairs, their boots soft against the worn wooden planks. The moment they stepped into their room, a soft patter reached Ezra's ears. He glanced toward the window where droplets of rain traced uneven paths down the glass. The rhythmic sound was soothing, an easy lull that promised a restful night.

She stretched, eyeing the bed. "I'll take the floor."

He scoffed. "Ridiculous. I'll take the floor."

She shot him a dry look. "You paid for the room. For the week, even! You take the bed."

He folded his arms. "You're the one always carrying heavy armor. You take the bed." They stood in silence for a moment, a battle of wills waged in the quiet space between them. With an exaggerated sigh, Adinah grabbed the blanket off the bed, tossing it unceremoniously onto her own bedroll.

"Fine. Do what you want, but I'm taking the floor."

Ezra barely bit back a smirk as she stubbornly settled herself, shifting until she found a comfortable spot and buried herself in blankets. *It would be easier to find a comfortable spot if she just took the bed.* He, too, though, took his place on the floor opposite her, his own bedroll arranged with only slightly more care. The rain continued its steady rhythm against the window, a soothing counterpoint to the steady rise and fall of Adinah's breaths.

He stared at the ceiling a while before closing his eyes. It was a peculiar thing, this strange and delicate balance between them, but somehow it felt right.

Something was wrong.

In his dream, water curled at his ankles, cool and creeping, spreading in widening ripples with every breath he took. He stood in an endless stretch of dark water, moonlight catching at its surface like liquid silver. The tide surged around him, first a gentle lap against his skin, then a steady pull, dragging him deeper. He tried to move, to step back onto solid ground, but there was none. There was only the water, rising higher, seeping into his clothes, his skin, his lungs—

He woke with a start.

His breath hitched as he blinked against the dark, heart hammering in his chest. The sensation of dampness clung to him. A chill spread across his back where his bedroll met the floor, and as awareness settled, he realized with growing unease that the dampness wasn't imagined.

He pushed himself up onto his elbows, frowning as he ran a hand over the blankets beneath him. Wet. Not soaked, but undeniably damp. He turned his head toward Adinah's bedroll. Between them, dark against the wooden floor, was a growing puddle of water. He sighed, rubbing a hand over his face. *Wonderful*, he thought.

Tilting his head back, he squinted up at the ceiling, following the soft, rhythmic patter of water droplets. Sure enough, a leak had sprung in the night, and their sleeping arrangements had the misfortune of being directly beneath it. He let out an exasperated sigh, resigning himself to the necessary course of action. Shifting onto his knees, he reached out and, very carefully, shook Adinah's shoulder.

The reaction was immediate. She jolted awake, hand shooting out in a blind, instinctive motion, and he barely jerked back in time to avoid a fist colliding with his face.

He raised his hands in quick surrender, voice low and firm. "It's just me."

She blinked blearily, her breath slowing as recognition settled over her sleep-hazed expression. "Ezra?"

He rolled his eyes. *Who else would it be?*

"Yes," he said, dropping his hands. "And while I admire your reflexes, I'd rather not be rewarded with a black eye."

She exhaled sharply, rubbing her face. "What–"

"The ceiling is leaking," he supplied, already shifting to gather his blankets. "We need to move before we're both properly soaked." She muttered something under her breath that was probably not very kind. She sat up, squinting at the puddle forming between them. With a groggy sigh, she threw off her own damp blanket and stood, stretching stiff limbs before helping move their things out of harm's way.

It was late–or rather, far too early. The room was steeped in heavy darkness, broken only by the faintest glow of embers from the lantern. When the last of their bedding was shuffled aside, they both stood there for a moment, staring at the lone bed in the room.

Adinah shot him a look, arms crossed. "To the hells with the water. I'll sleep on the floor."

"It's damp."

She shrugged. "I'll manage."

Ezra arched a brow. "And if the puddle spreads?"

She sighed through her nose, glancing between the bed and floor, visibly weighing her options. He could see the exact moment exhaustion won out over stubbornness.

"Fine. But if you start snoring or get too close, I'm rolling you off the mattress."

"I would expect nothing less." Without another word, they both climbed into bed, each settling on their respective edges. The mattress was large enough to fit them comfortably, yet they still clung to their corners as though the expanse between them were sacred ground.

He lay rigid on his back, staring at the ceiling, willing himself to relax.

64

He was tired. He should have been able to fall back asleep easily, but his body refused to cooperate. He was too warm despite the cool air drifting through the room. The blanket wasn't even heavy, but his skin prickled with heat. He swallowed.

Why am I so nervous? His palms felt clammy. He resisted the urge to shift, lest he somehow move an inch too close and disturb the equilibrium they had so delicately established. She had already gone still beside him, her breathing evening out, slow and steady. Meanwhile, his own pulse felt traitorous, stubbornly quickening and refusing to settle.

Why do I feel like I can't breathe? He shut his eyes. This was ridiculous. They were both fully clothed, simply sharing a bed because of an inconvenient leak. There was nothing untoward about the situation. And yet–

Why am I sweating like this? He exhaled slowly, forcing his muscles to unwind one by one. The room was quiet. Her breathing was a steady, grounding thing beside him. That, more than anything, eased the restless churn of his thoughts.

Eventually, as fatigue finally pulled at the edges of his mind, he let himself focus on the quiet rhythm of Adinah's breathing. The steady rise and fall, the soft, almost imperceptible sound of each exhale. A small, secret part of him found comfort in it, and sleep claimed him at last.

Ezra woke to the soft patter of rain against the window, a cool hush settling over the town in the early morning hours. The first thing he noticed was warmth–not just from the blankets, but from something solid and distinctly human pressed close. His breath caught, and as awareness fully returned, so did realization.

Adinah was beside him, her head tucked near his shoulder, their legs tangled loosely beneath the sheets. At some point in the night, the space between them had disappeared, and now he could feel the faint, slow rhythm of her breathing against his side.

Heat crawled up his neck. Very, very carefully, he began the slow process of untangling himself. He shifted inch by inch, willing the mattress not to creak, holding his breath as he eased his arm free without disturbing her. Finally, after what felt like an eternity, he succeeded, retreating to his side of the bed with an exhale of relief.

As if sensing the loss of warmth, she stirred. Her eyes fluttered open, hazy with sleep, before she seemed to become abruptly, painfully aware of their proximity. A flush bloomed across her cheeks as she shot to the far edge of the bed, nearly toppling over the side in her haste.

"Good morning," she blurted, voice a note too high, as if sheer politeness could erase the past few moments.

Ezra smothered a smile, schooling his features into something neutral as he sat up. "Good morning." Then, with a stretch and a roll of his shoulders, he pushed himself up. It was time to begin the day.

By the time they stepped downstairs, The Tired Fox was just beginning to stir. The scent of fresh bread and cooking breakfast mingled with the remnants of last night's ale. They exchanged a few brief words over a quick meal, deciding it would be best to split up to cover their preparations faster.

"I'll handle the potions," he said, adjusting his cloak. "You take your sword and armor?"

She nodded, already eyeing the street beyond the inn's doorway. "And the rations. If we're lucky, we won't need all of them."

"We should always prepare for the worst."

"Optimistic as ever," she murmured, a smirk tugging at the corner of her lips. "Alright then, we meet back here as soon as possible. I want to get going."

With a parting nod, they set off in separate directions. There was a welcome break in the rain as they left the inn, but the road was still slick and muddy. The town was just beginning to wake, shopkeepers pulling open their shutters, merchants setting up their stalls. Ezra walked at an easy pace, allowing himself to breathe in the morning air as he navigated the winding streets.

The potion shop, The Gilded Vial, was nestled between a blacksmith and a modest bookbinder's. Its sign, an ornate flask with gold leafing, swung gently in the morning breeze. The moment he stepped inside, the scent of herbs and alchemical reagents filled his lungs: sharp, bitter, and tinged with something almost floral.

Shelves lined the walls, stocked with bottles of varying sizes and colors. A wizened shopkeeper, a dwarven man with spectacles perched on the end of his nose, glanced up from behind the counter.

"Ah, welcome, welcome! Looking for something in particular today?"

Ezra offered a pleasant smile. "Restocking, mostly. Health potions, any other restoratives if you have them." As the shopkeeper began gathering the vials, Ezra let his gaze wander over the shelves until a flash of white tabard caught his attention.

A man had just entered, clad in a tabard almost identical to Adinah's, marking him as a paladin of Ptyraxa. He was tall and lean, with sharp features and blond hair neatly tied back. His posture was effortless, his expression calm and composed. Ezra, however, did not turn to face him directly. Instead, he kept watch through the reflections in the potion bottles, observing the way the man's gaze swept the room, the subtle way his fingers drummed against his belt.

Interesting.

Ezra kept his movements slow, his attention ostensibly on a bottle of shimmering blue liquid, while his mind raced. The man, whoever he was, did not interact with him, instead perusing the wares with a practiced nonchalance. It wasn't until the paladin stepped up beside him at the counter that Ezra allowed himself to glance up properly.

"Pardon me," the man said, his voice smooth and pleasant. Ezra, hoping to project an air of absentmindedness, gave a start, nearly fumbling the potion in his hand. He let out a chuckle, shaking his head.

"Apologies, lost in thought." The paladin smiled, bright and friendly. Too friendly. There was something about the way his lips stretched a fraction too wide, the way his teeth showed just a little too much. He had seen smiles like that before, something almost predatory concealed beneath a veneer of warmth.

"No trouble at all," the man assured him, placing his own selection of potions onto the counter. "Always a pleasure to meet another early riser."

Ezra hummed in agreement, stepping back slightly as if to give the man room. "Indeed. The morning holds a certain potential, wouldn't you say?"

The paladin inclined his head, turning his attention to the shopkeeper. Their exchange was brief, polite, and laced with pleasantries. Ezra, maintaining his affable demeanor, simply waited, offering no sign of interest beyond that of a passerby. When the man finally took his leave, stepping out into the now bustling street, Ezra was quick to make his own purchases before slipping out the door to follow him.

Ezra was careful, slipping into the flow of the morning crowd with practiced ease. He had no intention of being seen, and certainly no desire to draw attention to himself. He trailed the man at a distance, his movements calculated, always keeping to the periphery of sightlines.

Through gaps in the shifting crowd, he watched as the man entered a different inn, The Amber Hearth. Unlike The Tired Fox, this establishment was more subdued, clearly catering to merchants and travelers of means. Ezra lingered only long enough to see the mysterious paladin ascend the stairs before swiftly making his way back.

By the time he reached The Tired Fox, Adinah was waiting for him near the entrance, arms crossed, expression caught somewhere between irritation and concern.

"You're late," she snapped.

"I was waylaid."

Her brow lifted. "By what, a particularly gripping novel?"

Ezra smiled lazily, hoping she could see the intentness in his eyes. "I could tell you here, if you'd like. Or," he let his voice dip, the suggestion lingering between them. "You could let me steal a moment of your time upstairs."

Adinah blinked, thrown for the barest second before suspicion settled in her gaze. "That's… a new approach."

He tilted his head. "You wound me. Can I not be intrigued by a private conversation with a woman of striking prowess?"

She narrowed her eyes, then sighed. "Fine. But if you try anything, I'm throwing you out the window."

He laughed, stepping past her to lead the way. Once inside their room, he shut the door and immediately dropped the playful air, his voice quiet and urgent.

"There's a man in town wearing a tabard similar to yours. He's a paladin of Ptyraxa, or at least that's what he wants people to believe."

Adinah stilled, color draining slightly from her face as she sank onto the bed. "Who?"

"I don't know. Blond, sharp features. He's staying at The Amber Hearth in town." He took a careful step closer. "He gave me a smile that reminded me of something foul. Something's wrong about him, I just can't put my finger on it."

She exhaled slowly, running a hand over her face. "You think he's dangerous."

"I think we should be cautious." His voice softened. "If he doesn't sound familiar to you, we need to move. Now."

Adinah nodded, the weight of the moment settling between them. After a beat, her expression turned quizzical.

"Ezra?"

"Yes?"

"How do you know he wasn't a paladin of Ptyraxa? Plenty of people have disconcerting smiles. He doesn't sound familiar, but your conclusion is a bold one."

The corner of his mouth twitched upward. "He didn't comment on the dawn."

She blinked. "What?"

"I made an offhand remark about the morning, and he didn't give me some poetic sermon on renewal and holy light. Not one mention of duty or guilt! That's how I know he isn't a paladin, much less one of Ptyraxa."

She scowled. "You're ridiculous. Do you always reduce paladins to such stereotypes?"

He couldn't resist giving her a teasing wink. "Only when it makes you scowl like that."

Chapter 13

Adinah

The late morning passed in quiet, efficient preparation. Adinah moved with practiced precision, folding blankets, tightening straps, and rolling their bedrolls with careful, methodical movements. Ezra, to his credit, was just as meticulous, though she caught him once or twice absently smoothing the same edge of his robes as if lost in thought. Still, they worked well together, packing everything into neat bundles and securing them for travel.

Downstairs, The Tired Fox offered a hearty midday meal of thick stew, fresh bread, and warm cider. The warmth of the food chased away some of the lingering morning chill, though she knew it wouldn't last once they were out on the road. With their meal finished, they made their way to the stable. Tirin perked up the moment he saw them. His ears flicked forward and he let out a pleased huff as Adinah approached, rubbing along his broad neck with an affectionate pat. They finished securing their packs, double-checked the supplies, and after a brief stop to buy Tirin an extra blanket, they finally set off.

The road stretched ahead of them, winding southeast through sparse trees, farmland, and rolling hills. While Garrun estimated a three day journey on foot, Adinah was sure they could halve that with Tirin's steady gait. *Even so, definitely not a comfortable trip in this weather*, she thought miserably as she glanced up at the cloudy sky.

The drizzle began again not long after they left the village, a persistent mist that seeped into every exposed inch of skin. Their cloaks helped, but even well-oiled leather and sturdy wool couldn't keep out the bone-deep chill of autumn rain. The damp curled around her fingers and crept beneath her armor. She flexed her hands around the reins, willing the blood to return to them. They were quickly growing stiff, old injuries making themselves known with deep aches.

Ezra, riding behind her, was unusually quiet. She could practically feel the tension coiling in his posture. Normally, he was the one to fill silences, but today he seemed lost in his own mind. For once, she decided to break the quiet.

"So," she said, adjusting her posture in the saddle. "How do wizards rank themselves?" Behind her, she heard a soft exhale, something like amusement.

"Rank?"

"Like paladins or priests," she clarified. "You must have some sort of order."

He actually laughed at that. "I'm afraid not. Wizards are simply wizards. There's no official hierarchy or formal ranking system outside of the few remaining colleges."

Adinah frowned. "That can't be right. Some are stronger than others, aren't they?"

"Of course," he said, amusement evident in his voice. "But the most powerful wizards are known by reputation, not title. They take apprentices, they write tomes, and some have towers that conveniently appear or disappear depending on their mood." He paused. "A few blow themselves up in catastrophic magical accidents."

She snorted. "Efficient."

"Hardly. It's chaos, really."

She shook her head, adjusting her grip on the reins. "See, that makes no sense to me. With paladins, priests, and archivists, we all have ranks, earned through service and leadership."

"And how does one rise through these ranks?" he prompted, curiosity lacing his tone.

She considered it for a moment. "Time and experience, mostly. Years of service grant advancement. But the highest ranks? Those require a great work."

"A great work? Like finding the Dawnfire Heart?" He laughed. "You mean to tell me High Archivist Orlan has left his precious library long enough to find himself a relic?"

She forced down a smile, hiding her laugh with a cough. "Archivists must translate and preserve sacred texts and educate others on doctrine. The amount of work they must do is massive. Probably a third of the translated texts in the easternmost shelves of Morningstrike were done by High Archivist Orlan.

"For high priests, they perform miracles and spread the will of their god. Much of their work ties in nicely with the work of archivists, and it isn't uncommon to see high ranking archivists and priests working together to reach their goals."

"And paladins?"

She adjusted in the saddle again, the leather creaking beneath her. "Paladins… Well, ours are a little more dramatic."

"Oh? Do tell."

She smirked. "To achieve the highest rank, a paladin must complete a great work in battle. Reclaim a holy artifact. Vanquish a demon. Lead a charge against the forces of darkness. All very noble, very grand."

He hummed. "So, if a paladin wanted to advance, they'd simply go looking for an ancient relic or pick a fight with a demon?"

She rolled her eyes. "It's not that simple. The god and Their temple must recognize the effort."

"Ah, divine bureaucracy. How thrilling. I imagine most receive their rank posthumously?"

Adinah huffed. "Of course not. The dead are simply martyrs, or those that have failed. There may be honor in death, but there is not a promotion. What use are you to a god once you're dead?"

"Insult to the mortal injury, if you ask me," he teased.

"It's better than your chaotic mess."

He chuckled, but after a moment he let out a sigh. "Well, I must say, I'm quite glad I never entangled myself in your type of structured divine magic. Too many rules. Too many expectations."

She shook her head with a smirk, but didn't press further. They rode on, the rain steady against their cloaks, the cold clinging to their skin. At least the conversation had made the journey a little less miserable, and Ezra was finally sitting less in ominous tension behind her.

The day's journey stretched long, the steady rhythm of Tirin's hooves marking the slow passage of time. They pressed on despite the rain, the road dwindling beneath them as the sky darkened to a starless void. By the time they finally stopped to make camp, exhaustion weighed heavy in her limbs. The mist had thoroughly soaked the wood she found, leaving it too damp to catch even the smallest spark. She sighed, rubbing her hands together as she glanced at Ezra.

"Fine. I concede," she said, defeated. "Light the damn fire."

He grinned, all too pleased. "You wound me, as if relying on my magic were such a hardship. I did have fun watching your futile search for dry tinder, at least."

She huffed but didn't argue. With a simple flourish, he conjured a flame, coaxing it into something steady and strong. The fire crackled to life, orange light flickering across the damp clearing. Adinah stretched her hands out toward it, sighing in relief as the warmth seeped back into her fingers, chasing away the stiffness.

They settled in, eating a modest meal of dried meat, hard cheese, and a bit of slightly stale bread. The quiet between them was easy, interrupted only by the occasional pop of the fire and the rustling of the wind through the trees.

She leaned back slightly, glancing at him. "You know, you always seem different when you talk about Xernaea. A little distant, I suppose."

His expression stilled. He looked into the fire, his fingers flexing slightly where they rested against his knee before moving to fidget with the fabric at his waist.

"Ah. That." He let out a soft breath, shaking his head. "I figured you would ask about it eventually. Where to even begin?" She waited, giving him the space to find the words.

"I suppose," he started slowly, "for a very long time, I believed that power and skill could earn Her attention. That if I proved myself, I could not only gain Her favor, but perhaps something else I was working toward." He laughed quietly, but there was no humor in it. "I was foolish."

His voice was steady, but there was something beneath it, something she couldn't quite name. It was regret, maybe, or sorrow so deeply embedded that it had long since turned into something else.

"I wanted to be Her equal," he admitted. "I thought if I harnessed the very essence of the arcane, mastered it and bent it to my will, that She would look upon me and–" He stopped himself, pressing his lips together before shaking his head. "It was hubris. She punished me, as She should have. For a time, She even took my magic from me. I was nothing." His fingers continued to work the near threadbare piece of material, as if recalling the ache of that loss. "I had to claw my way back, prove I could wield magic without the arrogance and anger that had nearly consumed me. In time I did, but I lost something in the process."

Adinah listened in silence, watching the way the firelight cast shadows across his face. His normally bright, hazel eyes had gone dark, as if swallowing even the reflection of the firelight.

"The one thing I do envy about other divine magic, for all its bureaucracy, is that the faithful always know where they stand," he murmured. "I lost sight of that, of my own mortality. I–" He let out a breath, shaking his head again. "It doesn't matter now."

But it did matter. It mattered in the way he spoke, in the way his hands tensed and relaxed, in the way he looked away as if the fire held answers he could no longer reach. Before she could say anything, however, the mist became a cold, unrelenting downpour. The fire hissed out as Ezra jumped in surprise, leaving them in near darkness.

"Brilliant," he spat. "We'd best retreat before we drown." Before she could run to her own tent, he took her by the arm and pulled her to his. She protested until she found herself inside.

"I was trying to say," he started loudly, stepping in after her, "that my

72

tent is better suited for tonight. It's enchanted to stay dry. Sigils and all that." He pulled off his wet robe, trying to dry his tunic on a spare blanket. "You must not have heard me over the deluge."

Her face grew warm. "No, I hadn't." She shifted nervously. "But it does make sense. Thank you." She meant it. The idea of water coming in through her tent was far from desirable. They turned in, both exhausted by the day of travel.

As she lay there, her mind replayed his words. She wondered how lonely it must have been, what it must have been like to reach so high only to fall. That he had done it to himself, though, somehow felt like the cruelest part of all. She wondered if, had things been different, if the temple had been structured differently, if she would have ever done the same in her own ambition.

After a while, she began to notice that the tent, though spacious, felt impossibly small. The silence inside was so thick even the sounds of the downpour couldn't cut through it.

She stared at the tent's ceiling, heart hammering, her pulse a rapid staccato against the quiet hush of rain outside. She was acutely aware of every breath she took, of the way her chest rose and fell just a little too fast, of how close he was—close enough that she could hear the subtle shift of fabric when he moved. The tent carried his scent, parchment and sandalwood, as if it had seeped into the very canvas over time.

It should have been nothing. It should have been the least of her concerns, yet it wrapped around her, something deep in her chest tightening, a breath catching before she forced it steady.

Her nerves burned, not just from tension, but from something electric that left her restless. She felt too warm despite the lingering chill. Adrenaline licked at her veins, irrational and unnecessary. *Why now? Why him?*

Eventually, exhaustion won. Warmth, real or imagined, lulled her under.

Chapter 14

Adinah

Adinah awoke to an empty tent. She blinked groggily against the soft morning light filtering through the fabric, momentarily disoriented by the silence. The warmth left behind in the bedroll next to her had already cooled, though the scent of parchment and sandalwood still lingered faintly in the air. She stretched, sore from the damp cold of the previous night, then ducked outside.

The world was a haze of soft grey-blue. The mist had finally thinned, revealing a landscape still soaked from the night's rain. The air was chilly and the ground squelched underfoot, but the storm had passed. Morning, thankfully, had come.

A few feet away, Ezra stood hunched over a tiny, flickering cookfire. His brows were furrowed, and he held a bent fork like it was a weapon, poking anxiously at a small skillet suspended over the flames. The contents sizzled questionably: some mixture of oats, dried fruit, and what might have been preserved milk. It was congealing. She bit back a laugh.

He noticed her then, straightening abruptly. "Ah. Good morning. I was… attempting breakfast."

She stepped closer, rubbing her arms for warmth. "Attempting, huh?"

He sighed, looking down at the mess in the pan. "It was meant to be a warming porridge. I followed the proportions exactly. Well, approximately."

"Is it supposed to smell like that?"

He gave her a wounded look. "That's the dried apples. Probably."

She snorted, and he chuckled despite himself, though his ears turned a little red. "I appreciate the effort," she said gently. "It's endearing."

"Endearing," he muttered, looking back at the pan. "Not exactly the praise I strive for in the culinary arts."

Still giggling, she reached for her own supplies. Together, they salvaged what they could, managing a simple breakfast of hardtack,

74

cheese, and some of Ezra's sweetly charred porridge, which, surprisingly, wasn't entirely awful. They packed up slowly, wringing out fabric, shaking out cloaks, and letting boots sit open in the weak sun, hoping to coax a bit of dryness from them. The mud clung to everything, but the clear sky gave hope. As they loaded Tirin, Adinah sighed dramatically.

"I wish my tent could just stay dry all the time."

Ezra looked up from securing a saddlebag. "Would you like me to enchant it?"

She paused. "You can do that?"

He blinked. "Well, yes, of course. It's a simple enough enchantment. I assumed, since mine was done–well, I suppose I didn't realize you didn't know."

She gave a dry laugh. "Guess I figured that was just for wizards."

"Not at all, provided you have a wizard to set the enchantment for you," he said, clearly pleased to be of use. "Next time we make camp, I'll ward it. Should last a while, unless you dunk the whole thing in a lake."

She gave him a grin, one that lingered even as they mounted and rode out. The road was still damp but travelable, winding through low hills and sparse trees. Conversation ebbed and flowed, comfortable in its rhythm. Near noon, Ezra glanced at the horizon.

"How will we know the ruin when we find it?" he asked.

She hesitated, frowning. "Surely we'll know it when we see it."

"An inspiring strategy."

She shifted uncomfortably in the saddle, suddenly self-conscious at her own lack of plan. "You're free to come up with a better one."

"I'm a scholar," he said loftily. "Not a tracker of lost Ptyraxite ruins." They laughed and the road unwound further beneath them.

The rest of the day passed uneventfully. As evening approached, the terrain began to shift. Crumbling stone walls peeked from the tall grass, overgrown and half-swallowed by time. Moss blanketed fallen pillars and scattered fragments of what had once been architecture. By twilight, they set camp near what looked to be part of an ancient foundation. Adinah recognized the faint carving of the symbol the stonecutter had shown them etched into a piece of fallen stone, half-buried in the earth.

They scouted nearby, hoping for something more dramatic, but the forest had reclaimed most of the ruins. When night fell fully, they gave up the search and built a small campfire. The howl of wolves echoed in the distance: not too close, but not far enough to ignore.

"Shifts?" he asked, casting a wary glance beyond their camp.

She nodded. "I'll take last. Wake me when it's time." Adinah expected him to argue, his own exhaustion evident in his features, but after a moment he nodded and took a place by the fire.

The night passed slowly. Nothing came of the wolves and no threats stirred as stars blinked through patches of cloud cover. When he woke her gently a few hours later, she pulled her cloak tight and settled near the embers of the fire, watching the forest breathe. A few times she caught herself nearly dozing, but she managed to rouse herself enough to continue watch.

Some paladin you are, she scolded herself, *falling asleep like you're new to this. You've held the Oath for fourteen years now. Pull yourself together.* There was no way she was going to fail Ezra–or, more importantly, Ptyraxa–when she was so close to finding the ruin.

Theoretically close, anyway.

After hours of staring at the embers and pacing around the camp, the first hints of sunrise touched the eastern sky. A quiet, familiar pull tugged at her mind, something warm and urgent. She turned toward the broken sections of wall. The light hit it just right, catching the mossy edges and the faded symbol. But beyond it–

She blinked.

There was a shimmer in the air like heat rising from stone. Then a tall, vertical line appeared, an outline of something that had not been there a moment ago. Slowly, piece by piece, a structure began to emerge. It wasn't entirely physical yet, but slowly forming. Outlined by the dawn's light was a great temple, domed and radiant, its spires catching the dawn like mirrors. For a moment, she swore her heart stopped. After a breath, the urgency struck her again and she dove into Ezra's tent, shaking his shoulder.

"Ezra," she whispered, then louder. "Ezra, wake up. Now."

He blinked awake, groggy. "What is it–?"

"Look." She pulled him out of his tent, fingers trembling slightly as she gestured toward the rising shimmer in the distance.

He squinted blearily against the light. "At what?"

She was incredulous. "At what? The temple–can't you see it? Right there, past the old foundation. It's appearing."

He stared, then glanced at her, brows drawn. "Adinah, I see the stone and… the grass? Nothing's there." He looked concerned. "Do you maybe need a quick nap before we–"

"You don't see it? It's right there!" She blinked, looking back at the mirage-like vision of the radiant domes and gleaming arches growing clearer with every breath. "Gods, we don't have time for this. Just trust me. We have to go now." Still half-asleep, he fumbled as she thrust his bag into his hands.

"Quickly, quickly, just move. We're going." She grabbed her own bag before taking one of his hands in hers.

"Adinah—"

"Now, Ezra." She didn't hesitate. The temple shimmered, still half-formed, like a dream made real. She sprinted, dragging him behind her, hearing his curses as his tired feet stumbled over rocks and tree roots. As they approached, the half-illusory temple loomed, a silent and ethereal monument. Only a few yards from the base, large double doors formed, though still slightly transparent, revealing the landscape of trees beyond. Adinah reached out, pressing her palm against the door.

It swung open without a sound. She practically leapt through them, more determined than ever. She felt Ezra's hand break free from hers as he fell when he crossed the threshold, swearing as he hit the floor.

The moment they were completely free of the entrance, the heavy doors slammed shut behind them, leaving them swallowed by the silence of the temple antechamber.

Chapter 15

Ezra

Ezra hit the floor face-first.

The stone was cold and unforgiving, dust grinding into the cut on his cheek. The impact stole his breath and for a long second he stayed there, half-stunned, blinking against the sudden dark. The last thing he remembered before falling was the flicker of something impossible: a door where no structure had stood just moments before.

And then the door opened. On Adinah's word, on her certainty. And he'd followed her. The echo of it slamming behind them still rang in his ears.

"That can't be good," he muttered into the floor. With a groan, he pushed himself upright. His hands scraped against stone etched with faint inlays–sunbursts and radiant lines, dulled with age but unmistakably Ptyraxite. His knees protested as he stood, and when his vision adjusted, it nearly stole the breath right out of his lungs.

They stood in a vast antechamber, the kind of place that swallowed noise and space in equal measure. It was built like a cathedral but held the weight of a fortress. The vaulted ceiling soared above, lost in shadow, and high along the rear wall, above and around the doorway through which they'd entered, stood tall, narrow stained glass windows. They glowed faintly from the early morning light outside.

Each pane depicted radiant scenes of Ptyraxa, arms open to greet the dawn, golden rays bursting behind Him. Paladins flanked Him in each window, arrayed in armor of rose gold and alabaster, their weapons raised in defense or reverence. Smaller motifs repeated like a pattern: sunbursts, lotuses, and chalices overflowing with light. Crimson and gold draperies framed the walls, lush fabric hanging in thick folds from ceiling to floor. The whole room smelled faintly of incense, old stone, and dry parchment. The temple was beautiful, holy, and entirely untouched by time.

He let out a slow breath. "Well, this isn't how I thought today would

78

begin."

Adinah has already crossed into the center of the room. She stood still, face tilted up, her expression undone by awe. *Rapture*, he thought, *that's the word.* In the soft light, she looked different, almost otherworldly. She was awash in reverence, in something he didn't fully understand but didn't dare disturb. He moved quietly to her side.

"Are you alright?" he asked, placing a gentle hand on her shoulder.

She nodded slowly, her voice low. "This place… It shouldn't be here. Not like this, not whole."

There were six plain doors, three wooden ones with iron handles on either side of the chamber. The only ornate door stood at the far end of the hall: double doors carved with elaborate sunrise patterns, flanked by engraved columns.

They chose the leftmost side door. It opened without resistance. Inside was a small, domed, circular study. Shelves of books lined the walls, and a wide desk sat at the center beneath a dusty chandelier. The air smelled heavier here, tinged with ink and age. Scrolls rested in bundles atop the desk, and tomes leaned precariously against each other like they hadn't been touched in centuries. Adinah wandered toward the shelves. Ezra lingered by the desk, fingers ghosting over a leather-bound volume cracked with time.

Then came the thud.

A single book hit the stone floor behind them. They both froze. He turned slowly. The book lay open in the center of the room, well away from any shelf. Too far. It would've had to fall, then fly. She crossed to it, kneeling. Her hand hovered before she touched the page. He joined her, crouching to read. The illustration was unmistakable: a radiant, flame-like gemstone, pulsing with inner light. Even though he'd personally never seen it, he was certain this was the Heart. Adinah's awed expression only served as further confirmation. He turned to read.

"It is said the Dawnfire Heart was a shard of the first sunrise, carried into the world by Ptyraxa's chosen. It burns with celestial flame, capable of purifying any darkness it touches. Wielded righteously, it grants the bearer immense restorative power, and can cast back curses and shadow alike. In the wrong hands, its light can sear, destroy, and unravel.

Some accounts claim the Heart does more than heal—it empowers. When carried into battle, it bolsters Ptyraxa's magic, amplifying His blessings, wards, and paladins' strikes alike. The faithful who wield it are said to shine like the breaking dawn, their strength renewed with every invocation. Under its light, miracles are not only possible, they are inevitable."

"Convenient," he murmured, frowning. "Almost suspiciously so."

Adinah's expression was taut. "Someone wants us to find this, or believes we should."

The unease pricked at him now, colder than the stone under his feet. "We should check on Tirin," he said as he stood, shifting his weight uncomfortably from foot to foot. "I swear, if the door is gone outside…"

They returned to the antechamber. The door still stood where they entered, massive and sealed. He stepped forward and tried the handle, but it didn't budge. He pulled harder. Nothing.

"Well," he said grimly. "That's not promising." She stepped forward, pressing her palm to the wood but finding no give.

"We're trapped?" she asked, voice low.

He nodded once. "Appears so."

She took a breath, then squared her shoulders. "Then we keep going. There must be more Ptyraxa wants us to find."

He looked away before rolling his eyes a bit. *If Ptyraxa sent us here, surely He wouldn't trap one of His chosen. That wouldn't make sense.* The longer he thought, the more frustrated he became. *Adinah can't do much stuck in a dusty old temple.* Realizing she was already wandering toward another door, he moved to follow her.

Another small room branched off the front hall, almost hidden. Inside was a mess. Shelves were overturned, holy texts scattered across the floor. Ceremonial candles were smashed or crushed as if trampled. Robes were shredded at the seams, tossed like refuse. If the other area of the temple was any indication, the room had once been organized with care, but now looked ransacked.

He remained near the threshold, struck silent by the sight. She moved forward slowly, kneeling amidst the chaos. She lifted a broken sunburst talisman in one hand, much like the one he'd seen her wear, her face tight with emotion.

"This wasn't time or weather," she said. "Someone did this. Possibly recently." He watched her closely. Her reverence had been replaced with something quieter. Anger, maybe, or sorrow. Whatever the feeling, it darkened her face and he could see the divine light flicker in and out of her eyes.

"No faithful of Ptyraxa would treat these objects this way," she continued. "Even if the place was abandoned. We care for holy things, preserve them. We honor them." The words hung in the air.

"Did anyone else enter?" he asked.

She shook her head. "No. I heard nothing last night other than the wolves. Gods preserve me, I didn't even see the temple till dawn."

He crossed his arms. "Then someone beat us here. Maybe they never left." Silence filled the space again. Dread rooted in the walls now, deeper than the chill of the stone.

She stood, eyes hard. "Someone has defiled this place."

Ezra met her gaze. "Then let's find out why." She walked by him, back into the antechamber.

The door creaked shut behind them, muffling the scent of wax and crumbled vellum. He exhaled through his nose, fingers brushing dust off the hem of his robe. Her expression was unreadable, jaw tight. There were four rooms here left to explore.

"Which one looks least likely to be cursed?" he asked, squinting up at the massive stained glass.

Adinah glanced at him. "You're the expert on arcane doom. Pick your poison."

"Charming," he muttered, pushing the next door to his right open. The room beyond was wide and circular, a mediation chamber by the looks of it. Pale cushions ringed the floor in deliberate spirals and dozens of low-burning candles encircled the perimeter, though no heat rose from them. He moved to inspect one and frowned.

"They're cold," he said, touching the wick. "Like they've been frozen mid-flame."

She crouched, fingers brushing one of the cushions. "They're warm."

"So something's still sustaining the enchantments," he murmured, more to himself than her. "Which implies—"

A hum trembled through the floor beneath their boots. It was a pressure, like something buried deep beneath the stone awakened. A flicker of hope sprouted in his chest, but it wilted when she straightened uncomfortably, her expression uneasy.

"We should keep moving," she said, already turning to leave.

They tried the next door, finding a sleeping quarters. Rows of cots, each perfectly made, lined the room. They were covered in white and gold linens, unwrinkled, flawless other than the slight accumulation of dust. Some had personal effects still folded at the foot: bracelets, a single comb, and a single weathered journal. Ezra flipped through the book, finding only blank pages.

"They must have left in a hurry," Adinah said, voice hushed. Her hand lingered near her sword.

The next room had been a garden once, or something like one. Stone planters lined the floor and walls, their roots petrified in place. Some plants had browned a bit at the tips, frozen mid-wither. In the center stood a fountain, dry but intact, its basin filled with water. Neither of them dared touch it.

The last unexplored room was narrow and long, lined with arched shelves. A refectory, or perhaps a laundry. Folded robes rested in neat stacks: some ivory, others dyed deep crimson and stitched with sunburst emblems. The cloth was entirely untouched by time. A few table linens had been left in a corner, faded but whole. Ezra ran his hand across the nearest robe.

"Clean," he commented. "Almost annoyingly so."

She gave him a side-eye. "You thinking of freshening up?"

He smirked. "Tempting. I think I'd look rather handsome in these colors."

She rolled her eyes as they turned to head back to the antechamber. The last doors were the large ornate ones at the end of the hall. Adinah drew her sword as they approached, slowly stalking toward them as if she was approaching a waiting enemy. She stopped a few steps from the doorway, blade ready, and gave him a nod. Returning the gesture, he tried to open the doors. These, too, were completely frozen in place.

"Maybe we missed something," he reasoned.

Adinah's worried expression did not give him hope. "Maybe. I suppose we can wander a bit, or come up with a plan." He nodded, and the two set off to comb back through the rooms again.

When they first arrived, the sheer amount of light had astounded him. It felt like a warm blessing, the way it filled the high-vaulted rooms and corridors of the temple with a golden haze, as though dawn had paused mid-breath and refused to move on. The temple contained no torches or lanterns, relying solely on the pure, warm clarity of morning sunlight spilling through stained glass windows that showed no clear view outside.

By the second day, it grated on him. There was no sun, or at least no source to trace to indicate the sun existed. The light didn't bend as hours passed, didn't shift angles or color as it should have. There was no afternoon lull or golden hour. The entire temple was caught in endless brightness, suspended in time.

He and Adinah stopped trying to measure hours. Sleep came in fits, if at all. His internal sense of time, a usually precise instrument honed by years of study, had long since unraveled. She didn't say much about it, but he could see the tightness of her jaw and the way she rubbed at her temples whenever they stopped moving for too long.

The temple itself was vast, stretching even beyond the rooms they'd first explored, its halls echoing with too much silence. Over time, they'd found other doors, some hidden behind tapestries. They passed murals in brilliant crimson and gold, each depicting a stylized warrior figure wreathed in flame. Some were etched into marble, others carved into obsidian, all of them faceless. The farther they explored, the stranger the rooms became. Some were full of statues locked in eternal battle, while others housed long-dead relics arranged like offerings on dusty stone plinths.

One room was filled with mirrors, but none of them showed their reflections, just flickering glimpses of other unfamiliar places, the blood-red sky the only commonality. Another room had a tree growing in the center, its branches blooming with flame-colored leaves that felt warm to the touch.

"Something here remembers her," she said quietly after they left the room. "It feels like Elidane is watching, or maybe Ptyraxa."

"Maybe both?" he offered. She shrugged, continuing their aimless wandering.

That night, if it was night, they found a dining hall. A long table stretched down its center, polished wood gleaming. It was set with goblets and bread, fresh fruit, and roasted meat still steaming gently. No sign of life anywhere, nor signs of flies or decay.

Ezra stared at the spread. "It's fresh."

"That's the problem," she reminded him. She only let them take what they absolutely needed, mostly bread and dried fruit. When they got hungry, they'd carry food back to whatever side chamber they'd chosen to rest in. She refused to let them eat the meat or touch the wine, and despite his hunger, he didn't push.

Chapter 16

Ezra

They didn't speak much after the second-or third?-day. There wasn't much to say. They were tired, the temple's silence fraying at the edge of conversation, seeming to dull everything.

It was during one of those endless, artificial "mornings" that Ezra noticed how hollow Adinah's eyes looked as she leaned against a pillar, half-asleep on her feet. She hadn't said a word in at least an hour. Her hair was tangled, the gold parts of her armor dulled by accumulated dust. Even her normally upright posture looked cracked.

He felt it too, like something behind his eyes was unraveling, as if his thoughts had turned to slurry.

"We're going to lose our minds in here," he muttered aloud before he could stop himself.

She blinked at him, then, surprisingly, she nodded. "Yeah," she said. "We might."

They stared at each other a moment longer. He glanced around the room they'd stopped in, a small space near the east wing with a broken altar at its center. There were no windows here, but the same soft, golden light glowed from unseen sources. He stood and stretched, then began taking his outer robe off. Behind him, Adinah made a rather undignified noise.

"Just trust me for once," he said. "I'm rather desperately improvising here. If we can't get some proper sleep, we're going to break. Help me drape this over the altar."

She looked at him, face a deep scarlet, expression somewhere between skeptical and amused. She helped him anyway, and together they strung his robe and a few stray cloths they'd found from the fallen stone. He stacked his pack to hold one edge down and she'd used her pauldrons and sword to hold the other. By the end of it, they'd made something loosely resembling a tent.

84

"Is this a wizard thing?" she asked wryly as they crawled inside, adjusting the edges to close out as much light as they could.

"It's a survival thing," he replied, settling onto the floor with a long exhale. "Though I do like to think we invented blanket forts as a prime location for young arcanists to study."

She gave a soft laugh and sat beside him, legs folded, as she took off the rest of her armor. In the dimness, her face looked softer, her eyes less hard. They sat in silence for a while, shoulders close but not quite touching. He exhaled slowly and let the quiet wrap around them.

"It's strange," she said eventually. "I don't usually have trouble sleeping. Even in places like this."

Ezra looked at her. "Is this a typical thing for you? Abandoned temples, cursed unending light, haunted architecture?"

Her lips curved into a reluctant smile. "More than you'd think."

He huffed. "I'll take your word for it.".

"Do you think it's affecting us?" she asked quietly. "The light, I mean."

He hesitated, then nodded. "Definitely. You look like death."

She gave a short, dry laugh. "You're not winning any beauty contests either."

"I could," he said, mock-wounded. "With enough rest and proper lighting, anyway."

Another soft huff of breath. "This isn't what I expected, you know," she said. "From this mission. From you."

He turned to look at her, brows raised. "Oh?"

"I thought you'd be more of a liability," she admitted. "Dead weight. Pretty and clever, sure, but… useless in a fight."

He blinked. "That's oddly flattering."

She shrugged, and for the first time since they entered the temple, her mouth lifted in something close to a real smile.

"You're not useless," she said, refusing to look at him.

"Careful," Ezra said lightly. "That almost sounded like a compliment."

"I'm tired," she muttered. "Don't get used to it."

"You know," he said after a moment, "you're not what I expected either."

"Because I'm not quoting scripture at you and burning things?"

"No, because…" He hesitated. "You've clearly got this way of carrying yourself, and paladins in general have a certain reputation. All steel and command. But you are surprisingly tolerable."

Adinah snorted. "That's the nicest thing anyone's said to me in weeks."

They both laughed. It wasn't loud, but it was real. They made eye

85

contact and the laughter stopped. This close, he could practically feel her breath. He saw her eyes flick down to his lips, then back up to meet his gaze. For a moment, he wondered if he should kiss her.

"You're staring," she said.

He smiled. "Guilty as charged, and yet I find myself entirely unrepentant." Tension crackled between them, and it took every shred of Ezra's will not to lean in.

Desperate to gain some distance, he laid back on the floor, staring up at the darkened ceiling of their makeshift shelter. She remained upright a little longer, then finally lowered herself beside him, not quite touching but close enough that he could feel the heat of her.

Neither of them moved to close the gap.

"Do you think we'll find her?" he asked quietly. "Elidane, I mean?"

Adinah was silent for a long time. "Yes," she said. "I think we're already in her memory. Her echo."

"Do you think she'll listen?"

"I don't know." Another long pause.

Then he whispered, almost to himself, "I hope she doesn't hate us." Beside him, he felt her exhale, long and slow.

"I hope so, too."

Eventually, they slept, and for the first time in days, light didn't reach them.

There was no way to estimate how long they slept, but when he awoke, he noticed the color had begun returning to Adinah's face, the hope and determination shining in her eyes again. She stretched, carefully putting her armor back on.

"Are you ready to see if we're allowed to leave yet?" she asked as she slid out of their makeshift shelter. He followed her lead, putting his robe back on and helping her fold the cloths they'd used, laying them neatly on the broken altar.

"We can always try," he said. "The worst thing that can happen is we're still stuck here. At least we're not stuck here alone."

"That's true, and I am doubly fortunate to be stuck here with such an accomplished crafter of blanket forts."

He cleared his throat to cover his laugh. "Paladin, was that an attempt at an actual joke? I'd suggest marking the day on the calendar, but I can't even pretend to know the date." She rolled her eyes, but the corner of her mouth twitched up in the ghost of a smile.

The walk back to the antechamber wasn't a particularly long one, but every step increased the tension. He could still remember the look on her face when she'd tried the front doors, the look of desperation that clouded her features.

When they reached the antechamber, she took a deep breath and tried the great wooden doors again only to find them still stuck firmly in place. The despair covered her face again and his heart sank. He reached out and touched her shoulder encouragingly.

"It's not over then, I suppose," he said, "but there's still another set of locked doors we can try." She looked up at him, holding his gaze a long moment before turning to the ornate doors at the end of the hall.

He followed her in silence, their footsteps echoing off the walls despite the tapestries. His eyes, though still wary, kept slipping back to her. Here, as a paladin and faithful follower of Ptyraxa, she should have felt completely at ease, but she seemed to be walking ahead with a purpose that was increasingly fragile.

She stopped before great double doors at the end of the hall. These were carved in sunrise patterns, flanked by proud columns that reached like arms into the vaulted light above. As she stepped forward, barely more than an arm's length from them, the air changed.

Voices?

A low murmur rose all around them. It wasn't one voice, but hundreds of layered tones, the sounds of a congregation gathering. Laughter, soft prayers, footsteps, and rustling fabric wove together to form the unmistakable sound of life, of community, of a temple in motion. Ezra's breath caught in his throat, skin prickling. He turned to Adinah, whose eyes had gone wide.

The doors before them blew open. Wind surged from behind them, impossibly warm. It was like a spring breeze warmed by the first light of morning, carrying the scent of fresh air, sun-warmed stone, and blooming jasmine. It rushed past them and into the hall beyond, as though inviting them forward. The hall ahead seemed to brighten and he blinked against the light, reaching out instinctively to grab Adinah's hand as they stepped through the doorway.

The main worship hall defied logic. It was vast, far beyond what Ezra had ever seen in another temple. The ceiling arched so high above that the upper rafters vanished into gilded haze. Pale gold light filtered through windows hidden in the upper eaves, diffused through thin clouds of dust that danced like motes of flame.

The central aisle stretched forward like a royal procession path, lined in an embroidered runner of deep crimson and gold thread, edged in subtle lotus patterns. Time had dulled the fabric, but it had not undone it. It bore barely a hint of dust, as though some unseen hand kept it from decay. Pews–long, elegant rows of whitewood–lined either side of the runner. Their designs were old but lovingly crafted, backs carved with scenes of sunrises over waves and open hands cradling flowers. Something, however, had marred them. The pews closest to the aisle had been knocked askew, some broken where force had split them. Cuts marred the arms and backs.

Sword marks, he recognized, dread settling in his stomach. Scorch marks blackened a few of their once-polished surfaces. Whatever reverence this place once knew had been shattered.

In stark contrast, at the far end of the hall, light reigned.

Stained glass filled the entire apse wall. Massive panes of colored brilliance rose in triumphant arcs, each depicting a piece of Ptyraxa's creed: rebirth, healing, righteous wrath, dawn over darkness. The centerpiece was unmistakable. It was the Dawnfire Heart, stylized and immense, cradled in open palms, shining with layered flame and celestial radiance. Its brilliance turned the whole room to gold and rose and amber.

Beneath that central window, directly in the shaft of brightest light, stood a greatsword. It was embedded into the stone itself, sunk near to the hilt, its blade clean and gleaming as though newly forged. The pommel was a blazing sunburst, each ray crafted from sun-gold and pink quartz, catching the light like fire.

For the first time in his life, Ezra felt small. It wasn't in the way of shame, but in the way of witnessing something true. This was something ancient, beautiful, and sacred. The magic he knew–book-bound, controlled, shaped by will and logic–could not compare to this, at least in presentation. This was something else. He couldn't breathe for a moment, only stare.

I suppose this explains the drama of Ptyraxites, he thought dryly. Adinah, standing beside him, didn't speak. She simply watched. But after a long pause, her shoulders began to tighten. She turned sharply, pacing a few steps, looking around with frustration that grew sharper with every passing second.

"Why would it show us all this and not tell us what to do?"

Ezra blinked, startled. "I–what?"

She spun to face him, brow furrowed, voice tight. "You're the one always talking about reason and patterns. Well? Where's the logic now? What in the gods' names do you think we're supposed to do with this? A temple no one's seen in centuries opens up like it knows our names, leads us to a stupid sword in a hall big enough to house every Ptyraxite in Viremor and nothing else. Nothing! No guidance, no voice, not even a damned whisper!"

He opened his mouth, baffled. "Adinah, I–"

"If this is divine, then where is Ptyraxa's voice? Where's the guidance? If we're supposed to stop what's coming, why doesn't He say something?"

The heat in her words hit him square in the chest. He felt it twist, unearned, but it still struck home.

He snapped back, too sharp. "Maybe gods don't spoon-feed answers, paladin. Maybe they expect their chosen to think." He regretted the words the moment they left his mouth. He saw it in her face, the way she flinched ever so slightly like he'd cut her deeper than she'd expected. His chest hollowed out.

"Adinah," he said quietly, "I didn't mean that. I'm sorry. I just–" She had turned away, arms crossed, her head bowed low. Her shoulders shook once. He hesitated before continuing.

"We both want the same thing, Adinah. Answers. I don't think we're going to like what we find. Those cuts in the pews? Something happened here and we need to be ready. We can't be ready if we're fighting each other." He took a slow breath. "I am not your enemy."

She didn't reply. She moved, slowly, to the nearest intact pew and sat. Her eyes shimmered with tears.

"Why won't He answer?" she whispered. "If not now, then when? What else does He need me to do? I have given everything. Fourteen years of everything." She looked up directly at the great window.

"Please," she said, her voice raw. "Give me a sign. Anything."

Silence. Not even the wind stirred.

Ezra swallowed, throat tight. Watching her like that, gutted and desperate, made something in his chest ache. It felt protective and guilty. He rubbed the back of his neck and took a breath. Then, with a sheepish sort of wince, he glanced toward the sword, the stained glass, and the impossible room around them.

"Well," he sighed, "if gods are being tight-lipped today, maybe we call on someone a little more talkative."

She looked up, brow furrowed, and wiped her eyes with the heel of her hand. "What?"

He cleared his throat, self-conscious, then raised his voice slightly. "Elidane? If you're anywhere near and listening, we could really use a hand right about now."

The words hung there, awkward and strange in the sacred space. He felt like an idiot. Deep down, though, he felt like someone heard.

The heavy sound of doors closing echoed through the worship hall like the sealing of fate. Ezra flinched and the silence that followed felt thick and deliberate, like the hush of an audience awaiting a performance. He turned.

At the far end of the hall, where they'd first entered, stood a proud, elegant figure. He was certain she wasn't there before. There, regal and motionless, stood a woman in radiant full plate polished to mirror-brightness, the kind of armor forged as much for ceremony as for battle. Her golden pauldrons had sunburst motifs, her breastplate was etched with a blazing heart, and her cloak hung from golden clasps shaped like twin wings. The tabard beneath bore Ptyraxa's dawn sigil, embroidered in real thread-of-gold.

Her face was strong, noble, with high cheekbones and a resolute jaw softened by the faint curve of a once-kind smile. Her skin was a warm bronze, glowing faintly with the same inner radiance that limned her armor. Her hair was braided back in a warrior's plait, the color of burnished copper, and her eyes were a striking gold. She looked like someone carved from sunlight and memory.

Everything about her screamed high rank, divine authority, and unyielding purpose. A high paladin. Her body shimmered faintly, however, and her skin held no warmth. Her presence was silent, heavy, and still, like breath held in a cathedral. Ezra took a slow step forward.

"Adinah," he whispered, "I think that's her. That's Elidane."

Chapter 17

Ezra

The specter moved, walking with purpose, her bootfalls silent despite
the apparent weight of her armor. As she passed the pews, her head
remained high, gaze fixed straight ahead. When she reached the central
aisle, Ezra realized–too late–he was standing in it. She walked through
him.

Blistering heat shot through his chest like a brand. It didn't burn his
skin, but he felt the heat to his very core. It was like walking into the sun
itself. Every sense flared white for an instant and his legs nearly buckled
beneath him. When he blinked, she was already ahead, untouched and
undeterred.

As she moved, she spoke. Her voice was clear and calm, but rang with
power. Each resonant word echoed with ceremonial rhythm.

"I vow to guard the weak when they cry for mercy. I vow to lift
the fallen, though they bear the weight of their sins. I vow to walk in
morning's light, though darkness claws at my heels. I vow to strike down
evil without fear, without hesitation, and without hate. I vow to serve
Ptyraxa not as His voice, nor His blade, but as His hope."

Ezra felt the words settle like stones in his chest. She reached the front
of the room and knelt before the blade, knees hitting the stone without
a sound. Her gauntlets pressed reverently to the hilt of the greatsword
embedded in the floor. The stained-glass sun blazed before her, and for a
moment, the long shadow of her pauldrons cast shadows like great wings
upon the ground. She bowed her head and spoke her final oath.

"By the fire of the first dawn, by the breath of the Morning Lord, by
the tears of every soul I failed to save–I vow my soul to the light. Let it
burn within me until I am ash. Let me rise again with the sun."

Light exploded. The sunbeam over the sword intensified into divine
radiance. It spilled across the floor, golden and white, eclipsing everything.
Ezra shielded his eyes, heart pounding. When the light faded, she was

gone.

Silence fell like a dropped veil. He stood, blinking the brilliance from his eyes. Adinah remained seated in the pew, her expression unreadable.

"Are you okay?" he asked softly.

She let out a shaky breath. "Was that…?"

He rolled his eyes. "Yes, that was Elidane, I'm sure of it. Unless you know of any other mysterious High Paladins who vanished in this area and supposedly haunt the place."

She scowled before looking up at him. "Do you think I should try it?"

He raised an eyebrow. "Afraid you'll feel silly saying your vows in front of a ghost's sword in a magical temple no one's seen for centuries? Adinah, we are far past silly." That got the faintest twitch of a smile.

She rose, took a breath, and began walking slowly up the aisle. Ezra fell into step beside her, listening silently.

"I vow to guard the weak when they cry for mercy." Her voice trembled, then steadied.

"I vow to lift the fallen, though they bear the weight of their sins." She looked forward, but Ezra could see the flicker of emotion in her jaw.

"I vow to walk in morning's light, though darkness claws at my heels." No light flared and no magic stirred, but he kept walking beside her. She reached the front, her boots scuffing to a stop. She stared down at the greatsword embedded in the floor.

"I vow to strike down evil, without fear, without hesitation, and without hate." She lowered herself to her knees, placing her hands on the hilt as she looked up in wonder at the great window.

"I vow to serve Ptyraxa, not as His voice, nor His blade, but as His hope." Then, as he held his breath, she continued.

"By the fire of the first dawn, by the breath of the Morning Lord, by the tears of every soul I failed to save–I vow my soul to the light. Let it burn within me until I am ash. Let me rise again with the sun."

The light returned. It began as warmth around them before rising, glowing from the floor beneath. The glass above pulsed with golden light. Ezra instinctively reached out, his hand closing protectively over her shoulder, as the light swallowed them both. It burned, bright and pure and unrelenting, until the world seemed to vanish.

When the light faded, they were somewhere else entirely. The vaulted ceiling of the worship hall was gone. In its place stretched a dark chamber of smooth stone carved into sweeping lines and soft arches. Enchanted torches burned in sconces, casting flickers of gold across the walls.

Every surface was covered in engravings. Symbols of Ptyraxa, verses of devotion, radiant hearts and rising suns. In the center of the chamber stood a massive stone sarcophagus, twice the length of a man, sealed once by faith and stone, but now broken open. Adinah was still on her knees, so Ezra stepped around her to investigate the broken tomb.

Inside lay two bodies. One, unmistakably, was Elidane, her armor identical to the vision they had seen, though now dulled by age and stillness. The second was a woman crowned with silver and lapis. Her circlet was delicate but regal, etched with flame-shaped engravings. Her robes, though tattered, bore the crest of a kingdom neither of them had even thought of in well over a decade.

Adinah gasped softly. "That's the royal sigil of Nemysthra, but they haven't had a monarch in ages. She must've been the last, or very nearly."

Ezra frowned. "Elidane and a queen, buried together?" He looked at her quizzically, but before they could ponder further a screech split the stillness, coming from the shadows. As they turned, the figure of Elidane drifted forward from the darkness, half spirit and half flame, eyes burning with golden fury.

"You dare disturb this place?" she hissed. Her voice was like clashing steel, ringing with divine judgement.

"Graverobbers," she snarled. "You would defile her rest again?" She drew her greatsword from nothing, its blade shimmering with spectral fire.

Ezra pushed Adinah back, heart pounding. "No," he said firmly. "We're not here to defile anything. We were brought here. We saw your vow. We heard you! You led us here!"

Unmoved, Elidane raised her blade, a frightening specter of judgement and divine fury.

93

Chapter 18

Adinah

"I see you, servant of Ptyraxa," spat Elidane, eyes narrowing on Adinah. "But it was one of yours who shattered my tomb. You are not truly His chosen, just as the alleged 'paladin' who came before. You shattered my rest, rest meant to be silent and sunlit. My place beside Sereth will not be desecrated again!"

Adinah barely registered the name before Elidane surged forward. The air erupted in divine pressure. Adinah's instincts screamed. She turned just in time to see Elidane's blade arcing through the air, not toward her, but toward Ezra.

"Move!" she barked, shooting out her hand and grabbing him by the sleeve of his robe. She tossed him, which was easier than she anticipated, and she watched as he hit the ground hard, tumbling backwards with a gasp. She drew her sword, feeling the glow of divine fury burning in her eyes. She sank a bit, keeping her stance low and grounded. She stood between Ezra and Elidane, shoulders squared and her blade raised.

"I won't let you hurt him," she said, voice calm and deadly.

"He doesn't belong here," Elidane snarled.

"And yet he's the only one who hasn't raised a weapon," Adinah snapped back. They clashed, steel ringing against steel, light flashing as their blades collided. Elidane moved like a haunted memory: fluid, beautiful, and devastating. Adinah met her stroke for stroke, her own divine strength roaring in her blood.

"You should be kneeling, girl," Elidane hissed as their swords locked. "I was chosen before Ptyraxa ever knew your name."

"And yet you're the one desecrating His temple with your wrath," Adinah gritted out. She shoved forward. "Ptyraxa doesn't call His faithful back to punish the innocent."

That earned her a snarl and a flurry of strikes that forced her into a brutal defensive rhythm. Sparks danced around them. Ezra scrambled to

94

the edge of the chamber, visible just at the corners of Adinah's vision. He was wide-eyed, his lifted hands glowing with the traces of magic, clearly debating how to intervene. Elidane's head tilted like a wolf scenting blood.

"You," she hissed softly, voice laced with venom as her eyes locked onto Ezra. "You are no follower. No blood-right here. You've no reason to be in this sacred place."

Adinah's stomach sank. "Wait! Don't–!" she called, but Elidane had already turned. She advanced with a predator's grace, ignoring Adinah entirely. Ezra's hands flew up, summoning a shimmering wall into being just in time to absorb the brunt of her next blow. Still, her blade clipped his side, tearing through robe and skin with a hiss of pain.

"Ezra!" she shouted, feeling as if everything slowed. Inside her, something snapped. She screamed, a primal sound that seemed to come up from her very soul. Eyes alight, she surged forward, incandescent and terrible, her sword singing with divine fury.

She met Elidane in a maelstrom of strikes. Gone was the finesse; this was wrath. Her blade moved with righteous purpose, her muscles burning with effort. Elidane was tireless, beautiful, and merciless. They spun in a circle of golden violence until even Adinah's arms began to shake.

She was tiring. Elidane was not. Suddenly, instead of pressing the advantage, Elidane turned toward Ezra. She flicked her wrist, golden energy flaring into a whip of blinding light, and hurled it at him.

Adinah didn't think. She moved. She threw herself in front of Ezra, slamming into him hard enough to knock him to the ground. Her arms wrapped around him protectively, and pain unlike anything she'd ever known tore through her.

It was white-hot, an agonizing spear through her soul.

She heard herself scream before everything went black.

She floated: at least, that's what it felt like. There was nothing; just darkness, pain, and the ache in her soul. A hand seized her shoulder roughly. She flinched, preparing herself to plead with Khoravae.

"Get up," a voice snapped. She knew that voice.

"Get. Up. You are not done." Ptyraxa's voice wasn't the gentle warmth she'd hoped to hear in death. It was a command. She tried to speak, but her lips wouldn't move.

Please, she thought, trembling even in spirit. *It hurts. I can't... I want to rest–*

"You don't get to decide how your story ends," He growled. *"I do, and I say it does not end here."*

Please. I tried–

"You failed once. You do not get to fail again and remain in My light."

95

The words cracked like thunder in her mind. *Fail again.* It was almost cruel, the way He said it, like a knife of guilt twisting through her.

"You have a bit of time to escape before she comes back," He said. *"That's all I can give. Do not waste it."*

Adinah gasped. Pain slammed back into her body like a tidal wave. Her skin burned. Her ribs ached. Her breath rattled. Someone was shaking her. She felt hands cupping her face and heard a distant voice, low and ragged.

"Addi. Come on, please."

She blinked, the world swimming into focus. Ezra. His face was pale with fear, lips trembling.

He cradled her with careful, shaking arms. "Gods, Adinah," he breathed, on the verge of weeping. "I thought you were dead. And I–" He exhaled sharply, pressing his forehead to hers, "I am growing rather tired of the universe trying to take you."

Her hand found his sleeve, squeezing weakly. "Still here," she croaked, throat raw.

He gave a broken laugh, brushing her hair back. "Don't do that again."

"I'll try not to," she murmured. He helped her sit up. Her body screamed in protest, but she breathed through it.

"What happened?" she asked, voice still raspy.

"When you got hit, everything went bright. It was blinding. Then Elidane was gone, no trace of her. The room was quiet. I–" his voice faltered, "I thought I lost you."

She shook her head, dazed. "I'm okay."

He gave her a wry smile. "Good. You should know by now I'm very against the whole 'noble sacrifice' bit, and I believe it was you that said death came with no promotion."

She felt sick at his words, but after a moment she rose shakily to her feet, feeling over her armor. She was bruised, her armor dented, but she was alive. She turned, scanning the room, and a discarded item in a corner caught her attention.

She tried to hurry over to it, nearly falling in the process. Ezra caught her and wrapped a supportive arm around her waist, encouraging her to lean on him. They crossed to the corner and found a symbol on the ground, a pendant on a broken chain. It was twisted and cruel, a stylized flame with a black core. Even without touching it, Adinah felt the evil radiating from it.

"That," she whispered, pointing, "doesn't belong here."

Ezra eyed it warily, as if expecting it to generate another specter. "What is it?"

"I don't know," she murmured, picking it up with a cloth and wrapping

96

it up. "I bet it's part of what's poisoning this place. It shouldn't be here; no wonder they can't rest."

They didn't need to look long before finding a hidden stair behind a tapestry, the way narrow and half-collapsed. With Ezra's support and some divine light to guide their path, they made their slow ascent. The way was long and winding, dusty with forgotten years. Faint murals on the walls depicted the rise of a paladin and her companion. Sereth, her name had been. The story ended abruptly near the top.

As they emerged into the soft amber glow of the main temple hall once more, Adinah sagged with relief. The air here was clearer, less choked by rage and corruption.

Ezra steadied her, glancing around. "It appears we're safe for the time being."

She nodded slowly, catching her breath. Across the great hall, she spied a door in a shady part of the wall. She glanced up at Ezra in a silent plea. Wordlessly, he helped her walk to the door, slightly standing in front of her as he opened it.

Inside was a small living area, no space for much other than a large bed, a storage trunk, and a small writing desk. On the desk sat a leather-bound book, ancient but lovingly kept, free of dust despite the disuse. She sat in the desk chair, Ezra just behind her, hands gentle on her shoulders. Opening the cover, she saw a name in neat script.

Elidane Starcrest. Adinah read in silence, heart growing heavy. Entries detailed her faith, her rise to high service, and her travels to see Sereth. Near the end of the entries was a particularly well-worn section, where the spine was broken, as if the book had been opened many times to this particular page. Elidane's penmanship was slightly different here, too, as if she'd hurriedly scrawled this entry in low light.

"I should be tending to the altar. I should be praying. My thoughts, however, are restless, circling the same name like vultures over a battlefield.

Veylan.

He was once our greatest pride—Ptyraxa's favored, a High Paladin who made even the most wayward believe in light again. I watched men and women kneel beside him not because he demanded it, but because he inspired it. Because he carried the Dawn in his voice.

And now he is gone. Not dead. Worse. Cast out.

Ptyraxa turned His gaze from him, withdrew His favor. I felt it happen that day. A silence fell like frost, the sun dimming around him. His blade lost its glow. The prayers went unanswered and his miracles were gone.

He did not weep or beg. He simply nodded, as if he had been waiting for this moment.

'I asked too many questions,' he told me once, when I found him alone in the cloister gardens. 'And He doesn't like to be questioned.' I asked him what he meant. He only smiled—a bitter, faraway thing.

'Why should we kneel forever? Why must we beg for scraps of light when we could be equal to them?' Equal to the gods...

I told him that was not our path, that power without purpose is corruption, and that the Morning Lord would never turn from one who still walked in truth. He looked at me without fury or pleading, just sorrow.

'I don't think He knows what truth is anymore,' he said. That was the last time I saw him as I remembered him.

Since then, I've heard rumors of lost pilgrims and ruined sanctuaries, of a knight in crimson and black, seeking something unknown.

He left behind something in my dreams. A whisper, maybe, or a warning. I don't know what he's looking for, but I feel in my bones it is not salvation. I do not know where he walks now. I only know the gods do not watch him anymore, even as he haunts me."

Adinah felt sick as the suffocating feeling of dread seeped in. Moving almost too suddenly for Ezra to help her, she pushed back into the main hall, making her way toward the vestibule as quickly as she could manage. Her hand still faintly trembled from the journal entry. Anxiety coiled in her chest, making her armor feel as if it was pressing in on her with each shallow breath.

Veylan. The name echoed like a bell in her head, low and haunting. She tried to push it away, bury it beneath some kind of levity, anything to shift the unbearable weight from her shoulders. She glanced sidelong at Ezra, almost managing a crooked smile at him.

"Think that imposter paladin looked old enough to be Veylan?" she asked lightly, though her voice barely carried. It was a weak attempt. The humor wasn't there. She felt it crack and fall flat the moment it left her lips. He paused, looking up at her without amusement or surprise. His eyes held something heavier, worry etched deep in the corners as if he could see right through her.

"No," he said softly, "and I think you know that."

The silence that followed was thicker than before. She looked away, her mouth pulling into a line, jaw tight. A thousand things rose to her tongue—deflections, excuses, prayers—but none of them made it out. Her throat closed around the words before they could take shape. Ezra's voice, low and careful, broke through again.

"Come on," he said gently, stepping forward. "We should go. This place is done with us."

98

Adinah didn't move. Her legs refused. Her body felt like it was buried in the temple's stone, sunk beneath layers of fear, sorrow, and failure. She had failed in that tomb. She had let her emotions take the reins, lost herself to divine fury, and nearly died. Even worse, Ezra had almost died. She'd seen it in that flash of light. *If I'd been even a heartbeat too slow—*

A warm hand touched her arm, lightly at first, then firmer, reassuring.

"Addi," he said, quieter now. "We're still here. Let's go."

He didn't press. He just stood there, letting her lean on the steadiness of his presence. She exhaled slowly. Her knees trembled as she moved to follow him, step by reluctant step toward the front of the temple. Ezra pushed open the doors to the antechamber, and Adinah felt her stomach flip. The tall doors, covered in carvings of Ptyraxa's rising sun, loomed before them, still sealed shut.

She stopped, hands balling into fists at her sides. She tried to swallow but her throat felt dry and raw. Her breathing grew shallow again, tight and fast, as her hands started to shake.

No, she pleaded with herself. *No, not here, not now—*

She didn't even realize she was trembling until she felt Ezra's hand reach for hers. His fingers slid between hers with hesitant care, as if giving her a chance to pull away. She didn't, though she felt the contact break something in her. When he spoke, his voice was thick—not just with concern, but with something deeper and harder to name.

"Elidane," he pleaded softly, eyes fixed on the doors. "Sereth. Let us out. Please."

His thumb brushed lightly across the back of her hand, sending a wave of heat up her arm to break through the crushing dread.

"And be sure to fasten the latch behind us," he added with a humorless grin.

For a moment, nothing happened. The silence was so complete that Adinah could hear the frantic rhythm of her own heartbeat and the ragged edges of her breath. She squeezed her eyes shut.

A soft click broke the silence and the door creaked open, slow and deliberate, light pouring in through the widening gap. She opened her eyes to dawnlight. True, brilliant morning sunlight spilled across the stone floor, flooding the antechamber of the temple with gold. The warmth of it touched her face, her neck, her shaking shoulders. She couldn't move.

Ezra gave her hand a small squeeze and stepped forward, gently pulling her with him. Together, they passed through the door and out into the fresh morning air. Behind them, the temple doors groaned closed, the soft sound of the latch sealing echoing in the morning. Adinah turned her face to the sun and broke.

The tears came without warning, a sudden and overwhelming storm.

Her legs gave way beneath her and she dropped to her knees in the grass, sobbing so hard her entire body shook. She pressed her hands to her face, trying to hide it, but she couldn't. The flood had started and there was no stopping it.

Ezra was beside her in an instant, kneeling and wrapping his arms around her. She buried her face in his chest, sobbing raggedly into the rough fabric of his robes. His hand cradled the back of her head, the other rubbing slow, comforting circles between her shoulder blades.

"It's alright," he whispered, voice rough with emotion. "Let it out. I've got you."

"I thought–" her voice broke. "I thought Ptyraxa was turning from me, too." Ezra held her tighter.

"I can't fail again, I can't–" She gasped between sobs. "I thought I was going to lose you. I–I thought because of me–"

"You didn't," he murmured. "I'm here."

She clutched his robe tighter, her fingers twisting the fabric. "But if I'm not enough, if He turns away like He did from Veylan… What if I'm already failing and I just don't see it? He said I failed once already, what if I somehow already failed again?"

Ezra didn't try to argue with her. He didn't tell her to stop crying, or that she was being foolish, or that it would all be fine. He just held her. It was enough.

Her sobs slowly softened into hiccupping breaths, her face still buried in the warm scent of sandalwood and parchment. Even in the haze of her grief, it wrapped around her senses, blotting out the dark places in her mind. She felt the steady rise and fall of his breathing, the way his arms didn't loosen even when her tears soaked through to his skin.

"You nearly died," he said softly when her breathing began to steady. "I kept thinking how quiet and dim the world would be without you in it. I do not care for dark and silent spaces."

She buried her face harder against his chest, feeling her face flush. She wanted to tell him he was being ridiculous, that he shouldn't worry about her, but she couldn't find the words.

The campfire embers still occasionally crackled as morning light wrapped around them both, warm and golden and new. For the first time since the tomb, she felt the faintest flicker of warmth deep in her chest, fragile but real.

She would rise again and she would not fail.

Chapter 19

Ezra

The worst of the storm had passed, but the ache in Ezra's chest only deepened as Adinah's trembling breaths quieted, her sobs tapering to shallow exhales. She wasn't crying anymore, not properly, but the silence that followed somehow felt heavier. Her tears had soaked the front of his robes, her armor damp where it pressed against him. Still, he held her close, arms wrapped gently around her, one hand rhythmically brushing the back of her neck in quiet, steady strokes.

He'd thought heartbreak was for poems and ballads, nothing more than a metaphor. It was something artists composed when they didn't have words for the ache of living. For a while, he thought he'd found his own heartbreak when Caedmon cast him aside after he'd been separated from the shred of divinity he'd nearly attained. Now, though, watching Adinah unravel–watching her, the strongest person he knew, break under the weight of divine silence–it made the ache so much more real than it had ever been. It became tangible, like a stone lodged in his chest, grinding against his ribs every time she exhaled.

He would have cursed Ptyraxa if he thought it would help. *If it wouldn't damn the both of us,* he thought.

For a long moment, they stood there in the early morning light. Dew clung to the grass, glistening like glass under the rising sun. Birds chirped in tentative, melodic fits as life slowly reclaimed the edges of the world. Still, he did not move. She eventually shifted in his arms, her voice scratchy and worn.

"I'm fine," she murmured. It wasn't convincing.

"You're not," he said softly. "You're injured, emotionally and otherwise. You need time, and maybe even a proper healer."

"I'm too weak to argue the point," she said, a tired attempt at levity that didn't reach her eyes.

He pulled back just enough to meet her gaze. "We're going back to

101

town." He helped her to her feet and they started to break camp, but it didn't take long to realize she wouldn't make it. The second they started packing, she faltered halfway through lifting a saddlebag, a hand pressed to her side, wincing sharply.

He didn't hesitate. "Then we're staying," he said, gently taking the pack from her. "You're not riding in your condition." She opened her mouth, no doubt ready to protest, then exhaled and sat down heavily on a nearby stone.

"That's… fair." He could see the desire to protest in her face, but she didn't press the point.

He set to work immediately, ensuring his tent was ready. It was already standing from the night prior, and the waterproof enchantment made it ideal in case of a sudden shower. He started modifying the space for her, padding a bedroll with an extra cloak from his bag and adding folded blankets for cushioning. He didn't check to see if he had enough room for himself. He didn't particularly care.

It's the least I could do after all she's done.

When he stepped back out, he found her dozing lightly, still seated, head tilted just enough to suggest she hadn't meant to fall asleep. Her armor was unbuckled and pushed halfway off, revealing the mail and linen beneath. Her dark lashes rested against her cheekbones, a light bruise beginning to bloom near one eye. He wondered why he hadn't noticed before.

She looked fragile. Not weak, never weak, but she did look human, somehow more real than she had before. He swallowed around the tightness in his throat, quickly turning away. He gently roused her, helping her to his tent to settle. She had a pronounced limp now, likely from the injuries fully setting in after the adrenaline faded. When she was tucked on the bedroll, burrowed into a mess of blankets, he went to her bags.

As quietly as he could manage, he pulled out her tent and got to work. He pulled a spool of thick thread and a needle out of his satchel before taking a seat in a nearby clearing to work. Slowly, meticulously, a sigil began to take shape in the seam of the tent's entrance. Rather than do a simple ward, which would wear off in the span of a few days, this would be a lasting fix. He poured himself into his work, focusing on the precise, delicate craft. Hours went by around him, shadows shifting and lengthening as the day trudged on.

They'd missed lunch completely, but the gnawing in his stomach reminded him of dinner. After the previous failure of breakfast, he decided to make something much simpler. He was grateful to find enough vegetables and dried meat in their packs to make something respectable: a simple stew, which he let simmer over the fire as he continued his handiwork.

By the time she emerged, hair mussed and eyes shadowed with exhaustion, he was finished. He folded the fabric quickly, tossing his needle into his satchel.

"Dinner?" he asked, almost surprised at his own voice. *Have I really said so little today?*

She nodded, sitting down by the fire. To his surprise, she didn't sit across from him where she typically did, but beside him. The unexpected proximity made him still for half a heartbeat, but he forced himself to keep breathing. She sat so close her knee brushed his, her warmth a quiet comfort. They shared the stew in silence, gazing into the fire. She leaned her head toward him ever so slightly. He didn't dare move, letting her rest against him.

The sun dipped beneath the horizon, a chill settling into the air, the stars dusting the sky in flecks of silver. A sacred, soft silence stretched between them; for once, he did not feel the need to fill the evening with idle chatter. He was content to hear her breathing, thankful it was there to hear.

By the time they were ready to sleep, only one tent stood. He didn't mention it, and neither did she. He took the other bedroll and laid it outside, more than willing to sacrifice his own comfort. He wouldn't risk making her uncomfortable. She crawled into the space she'd slept in earlier, curling into the bedding he'd arranged for her, eyes already drifting closed. They lay like that for a long time before she stirred, peeking outside of the tent.

"Ezra?" Her voice was slurred with sleep.

He turned his head slightly. "Yes?"

"I don't want to sleep alone," she whispered. "Not tonight."

He wasn't entirely certain she was awake, and wasn't entirely certain he was either. Still, the statement struck something deep in him. The words were simple, and it was such a small thing, but his heart stuttered in his chest as warmth bloomed behind his ribs. Dizzying.

He barely hesitated before dragging his bedroll back into the tent, moving blankets as he went, until barely a hand's breadth separated their bedrolls. She reached out blindly, fingers brushing his tunic. Then she sighed and curled in, already half-asleep.

Ezra lay still, blinking up at the sloped canvas of the tent, heart hammering in his chest. He didn't sleep for a long time.

Eventually, lulled by her soft breathing, the comfort of her presence beside him, and the quiet crackle of the fire outside, he let himself drift. He still felt on guard, watchful, but he was peaceful in a way he hadn't been in a very long time.

She was safe. And that was enough. He slowly drifted off to sleep.
He did not sleep well, however.

He tossed and turned within the confines of his own mind. At first it was shadows at the edges of his dreams, the vague sense of being hunted and watched. Then came the cold, starting as a breath on the back of his neck before turning into a gale, slicing through him like knives. The sky above cracked, no longer blue or black, but a sickly red, split by ash and flame. The world was burning. He was burning. In the center of the inferno stood Adinah.

Blood soaked her armor, glinting dark and wet under the corrupted sky. She was on her knees, sword driven into the earth to hold herself up, golden eyes flickering but unfocused. Her olive skin had lost its warmth, gone pallid and waxen like she'd been carved from marble.

He ran to her. The ground shifted under him, slick with ash and bone. His feet refused to move fast enough. The distance between them grew with every step.

"Elidane," Adinah whispered, voice faint. "She was right. Ptyraxa was right."

"No—no, no, stay with me!" Ezra cried, panic rising like bile in his throat. He dropped to his knees, cradled her face in his hands. "You're alright, I've got you, just hold on—"

A blade burst through her chest. He screamed.

It wasn't real. It couldn't be real. He reached to pull the sword free, but it burned at his touch, radiating corruption and warped holy fire. It hissed against his skin and Adinah slumped forward against him, lifeless.

Her head lolled back, her vacant eyes staring through him. She was completely still.

"No," his voice cracked, broken and shuddering.

Blood coated his hands, ran down his sleeves and soaked into the ground around him like it belonged there. Everything was red. The wind howled louder. Shadows danced, whispering his name with cruel delight. The light began to change and a presence, cold and familiar, coiled in his mind.

"This is the cost of power." It was Xernaea's voice, thick with judgement. *"You seek the stars and forget the weight of flesh."*

He shook his head, clutching Adinah tighter. "She's not—she shouldn't have—she didn't deserve—"

"And yet she suffers," the goddess' voice continued. *"Because of you."* The firestorm above twisted into a spiral, an eye of divine fury watching him.

"Your greed will consume you, and she will be the one to pay for it."

A new sound, a chorus of screams, rose in the wind, promised echoes of a grim future. Visions of Adinah dying, again and again, ran through his mind. Falling to a dragon, or a blade, or to one of his spells misfired. Every death traced itself back to him, branding itself on his soul.

He screamed again, hoarse and ragged, shaking her body like it would wake her. It didn't.

Chapter 20

Ezra

He startled awake with a gasp, breath caught painfully in his chest. The tent was dark, but safe and quiet. The dream's cruel remnants echoed in his mind like a dirge, but the reality in front of him was grounding.

Adinah was very much alive and warm, curled against him in sleep. Her forehead was lightly pressed against his neck, her hand still clinging faintly to the front of his tunic. Her hair brushed against his arm and her breath stirred against his skin. He didn't move.

He couldn't risk breaking the illusion. He closed his eyes and breathed through the aftershocks of terror. Her presence and the steady weight of her body pressed against his anchored him. The ache in his chest, the one that started when she collapsed under Elidane's attack, throbbed differently now. It felt less like pain and more like a sick promise. He clenched his jaw and whispered a silent vow, one he could only keep by force of will.

No matter what power I'm offered, I will not be the reason she suffers again. With that quiet vow, he let her breathing lull him back to sleep.

When he next opened his eyes, daylight filtered softly through the seams of the tent. The space beside him was empty and cool. He sat up slowly, blinking sleep from his eyes, and reached a hand out as if to touch where she'd lain. It wasn't even warm anymore. The flap of the tent had been drawn back, allowing the scent of morning grass and lightly charred food to drift in.

Outside, he found her already moving. Her armor still looked heavy on her frame, but she was upright, her eyes just as sharp as they'd been at the start of their journey. Tirin was nearly fully packed. Her bedroll was lashed in place, and he saw both of their canteens secured. A simple breakfast of fire-warmed bread and spiced root mash was laid out, two portions arranged neatly. She didn't look up when he stepped closer.

"Good morning," he offered carefully, voice soft.

She gave him a nod. "Morning." Her tone was calm and practiced, but he could feel something was wrong. She wasn't looking at him, not directly, even when she passed him his food.

They ate quietly, seated across from each other with the fire between them little more than a smoldering memory. Ezra stole glances at her, noticing the lines in her face were harder than they'd been the night before. Her hands flexed with tension as she picked at her food.

"Addi," he started after a long moment, "you're distant this morning."

"I'm tired," she said flatly.

He frowned. "That's not all it is."

"I said I'm tired." She turned her body away from him a bit, as if physically trying to end the conversation.

He leaned in slightly, voice lowered. "You're not usually this quiet unless you're brooding, and I know you're not fond of that word–"

"Stop." The word was sharp. She set her food down and stood, arms folding tightly across her chest as she turned away fully.

He rose slowly. "Adinah–"

"I don't want your pity." The words landed like a blow.

She kept her back to him, but her voice trembled. "I know you mean well. I know you think you're helping, but I don't want to be pitied. I don't want to be seen as weak. I can do this; I have to. I can still find the Dawnfire Heart. I will find it, and I'll find it first, but I'm not sure I can if you're going to act like I'm fragile."

His heart clenched. "I'm not–"

She whirled on him. "Aren't you? You looked at me like I was glass yesterday, like one wrong move and I'd shatter. I just needed a bit of rest, that's all."

He took a breath. "I was scared." She faltered.

"You almost died," he continued, quieter. "I watched you fall, and even though I was right there, I couldn't do anything. Last night, the past few nights, haven't been rooted in pity. They've been rooted in panic, and last night added in grief. You mean–" He broke off, shutting his eyes. There were too many words fighting to be said, each phrase carrying its own potential consequences.

"I just didn't want to lose you," he said finally. "I'm sorry if I made you feel small. That was never my intention. If last night was a problem, or if I hurt you somehow, I apologize."

There was a long silence, the occasional birdsong the only break.

Then, barely audible, she murmured, "I thought last night was… pleasant." He looked up. She dropped her gaze to the smoldering embers in the center of camp, a faint flush touching her cheeks.

His throat felt tight. "Ah, yes," he replied, just as softly. "I did too, for what it's worth."

She cleared her throat softly. "We should ride back. If we leave now, we can make camp near the edge of the forest tonight and reach town tomorrow."

He nodded. "Let me finish packing." She gave a quiet hum of agreement, and together they packed and loaded the last of his belongings onto Tirin. The morning sun warmed their backs as they mounted, and he felt it burn away the weight of the dream.

The day passed in a gentle haze, the kind that made it easy to forget the days behind them had been full of ruin, blood, and things better left unnamed. The wind was warmer than it had been, brushing softly through the tall grass as if reluctant to disturb the quiet. Even the air seemed kinder.

By the time they made camp, dusk was leaning heavily on the horizon, staining the sky in deep reds and honey-gold light. Ezra helped set up camp with the rhythm of repetition: tent stakes hammered, fire lit, bedrolls shaken out. He had just started to loosen his boots when he noticed Adinah standing by the edge of the clearing with her arms crossed, watching him like she was debating something.

"You're not going to like what I'm about to say," she said.

He glanced up from his pack. "That's a strong opener."

She tilted her head. "You're learning how to fight tonight."

He blinked, waiting for her to change her mind. "We just rode a full day," he protested.

She shrugged one shoulder and bent to unbuckle her greaves. "All the more reason to stretch, then." He opened his mouth to protest further, but her tone had the finality of someone who wasn't asking for input.

"Why now, then?"

"Because I've seen the way you handle yourself–if you can call it that– in a fight. You were entirely reliant on your magic against the bandits and completely helpless against Elidane. I have to assume the latter is because your spells wouldn't work against a ghost."

"Usually ghosts just reform after a moment," he said, wounded.

"Nevertheless," she continued, "I want to be certain if you ever get separated from me, you won't fold like wet parchment."

He narrowed his eyes. "That's a vivid image."

"I'm feeling generous."

She stripped off the last of her armor and laid it neatly in her tent by her bedroll, the motion practiced and swift. Her tunic hung loosely against her frame. Without the weight of steel, she looked younger and lighter, a version of her only seen at the edges of twilight when duty was half-forgotten.

"I certainly can't get you ready to fight someone like Elidane," she said, stepping into the center of their makeshift camp. "But for regular people? This might at least keep you from getting kicked in the ribs."

He winced at the memory, then sighed, deciding it best to humor her. "Alright, what's the first step? Surrender?"

She grinned. "Stance." She gestured for him to join her and he reluctantly shuffled over, squinting in the dim firelight. She took his hands, rough palms warm against his fingers, and adjusted his arms into something resembling a guard.

"Left foot forward," she directed, nudging his foot with hers. "Weight centered." He did his best to do as she directed, though he suspected he looked more like a drunk duck than anything approaching dangerous. She circled him slowly, nudging a knee with her own, pressing his elbow down, and tilting his chin.

"Good," she said, "Looser in the shoulders, though. You're not bracing to be hit by a weapon."

He exhaled. "I'm not *not* bracing." She chuckled.

Adinah came to stand behind him, arms reaching past his sides as she corrected the angle of his hands. Her chest brushed lightly against his back with each movement, and his brain promptly forgot every word in the common tongue. She held his arms, guiding them gently through two consecutive punches.

She was very close, her voice low.

"Try the jab. One-two."

When she stepped back, he steeled himself and tried it. The effort was clumsy and hesitant, but she muttered something approving before stepping in to guide him again. She grabbed his arm, warm and firm, and he caught the faint scent of campfire smoke and salt. They ran the drill a few more times, his rhythm gradually steadying with practice. She let him move on his own, circling now like an opponent instead of a teacher.

"Better," she said, pleased. "Now, let's talk follow-through." She moved in suddenly, lightning-quick, and he jumped backward, nearly tripping over his own feet.

She stopped, raising her brows in amusement. "You've got to close the distance, Ezra. You can't win a fight from two towns over."

He straightened, defensive. "I'm not trying to hurt you!"

She smirked and a hot flush ran through him. "You think you could?" He narrowed his eyes. "I'm wearing a thin tunic, no weapon or armor, and I still think I could knock you on your ass with one hand." She grinned, stepping back. "Try again. This time, commit."

He set his shoulders, took a breath, and lunged. It might have seemed reckless, but he'd seen it in half a dozen bar fights: a move from a guard to

109

a grapple. *Since she'll be expecting punches, I'll have surprise, and I can use my size to my advantage*, he reasoned. His hands found her arms as he stepped forward into her space–

And suddenly they were chest-to-chest. The world stilled, his thoughts fizzling out like sparks.

Her breath caught audibly. Her hands instinctively came to brace against his chest to push him off, her fingers splaying over the fabric of his shirt. He could feel the warmth of her palms and the tension strung between them like a drawn bow. They didn't move, and Ezra wasn't sure if either of them remembered to breathe. His heart thundered in his chest.

Gods, surely she can feel that. He could barely think. She was looking up at him through slightly lowered lashes, expression unreadable but definitely not indifferent.

I could kiss her. The thought came so quickly and clearly it shocked him. The moment hung between them, adding to the scorching heat he felt lapping at his skin.

She moved, fast and sharp. With a twist of her hips and a shift of balance, he was suddenly stumbling backwards. He landed on the grass with a surprised *oof*, breath gone from his lungs. She stood over him, one brow cocked, hands on her hips. Her smirk was infuriatingly victorious.

"Well," she said. "You committed."

He stared up at her, still catching his breath. "You could have warned me."

"Your enemies won't, so you might as well get used to it now."

He groaned and covered his face with one hand. "You're enjoying this."

"Immensely."

He let his hand fall away and met her gaze again. Her expression had softened now, the firelight casting gold over the lines of her face. She looked at him for a moment longer than necessary, then stepped back and offered a hand. He took it. Once he was standing again, she didn't immediately let go. For a second, she just looked up at him, fingers still curled around his. Slowly, cautiously, she stepped forward, pressing her lips softly against his. He stroked her hand with his thumb, the tiny bit of movement sending sparks through him that put Xernaea's magic to shame. She backed away, blushing, looking up at him through her lashes.

"Well," she said, voice a little quieter now. "You didn't do terribly."

"I'll treasure that shred of praise forever. Truly."

She gave him a sidelong glance as she walked to her tent. "Goodnight, Ezra."

"Goodnight, Addi." He stood there for a long moment after she vanished into the flap of the tent, seeming not to have noticed his stitching

110

yet. He stared into the fire and tried to get his heart to stop its desperate thudding. He wasn't entirely certain what had just happened, but—gods help him—he already wanted it to happen again.

Chapter 21

Adinah

Adinah ducked into her tent and let the flap fall shut behind her. The quiet settled over her in a thick, weighted hush, too heavy and too close. She crouched to unlace her boots, but her fingers were clumsy, fumbling with knots she could usually undo in the dark.

Gods. She could still feel his breath. She could still feel the way her hands pressed against his chest, his body so close that every inch of him had been impossible to ignore. Her skin burned with leftover heat, each memory a flicker of flame along her spine.

Stupid, she scolded herself. *It was a training exercise. You're imagining things. You're the one who made it something else.*

The way his eyes had gone dark for half a second, however, and the way he had closed the distance first–she hadn't imagined that. She definitely hadn't imagined the way her body had refused to move, for once not from fear or fight, but from something far worse.

Desire.

She groaned under her breath and tugged off her boots with more force than necessary, one hand bracing on the canvas wall of the tent. She stripped down to her undershirt and trousers, crawled into her bedroll like she was trying to bury herself alive, and stared at the sloped ceiling above her.

The kiss meant nothing. That's what she told herself. It wouldn't happen again–not that anything happened–because it couldn't. She wasn't like that. She didn't lose control.

But the longer the silence stretched, the harder it became to ignore the sick ache curling behind her ribs. She'd almost lost him and nearly died to save him. She hadn't hesitated; she didn't even think before throwing herself between Ezra and Elidane. The pain had been blinding. She could still feel the echoes of it in the marrow of her bones, like it had scorched straight to her soul.

112

She rolled over onto her side, half-wrapped in her blanket. Her hand slipped into her pack, fingers brushing over the wrapped bundle nestled within. The amulet. She sat up and drew it out with a slow, steadying breath. The cloth she wrapped it in was thick. She didn't dare touch it directly.

Unwrapping the layers felt like peeling away something rotten. The closer she got, the more the air seemed to press in, as if the thing was breathing, waiting. The final fold came away, revealing the black-cored flame. She stared down at it, taking care to keep the fabric between it and her skin. Her eyes narrowed.

There were no runes. No names. No sigils of any kind. It seemed profane. Her gaze tracked each strange curve and unnatural groove. Somewhere, buried deep beneath the revulsion, a question gnawed at her.

Who did this belong to? It couldn't have been Elidane, that was certain. She wondered if it was the man from the High Paladin's journal, the one who was forsaken by Ptyraxa. *Impossible*, she concluded. There was no way a person like that would have made their way into the temple, especially since Ezra hadn't been able to see it. If Ezra couldn't see it, surely one cast out by Ptyraxa would have an even worse time.

It couldn't be a paladin of Ptyraxa, either, she reasoned. *None of His faithful would bring something tainted like this into a temple.* She pondered the amulet a bit more before deciding her curiosity would still be there in the morning.

She took a deep breath, wrapping it again. She found a scrap of fabric in her pack, a small strip from a clean bandage roll, and added it for good measure, tying it off with a cord. It went into her satchel, buried beneath a bundle of cloth wedged against her extra shirt. It was out of sight and out of reach, but certainly not out of mind. She laid back down, pulled the blanket over her shoulders, and stared at the ceiling.

Sleep didn't come all at once, but when it did—

She was warm. That was the first thing she noticed. She was warm and safe.

Ezra's arms were around her. She lay curled against his chest, her head tucked beneath his chin. His bare skin was smooth and warm, with just enough lean muscle beneath to remind her this was a man who'd sought the impossible, failed, and lived.

His fingers traced up and down her bare back. Her skin shivered beneath the touch, gooseflesh rising in the wake of each gentle sweep. She should have moved, should have said something, but she couldn't stop staring at him.

His eyes were soft in the low light, his hair mussed like he'd just

113

woken, or perhaps never slept. He looked at her like no one ever had before, like she wasn't untouchable. He admired her like she was beautiful, like she was sacred.

"Addi," he breathed, voice barely above a whisper. She tilted her head up, heart fluttering hard.

He kissed her.

It was slow and searing, sending heat licking through her bones. His mouth moved over hers like he already knew every part of her. One hand cupped the back of her neck, the other on her back to anchor her close. Her hands found his shoulders, trailing down the slope of his back, and–

She woke with a violent jolt. The tent was dim with pre-dawn light, her breath caught high in her throat, heart hammering hard enough to hurt. She was sweating.

"Gods," she whispered, pressing her palms over her face. *What in the hells was that?*

She was a paladin, a protector of the innocent. She wasn't supposed to think like that, at least while on a mission. Her dreams weren't supposed to leave her flushed and trembling and wanting...

She shut that thought down before it could finish. Outside, she heard movement. Fabric rustled, footsteps on grass. Ezra was stirring. Of course he was. She scrambled to sit up, wiping her face with the hem of her shirt, trying to will the heat out of cheeks. She couldn't face him like this, not when her body still remembered the weight of his arms, and definitely not when the kiss still burned her lips like Elidane's power.

She dressed quickly, muttering prayers under her breath to keep her voice steady. When she stepped outside, the sky was tinged with gold, the fire just embers. Ezra was crouched by his pack, stretching his back with a wince.

"Morning," he said, voice still rough with sleep. "You look like you didn't get much rest."

She froze a half second too long, then forced a shrug. "Didn't sleep well."

He studied her for a beat. "Still thinking about before?"

She blinked. "Yes," she said, too fast. Then, softer, "Yes. I keep seeing it. The blast. If I'd been slower–"

"You weren't." She didn't reply, just looked away. "You saved my life."

"It shouldn't have come to that." He didn't argue, just sighed and went to stoke the fire. She was grateful he let the subject drop as the two started breakfast. They ate salted oatcakes and dried fruit in near silence as the morning light grew stronger. The wind had picked up again, stirring the

114

grasses beyond the camp.

"So," Ezra said, licking crumbs from his thumb, "once we're back in Chembrus…" She glanced over. "I think we should check out that inn, The Amber Hearth. I saw that possibly-phony Ptyraxite there, remember?"

She nodded. "Makes sense. Maybe someone saw or heard something suspicious? Ptyraxites aren't very common in Chembrus, since most reside closer to Morningstrike Hall, but surely he couldn't have been that good of an actor."

"We're bound to find something there," he said. "I mean, assuming we don't get immediately thrown out for you boring patrons with your stories."

She gently punched his shoulder. "I am an outstanding storyteller, thank you. I even got some cheers!"

"I started this journey thinking I was safe with a paladin, and you're telling me I've been risking life and limb with a bard?" Ezra clutched his chest dramatically. "I ought to seek out safer companions!"

She grinned. "And yet you're still traveling with me."

He shook his head, but the corner of his mouth curled. "For now."

They packed in companionable, easy silence, giving her mind plenty of space to wander. The dream still lingered at the edge of her thoughts, taunting her. She shoved it down, burying it beneath her duty to find the Heart and keep them both from getting killed along the way. There were more important things to worry about than her wandering thoughts fueled by a lack of bedsport.

Adinah finished packing up Tirin's saddle, checking the straps while Ezra cinched the last bundle in place. She climbed up first and offered her hand without looking. He didn't hesitate, taking it and sliding onto the saddle behind her.

The sky had a muted gray cast, clouds scudding overhead, but the rain held off. They traveled through the morning without trouble. No signs of the divine, no lurking monsters, and no hidden temples calling them in felt like a welcome surprise after all they'd gone through. There was just the road, the wind, and the distant songs of birds in the treetops. They pushed on until early afternoon, the walls of the town rising up ahead.

"We'll be staying at The Amber Hearth then, right?" she asked as they trotted past the outer gates, through streets now busy with merchants and townsfolk.

"That was the original plan, yes, but I was thinking The Tired Fox. For the first night, at least."

She raised a brow. "Isn't that where we stayed last time?"

He nodded. "Yes, but The Hearth tends to attract wealthier patrons and merchants. We don't exactly look the part right now, so any espionage would be useless." She glanced down at her dented armor and travel-worn clothes. He had a point; they'd be entirely too obvious.

"The Fox is safer," he concluded. "Familiar, too. We can get something more respectable to wear, then move on to the Hearth."

She nodded in agreement. *I hadn't thought about the possibility of being too obvious.* Her ears flushed. *That could have been a humiliating oversight.*

They dismounted outside the inn, the carved wooden sign creaking overhead in the breeze. Inside, Thorman looked up from behind the front desk.

"Well now," he said, eyes flicking over them with a glimmer of mischief. "You two back again, eh? Just passing through or sticking around again?"

"Just passing through," Ezra said, brushing travel dust from sleeves.

Thorman nodded slowly, then gave a sly smile. "Still want two rooms? I have them available. Or do you just want the one again?" She felt her heart trip in her chest. She glanced at Ezra, seeing his tight jaw and unreadable expression.

"Two," he said after a pause, "since you have them both available." Adinah looked away quickly, pretending to adjust the strap of her satchel. Her thoughts raced.

Of course he said two, she thought. *Obviously. Why would he say anything else?* A traitorous part of her, though, began to whisper something foolish: *He knows. He knows about the dream somehow.* The heat in her cheeks was immediate and unwelcome.

She shook the thought off. It was irrational. He wouldn't be able to read her mind without her knowing; Ptyraxa prevented that. Still, the silence between them felt thick as he paid for the rooms. Thorman handed over the keys, brow raised in amusement.

Upstairs, their rooms were across the hall from each other. She stepped inside hers and lingered just past the threshold, oddly hesitant. The room was clean and simply furnished, the bed narrow and neatly made. It felt quiet, empty in a way she didn't expect.

Don't be ridiculous, she scolded herself. *It's just me being used to Ezra's constant chatter.* She dropped her pack and leaned her sword against the nightstand.

They had an early supper not long after, a meal of stew, bread, sharp cheese, and two mugs of something warm and spiced that settled in the belly like a hearthfire. Afterward, they wandered into the market quarter, passing shops with woven curtains and displays lit by ever-burning lanterns.

They split up at the tailor's, agreeing to find something decent for appearances' sake. The shop, Stitch & Thread, was a cozy one with bolts of fabric pinned up like banners and a half-dozen mannequins in various stages of dress. The tailor was a small, spry halfling woman with a sharp grin and spectacles on a chain around her neck.

"Well, don't you look like a sword in need of a scabbard," she said to Adinah, sizing her up. "Travel-stained, hard eyes, calluses. Let me guess, you want something that says 'I own a sword' but also 'I know which fork to use at dinner.'"

Adinah grinned. "You read minds better than most mages."

"I am a mage, love," laughed the halfling. "A mage of fabric. Now hold still, my dear. We're going to pin you up like a royal tapestry."

They bantered back and forth, playful and easy. The tailor was efficient, tugging and pinning and muttering, occasionally stepping back to frown in thought before making another adjustment.

She'd chosen a fitted tunic in a deep forest green, made of soft brushed wool that felt far nicer than anything she'd worn in months. The fabric had a subtle sheen under the light, and fine embroidery of simple, curling vinework in muted silver thread that ran along the hems and the high collar. It buttoned neatly up one side with little pewter fasteners, tailored to taper gently at her waist. Over it, the tailor added a sleeveless over-jacket in a deep charcoal. The trousers were soft but well made, dark slate and tucked easily into her boots.

It wasn't ostentatious, but unmistakably the sort of thing a noble's guard captain or minor dignitary might wear off duty. She didn't need to look wealthy, just not out of place. She admired the clothing, feeling like a woman again, rather than a weapon always waiting to be drawn.

"You can pick it up tomorrow," the tailor–Revinia–said with a slight bow. "Pleasure serving you today, Paladin Thorne." Adinah smiled, nodding at the halfling, and stepped outside. Ezra started walking by her to get his own clothing fitted.

"I'm heading back to the inn," she said. "I'd like to get a bit of rest somewhere warm."

He gave her a nod. "I'll catch up. I'm sure I'll be here longer than I'd like to be."

She chuckled. "Not a fan of finery? Could have fooled me."

He didn't look amused as he was eagerly led off by Revinia. She turned toward the street, already thinking of tea and an afternoon nap. Just as she passed the door of a tavern, however, she caught movement in her periphery. Someone leaned casually outside the door. She might've passed him by entirely, but his voice cut the air like a note on familiar strings.

"Well, well. I never thought I'd see you in a place like this."

Chapter 22

Adinah

She turned, already knowing the shape of him. Tall, lean as ever, with a little more sharpness carved into the angles of his face. His golden hair was tied back, neater than it used to be. His light brown eyes, almost gold in this light, still carried that glint that had once made her reckless.

"Dolran," she said, almost teasing. "Still loitering outside taverns, then?"

He gave a low chuckle, stepping out from the shadows. "Only when it yields surprises like this."

She folded her arms as if steeling herself. "You've aged. Less than I expected, though."

"You haven't aged at all," he said, his voice tinged with something like flirtation. "You're still wearing too much armor and carrying too much weight in your eyes."

She laughed quietly, a little rueful. "Still reading people like you've got a book in front of you."

"I used to be very good at reading you."

"You were good at making me want to be read," she said, a little softer than she meant to. She paused.

His expression shifted just slightly, softened, and the air between them changed shape. "It's been what?" he asked. "Ten years?"

"Twelve," she corrected.

"Long enough that I thought you'd forgotten me."

She shrugged, glancing away with a small, fond exhale. "I don't forget people like you."

"Gods," he said with a grin, "still dramatic."

"You didn't think I was dramatic when I broke into Orlan's study with you."

He held up a hand. "Correction: you broke in. I was dragged along under duress."

118

"You wanted that book on infernal history!"

"I just wanted to impress you."

That startled a laugh from her, and it lingered in her smile. She shook her head, feeling the pull of old trouble in the way he looked at her.

"What are you doing here?" she asked. "I didn't remember you being from this area."

"Passing through," he said smoothly. "Like always."

"You've always been so vague."

"No, I've been cautious."

She tilted her head, studying him in return. "What do you do now, Dolran?"

His smile flickered, just for a second. "I'm an adventurer. Nothing more." He stepped a little closer. "What about you? Still in the light of Ptyraxa?"

She hesitated a beat too long, weighing her response. "I'm still walking a path," she said. "Different terrain, but the same Dawn." His eyes lingered on her face.

The corner of his mouth twitched. "What about that man you were riding with?"

She stilled. "What about him?"

Dolran shrugged, his smile careful. "Just seemed close is all. Is he a partner?"

"Only in travel," she replied, more firmly than she meant to.

He gave a little hum. "You always were slow to warm up to new people."

She arched a brow at him. "That didn't stop you." That brought a glimmer of mischief to his eyes, and memories of their time together came unbidden: nights tangled in bedsheets, the sound of rain on temple roofs, and whispered promises between young fools. But the fire had cooled with time. She wasn't that girl anymore.

"I was persistent," he said after a long moment.

"Mm." She smiled just a little too long. "You were something."

He bowed his head slightly, still wearing that damnably charming grin. "Fair enough. I'll take 'something.'"

She stepped back, letting the space between them settle. "I should go."

"Of course," he said, not quite stepping aside. "But it's good to see you, Adinah. Really."

Her gaze lingered on his a second longer than it should have. "You, too."

She felt him watch her leave, eyes trailing her with that slow, familiar intensity. As she turned the corner, her heart beat a little too hard in her chest. Not because she missed him, but because she knew how tempting it could be to fall into heat disguised as history.

Ezra returned to the inn not terribly long after she did. She flagged him down as he entered, ordering him a cider as he slid into the seat beside hers. His mood seemed sour, and she wasn't sure if it was from the process of the fitting or the price. She empathized, having parted with two gold coins herself.

"Ran into someone I used to know," she said, hoping to lighten the mood.

He looked up. "Oh? Nice to see an old friend?"

"I suppose. It's been a long time." She sipped her own drink. "We were kids training together. Snuck off to smoke mistvine behind the shrine and drink stolen dwarven ale."

Ezra huffed a quiet laugh. "Tragic that I never knew the less reformed Adinah."

"Truly. I'm now on the straight and narrow, following the Dawn." He rolled his eyes a bit at the comment, but he smiled. They lingered for a while, sharing soft conversation and idle observations. The night crept in, exhaustion hastened by a day on the road, and they parted for their rooms.

It was the crash that woke her. Sharp and sudden–glass, maybe– followed by a thump and silence. She was out of bed in an instant, sword in hand, heart hammering. *Was that his room?* She couldn't quite tell in the haze of sleep. She rushed across the hall and knocked, quick and firm.

"Ezra?" A moment passed, then the door cracked and opened. He stood there, blinking.

"Are you alright?" she asked when he said nothing.

"Yeah," he muttered, rubbing his head. "I woke up from it, too. But it wasn't me."

She studied him a moment longer, then nodded. "Alright, just checking."

He smiled faintly. "Thanks, but after you taught me to fight yesterday, I'm sure I can take any ne'er-do-wells." Her ears felt hot. She wanted to disappear.

She nodded, turning back to her room, the silence pressing in around her. Crawling back into bed, she waited a moment to listen to any further commotion before she let sleep claim her.

The next morning passed in the slow, steady way only an old inn in a small town could offer. Sunlight slanted through the warped panes of the common room, catching the glint of dust in the air. Adinah stirred a spoon through her porridge as if the rhythm might wake her more than the bitter tea beside it. Ezra was quieter than usual, which meant his mind was already busy sorting through plans and questions. She waited until they'd eaten most of their meal before leaning back in her chair.

"We should stay here another night," she said firmly.

He looked up, eyes sharp. "Something change?"

"No," she said, stirring again. "But if we're planning to do reconnaisance at The Amber Hearth tonight, it's better we don't draw attention by coming and going. If things go sideways, we need somewhere to disappear to where we won't risk being overheard."

"Fair point," he said, glancing toward the stairs. "We should keep our same rooms, yes?"

She nodded. "Less fuss for Thorman."

"Then I'll let him know." Ezra rose, the chair scraping lightly across the floorboards. Adinah smiled when he didn't question her logic. She appreciated that more than she was willing to admit.

Later that morning, they returned to the tailor to collect their clothes. She lingered a little too long just outside the shop, her hand hesitating on the door handle. The outfit she'd chosen the day before had begun to feel impulsive. It wasn't improper, but definitely not her usual fare. Now that she was about to put it on for the evening, self-consciousness curled warm and stubborn in her chest. The tailor beamed when they entered, already pulling parcels down from hooks along the back wall.

"Ah, my dears! You're back." Adinah rolled her eyes but didn't suppress the small smile that tugged at her mouth. Ezra looked bemused. As they took their wrapped bundles and thanked the tailor, Adinah caught herself scanning the street. She didn't want to see Dolran, not really, but part of her expected to. She crushed the train of thought.

After lunch, they returned to their rooms to prepare for the evening. The Amber Hearth was known for its deep cellars, rare vintages, and clientele with coin to spare. It wasn't the sort of place a paladin and a wizard covered in road dust and suspicion could stroll into unnoticed.

She cleaned up the best she could. She heated water with a simple stone Ezra had enchanted for the purpose, stripping down to wash in the shallow copper basin in her room. The water quickly turned murky as she scrubbed herself red-raw, as if that might quiet her thoughts.

She thought of Dolran, his smirk and the way his voice dipped when he said her name. She remembered being nineteen, cloaked in night and nervousness, watching him spar until the moment his blade slipped and his power failed. She'd seen it happen, like someone had snatched the light out of him. There was no glow, no warmth, just the chill of rejection that passed through him like a ghost. He'd stood there, dumbfounded, and she'd stared at him like she didn't recognize him anymore.

The next morning, she'd been in the chapel before dawn as he packed his things to leave. She'd been in the chapel every morning after that, too. Her faith had always been a tether, but from then on, it had been a leash, too. One she kept tight to avoid a similar fate.

She slipped into her new outfit just before the sun began to dip again. Revinia had done incredible work. The fabric cut was flattering, somehow more feminine than it'd seemed in the shop, and for a fleeting moment she felt something unexpected. She felt pretty.

With a shaky breath, she opened the door to the hallway at the exact moment Ezra opened his. He stepped out and for a moment, her breath caught.

He wore a high-collared longcoat in a deep obsidian, tailored sharp to the waist, with brushed silver clasps that caught the light like moonlight on steel. Beneath it, a midnight blue tunic peeked out, layered over narrow black trousers tucked into freshly polished boots. His hair was brushed back; it wasn't really formal, just smooth enough to look intentional. He wore only a small satchel and a single dagger at his belt. The outfit made him look taller somehow. Quieter, too, maybe a bit more dangerous. Unfortunately for her, it also highlighted how infuriatingly handsome he was. She stared for a beat longer than she meant to.

"You clean up," she started, steadying herself, "annoyingly well."

He glanced over, a flicker of amusement in his eyes as they swept her frame. "Likewise. That color suits you." She turned her face slightly, not letting him see how that compliment landed.

She cleared her throat. "Ready?"

Ezra nodded, and together they descended the stairs, the two weaving their way through the Fox's patrons and out onto the evening street.

Chapter 23

Ezra

Ezra had always been good with words, but as soon as Adinah stepped into the hallway, dressed in that fitted tunic and trousers that hugged her legs just enough to make a man reconsider his priorities, he nearly lost the ability to form a coherent sentence. She looked like something out of a dream, equal parts elegance and danger, every inch the woman who could cleave a man in two and leave him grateful for it. He'd tried not to stare, honestly he did, but his voice came out lower than he'd meant it to.

"That color suits you?" He scolded himself. *A beautiful woman comes out to spend an evening with me, and the best compliment I can muster is on her color choice? No wonder my bed's been empty so long.* He spent most of the short walk to The Amber Hearth chastising himself, but he was acutely aware of every step she took beside him.

He thought, once or twice, about offering her his arm. *After all,* he told himself, *that's what a gentleman would do.* He knew better, though. Adinah had made enough of a point about not wanting to feel small, or protected, or handled like fine glass. She was steel wrapped in silk, and even in finery she walked like someone who didn't need saving. Still, he couldn't help the occasional glance, couldn't help the way his gaze lingered on the curve of her waist or the bounce of her curls.

He just hoped to the gods she didn't catch him looking.

By the time they reached the Hearth, the crowd had already begun to swell. Laughter spilled out of the doors with the golden light, and the scent of meat, spices, and sweet drink hung thick in the air. He instinctively moved a half step ahead, clearing a path toward the back wall where a small corner table stood unclaimed. He pulled out the chair for Adinah before catching himself, and she gave him a dry look that he met with a crooked smile. No words were exchanged, but the message was clear: she could seat herself just fine.

They both sat and ordered drinks before Ezra leaned in, dropping his voice.

"Alright," he started. "Here's how I see it. We can't stick together all night. We'll learn more apart. Different faces, different approaches."

She nodded. "We'll circle back here after an hour or so. Or sooner, if something happens."

"We should have a signal." His lips twitched. "Just in case one of us, probably me, needs rescuing."

She took a long sip from her drink, then arched a brow. "Like what?"

He considered for a moment, swirling the amber liquor in his glass. "How about 'we forgot the cask?'"

She blinked. "That's terrible."

"Which is exactly why it works." He grinned. "No one would ever say it unless something's wrong."

She chuckled softly, the sound almost lost in the din. "Fine," she conceded. "'We forgot the cask.' But hopefully you only expect intervention in the event of actual danger, not flirtation gone awry."

Ezra feigned offense. "You wound me. I'm a professional."

"You're a menace," she corrected, smirking as she finished her mead.

He raised his glass in mock salute. "To menace, then."

"To a quiet night," she countered. They clinked their glasses together softly, the moment lingering longer than it needed to. Then, with a brief shared nod, they rose and parted into the crowd.

Ezra found his target quickly, a brunette with honey-colored skin and a smile that could make saints weep. She was dressed in amber silks, gold thread shimmering at her cuffs, and her laugh had a musical lilt that caught him by the collar and dragged him in. He slid into a seat beside her with practiced charm.

"Evening," he said, easy and warm. "You don't happen to be one of the many people here tonight who know things they shouldn't, do you?"

She laughed. "Depends. Are you buying the next drink?"

They talked for a while, with him ensuring her glass stayed full. Her name was Mairen, and she was more than happy to indulge in flirtation, fingers trailing her glass rim as she spoke. He leaned in and listened close, offering sly smiles at just the right moments. When he directed conversation to interesting individuals she'd met recently, he found what he had been searching for.

"Oh, there's the most handsome Ptyraxite," she said, eyes lighting up. "He's staying here, though he keeps entirely to himself, which is the real tragedy." She inclined her head, gesturing toward the stairs. "Room right next to mine. He's in thirteen, I'm in fourteen." She winked.

Ezra knew better than to take the bait so early. "Why talk to me? You sound rather sweet on him."

She flushed a bright red. "No time, sadly. He looked pretty badly beaten the other night, limping up the stairs like he'd been thrown off a horse. I assumed I'd give him time to mend his broken pride, but the next morning? Fresh as a daisy."

He feigned surprise. "Impressive healing, then."

Mairen scoffed. "No one heals that fast. I figured I must've been mistaken, but it was definitely him that night. He's been twitchy since. Paranoid. Keeps talking about losing something sacred, some amulet or other. You know those paladin types: one lost trinket and suddenly the sky's falling."

"You don't say," he murmured, brushing her hand gently. "Sounds like he could probably use a bit of a calming presence, then."

Mairen caught the hint, her smile falling just a bit. "If he comes down tonight, I might have to. He doesn't usually stay down here long." She sighed. "Maybe this is the sign to make my move."

He let his hand gently brush hers as he stood. "You've been a pleasure, Mairen. Good luck."

She flushed a bit, her gaze dipping to her empty glass. "Don't be a stranger."

He turned just in time to see Adinah across the room, sitting alone, watching him with a look that hovered between dry amusement and reluctant admiration. He crossed over to her, carefully navigating around various merchants and affluent adventurers.

"Poor woman never stood a chance," she teased, raising her glass to him in acknowledgement.

"We'll talk later," he said quietly. She nodded, lips twitching like she was trying very hard not to smirk.

They moved to the bar, each keeping themselves open for conversation with others. Ordering another round, he kept his eyes on the room, occasionally glancing at the door and the stairs. After an hour or so, they'd spotted nothing suspicious, and their mysterious "Ptyraxite" was nowhere to be found.

As the evening wore on, Ezra found his gaze drifting more often. First it was to the way Adinah leaned her chin on her palm, then to the way her eyes glinted in the candlelight, then to the way her tunic clung to her hips.

He was definitely overserved. When his thoughts further edged into dangerous territory—*How would she sound if she let go? What would her hair feel like tangled in my fist?*—he decided it was time.

"We forgot the cask," he said into his cup.

She glanced at him, carefully studying his expression, and gave a small nod. "Let's go, then." She slid off her seat and started towards the door without waiting for him.

The walk back to The Tired Fox felt long in the crisp night, but the bite of the air was a welcome distraction that kept his thoughts straight laced. They hadn't spoken on their way back other than deciding to share their findings over breakfast. He tried not to appear grateful he would be turning into bed soon.

Just outside the Fox, she paused. "You go ahead to bed. I'll chat with Thorman on the off chance he's heard any gossip."

He nodded, bid her goodnight, and slipped into his room. Door closed, he stripped down and collapsed into bed, still flushed from drink and too much proximity to temptation. He closed his eyes, hand slipping beneath the blanket to soothe his arousal.

He tried to think of Mairen, of the curve of her shoulder and the flirtatious glint in her eyes, the promising smile that had lingered on her lips. She was beautiful and easy to imagine, but the longer he lay there, fist curled around the aching weight of himself, the more she slipped from his mind.

Adinah replaced her.

Gods, it wasn't fair how vividly his mind could conjure her. The way her tunic had hugged her figure, the slope of her waist beneath leather and wool. The strength in her arms. The fire in her eyes when she argued with him.

He bit down a groan, stroking himself slowly now, more deliberately. He imagined her standing over him, still in that green tunic, arms crossed, amused and unimpressed until she wasn't. Until her mouth curved into something darker and indulgent. Until she climbed on top of him, straddling his hips, tugging her leather riding gloves off with her teeth.

His breath hitched.

He imagined her voice, low and commanding. "Keep your hands to yourself, Ezra."

He would. He'd lie still while she undid his belt with maddening slowness, cool fingers grazing skin just enough to make him twitch. Her expression would be impassive, studying him like a puzzle to solve, until he said something that broke her composure. Something desperate. Something filthy. She'd smile then, just a little, before commanding him to remove her clothing, using her strength when necessary to keep him from going too quickly.

His hand quickened.

He imagined her thighs bracketing his, that first slide of her down onto him—tight, slick, and unbearably hot. His hips jerked upward involuntarily at the thought, a shudder racking through him. She'd be breathless and flushed, brow furrowed in concentration as she moved above him, using him, hands splayed on his chest to hold him down.

He'd love it. Gods, he'd beg for it.

He muttered her name under his breath, the closest he'd ever come to a prayer. His strokes grew faster, more frantic, driven by the images in his head: Adinah tossing her head back, Adinah riding him hard, Adinah dragging her nails down his chest and growling his name when she came.

He was close. Too close. Then–

Knocking. It was soft at first. Then louder. He froze, panting, sweat slick at the small of his back. The knock came again. It was more insistent this time, bordering on frantic.

"Fuck," he hissed, throwing back the covers, pulse still thundering in his ears. He dragged on a shirt with shaking hands and yanked up his pants, not even bothering to lace them properly. The ache between his legs throbbed like a cruel joke as he stumbled to the door and threw it open.

Adinah stood there, still in that same green tunic. Her face was sickly pale, eyes wide.

"My room's been ransacked," she said, a little too calmly. "Everything: my bags, my satchel, all of it. Torn apart." He opened his mouth, heart still pounding, but she cut him off, her voice lower and sharper.

"And the amulet," she hissed. "It's gone."

He blinked at her, letting her words sink in. "Oh, shit. Well," he said, trying to keep his breathing steady. "I'll be right there." He started to shut the door, but Adinah stuck her foot in the way.

She squinted at him suspiciously. "Ezra? Are you alright in there? You're sweating." Before he could answer, she poked her head in, looking around with her hand on her sword hilt. "If someone's in there threatening you, you should've–"

She glanced around the door as if trying to see if someone else might be behind it. Her gaze flicked down, probably to check for a crouching robber, and held there. Just for a second. She looked back up at his face, eyes wide, face flushing with unmistakable color. She didn't look again.

"I–" she started, clearing her throat as she backed into the hallway. "I'll wait here until you're more... appropriately dressed."

He wanted to die. No, to be struck down by a bolt of lightning from the heavens. Hells, he'd rather take Elidane on again.

"Right," he muttered shakily, stepping back and shutting the door with a muffled thud. His heart pounded in his throat. He was still achingly hard. Gods, he hadn't even finished.

He scrubbed a hand through his hair and turned from the door, biting back a groan. Mortification clung to him like a second skin. *What she must have thought,* he panicked. *What she must have known.*

And the worst part? She didn't even look disgusted. Just embarrassed, like she'd caught someone doing something she shouldn't have seen, but maybe, just maybe, hadn't minded the view.

Don't think about that, he told himself, fumbling with the ties on his breeches. *No more thinking about her. You had your chance already tonight.* But she was already etched into the inside of his eyelids: long legs, the way that damn tunic clung to her curves, and the shadow of muscle beneath the fabric.

Chapter 24

Ezra

By the time he stepped back into the hallway, decently dressed and pretending not to still feel half-naked, Adinah was standing beside his door with her arms folded across her chest. She gave him a polite nod as if the last thirty seconds hadn't been possibly the most awkward of his life.

"Come on," she said softly. "It's bad." He followed her without a word.

The door to her room stood slightly ajar, and inside it looked like a whirlwind had torn through. Clothes were scattered everywhere. Her packs were gutted, flaps open and contents dumped across the floor. Her bed was even stripped bare other than her holy text, the blankets tossed aside in a tangled pile. A few buckles glinted in the lamplight from her armor, but none of it had been taken.

It looked like someone had been searching, not destroying or blindly robbing. The thoroughness suggested someone rifled through with intent. The window hung half open, curtains stirring in the night breeze.

He stepped carefully over her pauldrons. "Looks like they left in a hurry."

"Or arrived that way," she said thoughtfully. "Or both, I suppose." She moved through the mess, checking each of her bags.

He started to step toward her, then hesitated. "I'll keep watch. Unless you want help, of course, but I figure you might not want another set of hands on your things."

She glanced back, visibly touched. "Thanks. I've got it."

He took position near the door, scanning the hallway, but kept one eye on her. She checked through what remained and returned gear to her bags. Her motions were slower than usual, though, tight with worry.

She broke the silence first. "I spoke to someone earlier at The Amber Hearth. An elf, friendly enough. He said there's a Ptyraxite paladin staying there in room thirteen."

He glanced over. "That tracks with what I've heard. The woman you saw me with for so long said the same, but I never got his name."

"Neither did I. Apparently he's quiet, keeps to himself. The gentleman I spoke with hears him pray every day."

"Oh?"

"Just the expected," she sighed. "Just asking for strength and guidance. Apparently he didn't get it, though. He'd left for a day, but came back in quite the state, covered in bruises and limping. The next morning he was perfectly fine. Not surprising, maybe, if he'd been up all night praying."

"Paladin healing is incredible, from what you've shown me," he agreed, frowning. "Still, healing that much damage in a day? You told me most wouldn't burn the energy just to fix themselves completely unless they had to."

"Exactly," she said. "That's what's bothering me. Most of us can't heal that completely even if we worked on it all night. The energy such an effort would require would be immense. We were always taught that our divine healing should be used as a last resort, and only as much as we need to stay alive, especially since healing is so taxing." They shared a look, quiet tension stretching between them.

"Maybe he had something to hide," he offered. "Though, of course, there is the chance he really is a Ptyraxite and we're pursuing an innocent."

"No," she said, shaking her head. "That's too much coincidence."

He sighed, nodding. "You're right, of course. A Ptyraxite you know nothing about, in an area where they aren't common, appears just before a mysterious Ptyraxite temple is desecrated, and the same paladin arrives in town looking rough?" He gave a humorless laugh. "Not impossible, but far too unlikely."

She tugged a scarf free from the edge of the bed and shook it out. "And now my room's been searched."

He nodded. "Which means they were looking for something."

"And they found it. Like I said, the amulet we found with Elidane is gone." Silence fell again, heavier this time. He hadn't recognized it, but clearly the symbol was important enough to someone to necessitate a burglary.

Eventually, when she'd done as much sorting and re-packing as could be done, they left the room and descended the stairs together, the hour late enough that the inn's common room had emptied. They made their way to a back hallway where Thorman's door bore a carved woodplate with his name. Adinah knocked gently. The innkeeper answered in a nightrobe, bleary-eyed but concerned the moment he saw her expression.

"Gods, miss–what's happened?"

"My room was broken into," she said calmly. "Everything was searched but nothing damaged. I don't believe anything's missing, but I wanted to let you know."

He pressed a hand to his heart. "I'll refund your room. Should I fetch the guard?"

"Please, let's wait until morning," she said gently. "There's nothing to go on, and I'd rather not cause a stir without reason."

"Of course, of course…" He rubbed his face. "I don't have another room to offer, I'm afraid. We've been booked by festival travelers. I can try to help you find another inn, though it'll be difficult at this hour."

Ezra cut in. "She can stay in my room. Safer that way anyway, and if someone's targeting her specifically, they won't be able to isolate her."

Adinah looked at him, surprised, then smiled faintly. "Safety in numbers."

Thorman gave a grateful nod. "Thank you both. Give me a moment and I'll get dressed to check your mount before you turn in–"

"No need," Ezra said. "I'll go."

Outside, Tirin was still tethered in the stable, unharmed and chewing contentedly on a bundle of hay. Ezra patted his neck and returned to the common room.

Adinah waited near the stairs. "Before we turn in, do you, um," she asked with a cough, "need to move anything around before I come in?"

He winced. "No. It's fine." She stepped in her room for a few minutes, returning with her bags, wearing her simple traveling clothes.

They entered his room together and she stepped lightly across the floor, laying her bedroll out neatly on the far side of the space. He mirrored her, intentionally leaving the bed untouched between them.

"You sure?" he asked, nodding toward the mattress. "You can have it."

She was already curling into the bedroll, pulling a blanket over her shoulders. "We'll both survive."

"You didn't mention the amulet to Thorman," he said after a quiet moment.

She sighed. "I didn't want to mention it if I didn't have to. I don't know if the person we're investigating is working with anyone else, and I didn't want to risk dragging yet another person into my mess."

"It makes sense, I suppose, but he still might have known something useful about it."

"If the two of us didn't recognize it, I doubt many else would. I'm not certain if the people who would recognize it would tell us anything, either."

"Fair enough." He wondered if she had other reasons for being tight lipped, but he doubted he'd get any other information from her until morning, at least.

He watched her a moment longer. She rolled over, pulling something small from her pack and clutching it to her chest. Before she could turn away, he saw it: her holy text. Seeing her hold it close like a ward made him swallow hard.

There was something sacred about the image of her like this, devoted and vulnerable, yet still braver than most he'd known. She'd faced down horrors without flinching, and here she was, clutching a book and laying her head down on a wood floor like it was a perfectly normal evening.

His earlier lusts burned in his chest like guilt. *She's got enough on her mind without me adding to it,* he thought, turning over in his own bedroll. He listened to her breathing slow, soft and steady. Outside, the wind rustled the shutters. He didn't sleep for hours. Every creak of wood or whisper of movement had him half-risen, eyes scanning the dark. When sleep finally claimed him fully it felt like a mercy, and he dreamt of a world in which he hadn't thoroughly embarrassed himself in front of her.

By morning, the inn's common room stirred with quiet clatter and the scent of hearth smoke and tea. Warm sunlight slanted through tall windows, streaking across the worn floorboards and catching the floating motes of dust in a golden glow. Ezra sat at a small table with Adinah, nursing a steaming bowl of porridge that tasted like it had been made hours ago and left to congeal.

She hadn't said much since waking. Her cloak was draped around her shoulders, hood pushed back, her hair still damp from washing. The dark circles beneath her eyes were more visible in the morning light, and he wondered if she'd slept at all.

They ate in silence for a time, until the front door opened with a brisk creak and two town guards stepped inside. The innkeeper spoke to them in hushed tones and pointed toward the two of them.

Adinah stood before they reached the table. "I'll speak with them."

Ezra didn't argue. He watched as she stepped away to offer her report: precise, polite, and brief. The guards asked a few questions. She answered them, but only what was necessary. She mentioned nothing of mysterious paladins, nothing of the man who might have healed himself overnight, and definitely nothing about Elidane or the symbol or the amulet that had vanished from her belongings.

Ezra kept quiet.

The guards left, promising to check around to other inns about possible break ins. After returning to his room to collect their things, they went to the stable, ready to leave the inn behind. Tirin greeted them with a soft huff. Ezra took his time gently scratching near his ears and along his neck

132

while Adinah loaded him with their gear.

The morning was clear and chill, with carts already rattling by as people milled about. They decided to seek out a room at The Amber Hearth, hoping to find their mysterious Ptyraxite on his way in and out. As they walked, they passed a few traveling minstrels tuning their instruments by the steps of a bakery, each of them dressed in the livery of various nobles.

"Must be something big happening," he murmured.

She followed his gaze. "Must be, with this many houses represented."

"A few autumn rite festivals happen in this region, but I don't know many close by that would attract nobility."

"Do you think it has anything to do with the theft?"

He thought for a moment. "Not unless the gods have a particularly cruel sense of humor. Seeking judgement against the landed gentry seldom goes well for the petitioner."

They reached the Hearth soon after, the inn as bustling as ever. The innkeeper, who introduced herself as Marla, stood behind the bar arranging bottles, her sleeves rolled up and her cheeks ruddy from the morning's exertion. She looked up with a bright smile as they stepped in, but her face dimmed with sympathy when they asked for a room.

"Ah, I'm afraid I've got nothing," Marla said. "Haven't had a room to spare in four days. Festival traffic's coming in early this year."

Adinah blinked. "Which festival?"

Marla leaned forward, elbows on the bar. "The Festival of the Amber Moon. Happens every year in Ravenglen, about six days east of here. Most folk stay here a few days before making the last of the journey. Easier to break it into smaller trips than doing the whole trip in one go, or so they say."

Ezra tilted his head. "Amber Moon... sounds familiar."

"It should," Marla said. "Biggest festival on this side of Viremor. Food, music, art, lots of parties. The regional nobility and the well-to-do show up for the masked ball on the final night, even those from as far as Larkspin."

"A masquerade?" Adinah asked.

"The Amber Masquerade," she confirmed. "It's held at the Torneval Estate. The manor belongs to this older mage named Caedmon Throneval. Bit of an odd duck, but a good soul. He opens the estate every year for the event." She leaned across the bar, lowering her voice to a conspiratorial whisper. "Between you and me, I've tried for ages to get in, but I've never secured an invitation."

Ezra's brow lifted, recognition rippling through him. Adinah noticed immediately.

"You know him." It was a statement, not a question. He tried to play it off, but the corner of his mouth betrayed him.

"Caedmon and I are… acquainted. We studied together once." He smiled, gesturing toward a bottle Marla was about to put away, eager to look anywhere but at the two women.

Marla grinned, handing him the fine red. "Well, there you go. You've already got an in. That's more than I've ever gotten!" Adinah gave him a sidelong look. He paid, thanking Marla as he tucked the bottle into his satchel and turned toward the door.

Once they were back into the street, Adinah tilted her head at him. "So, Caedmon Thorneval?"

"He's an old friend," he said, fingers rubbing the fabric tied at his waist. "We studied together once, long ago. He's a brilliant arcanist and absolutely obsessed with the occult. Spirits, interdimensional echoes, dead gods, you name it. He doesn't practice any of it, mind. Just studies."

Her eyes lit with mischief. "Do you suppose he might know anything about an amulet, if we asked him?"

He smiled. "He might, come to think of it. I'm sure I could pull some strings to get an audience. If anyone knows about strange relics or amulets, it would be Caedmon. He's got contacts in every mages' college and temple on this side of the Spine."

"You two were close then?" she asked.

He felt his ears burning. "Very."

She looked like she was fighting down a smirk. "Let's sleep on the idea of going to see him," she suggested. "We can decide if that's our best option. There's no need to be hasty." He nodded, and they ventured back into town in search of another room.

They spent the rest of the afternoon checking every inn and guesthouse in town. The answer was always the same: no vacancies. Even the stable lofts and half-floored attics were taken. By dusk, they found themselves standing on a quiet far road at the outskirts of town, where a kindly old farmer agreed to let them camp at the edge of his orchard. He'd even let Tirin have a place in his stables. Ezra gave him two silver for his trouble, and they promised to leave early the next morning.

They set up camp in a small clearing near the gnarled trees, the leaves shining silver in the moonlight. The air was cool and still, filled with the scent of earth and fresh apples. They made camp quickly and prepared dinner, sharing a plate of roasted potatoes and salted pork.

They sat close, trading the bottle back and forth between them as the stars came out. Eventually, somewhere in the middle of the bottle, Ezra broke the silence.

"Elidane's journal, what it said about Veylan," he started, taking a long drink. "It's been bothering me."

Adinah looked up from her plate. "Oh? Any reason?"

"Because I understood him," he said softly. She set her plate down.

"I wanted to be equal, to have the same control over the arcane the gods do," he continued. "Partially for the power, but also because I was tired of being ignored and overlooked. I wanted someone to see me, someone to think I was worth keeping an eye on."

He took another drink. "What if they don't watch me at all? What if no one does?"

Her voice was warm and firm. "They do."

He smiled without humor. "You don't know that."

"Then I'll watch over you."

Ezra blinked, startled. Her words weren't dramatic, just firm and quiet, the kind of promise you believed even when everything else seemed uncertain.

She smiled faintly. "I mean it. You're not lost. You haven't fallen the way you seem to think you have. And if you did, it's not a road you'd walk down alone."

It hit him harder than it should have. He looked at her, really looked at her. The firelight caught the curl of her hair, the softness in her expression, and the strength in her jaw. He swallowed hard.

She picked at a loose thread on her sleeve. "I've only known one person who was ever turned away by a god the way Veylan was. They weren't evil, though. I don't think they were evil."

She paused, then continued, "We were young, barely recruits still. One day they had their gifts, and the next they were gone. I still think about it sometimes. How lost they must have felt."

"I'm glad you'll never find out," he murmured.

"I can't guarantee that," she said nervously. "I suppose if I failed Ptyraxa, I could be cast aside."

He scoffed. "You shine too brightly to be cast aside. Honestly, it's like sitting beside the Dawn itself."

She let out a laugh, nudging him gently. "Silence, you heretic."

They both laughed, the sound fading into a silence that hummed with something unspoken. The humor gave way to warm tension, something that curled beneath the skin and made the air feel heavier.

His pulse jumped. He wondered what would happen if he was the one to lean in this time or if he touched her hand. He thought about asking her to spar again just to be close. If he asked her to bed, what would she say?

Before he could speak, she tucked a lock of hair behind her ear and said, barely a whisper, "We should turn in. Maybe tomorrow we'll find a room and make a decision about Ravenglen."

He watched her rise and move into her tent, her silhouette framed in moonlight. When he laid down in his own tent, sleep eluded him. He stared at the sloped fabric above him for a long time, but it offered no answers.

He wished she were closer.

Eventually, sleep found him, but in his dreams there was only firelight and the moment her eyes lingered on his, like a secret they hadn't yet dared to share aloud.

Chapter 25

Adinah

She woke to the smell of smoke. It was faint, curling beneath the edges of her tent flap, but strong enough to drag her from sleep. Her heart began to pound as she sat up and listened. Beneath the silence of the orchard, she heard distant shouting echoing off the surrounding stone and wood. Screams threaded through the darkness, piercing through her drowsy haze.

Her hand went for her sword as she pushed out of her bedroll and onto her feet. A faint glow came through the fabric, offering an orange silhouette of the town and trees. Peering outside, she saw fingers of flame reaching up toward the pre-dawn sky, their light reflecting off the dense smoke that rose to the heavens. Dread twisted its fingers into her stomach.

She threw on her mail before half-stumbling as she jammed her boots on and staggered from the tent. The breeze carried more acrid smoke, and she could now better gauge that the fire was coming from near the town square. It was far enough away to be safe, but close enough to demand action. She turned to grab her armor.

By the time she came back out of her tent, breastplate fastened and sword sheathed at her side, Ezra was already up and ready. His hair was still mussed from sleep, but his coat was on, the first threads of magic illuminating the tattoo on the back of his hand.

"They'll need help," was all she said. He nodded, eyes sharp, and they took off at a sprint and left their gear behind with Tirin.

The fire wasn't hard to find. By the time they'd reached the edge of town, a crowd had already gathered, some forming a bucket brigade and forming a firebreak, others merely gasping as smoke choked the air. A few guards directed people, but the chaos had clearly only just begun. The fire blazed out of the second floor of a building she recognized instantly.

The Tired Fox.

The flames licked the upper floor windows, blacking the wood and greedily licking skyward. Smoke poured out into the night air. Thorman was outside, screaming directions at evacuated guests. Ezra cursed and raised both hands as he called forth a pulse of magic. A wave of water erupted from the air itself, crashing across the flames and darkening the wood. It helped some, but not enough.

Adinah didn't hesitate. She plunged forward, pushing past onlookers and ducking beneath a low-hanging beam to slip through the main door. Inside, the heat hit her like a fist. The wooden beams groaned above, a chorus of creaks and cracks like dying screams. The ground floor remained mostly untouched, but smoke was curling down the stairs like a creeping specter.

"Anyone inside?" she shouted, voice already hoarse from the heat and smoke. No response.

She tore through the lower floor, finding overturned chairs, abandoned mugs. She nearly tripped over a boot lost in haste and a child's doll. The stairs up were half-burned, one side glowing with ember light. She made it up anyway, cursing with every step, hand over her mouth. The hallway above was a nightmare of smoke and rising heat. Most of the doors hung open or ajar.

She searched each room quickly, finding no bodies or movement. Near the end of the hall, her blood ran cold at the sight of a particular room. The door was blown inward, flames still licking the shattered frame. Scorch marks climbed the walls like veins. She didn't linger. She was back out seconds later, boots thudding hard down the stairs.

Outside, Ezra had cleared another wide swath of flames with a fresh wave of conjured water. A cheer rose from a few in the crowd. When she reached him between spells, she grabbed his arm, pulling him down to talk in his ear.

"It was your room," she said quietly.

Color drained from his face. "Are you sure?"

She nodded once. "The fire definitely started there. The door was blown inward. It's all gone."

He didn't respond right away, just turned to watch the remaining flames devour the second floor as people threw water, shouted orders, and dragged buckets. He was breathing hard, sweat covering his brow, clearly exhausted from his efforts.

The tattoo on the back of his hand glowed faintly as he raised his hands again, preparing to summon more water. She saw the focus in his face as he steadied himself, and before he could complete the spell she gently put her hand on the back of his. The tattoo was cool to the touch, sending little tingles up her fingertips. He looked at her helplessly as he let his hands slowly fall to his sides.

Once they were certain no one was trapped inside and the flames were coming under control, they slipped away from the chaos and back into the orchard. Their belongings were, thankfully, untouched. Tirin even seemed unbothered despite the scent of smoke. Neither of them said much. They knew what this meant: they couldn't afford to stay until morning.

She ran a hand through her hair. "We can't wait around anymore," she said. "I'd bet money someone lit that fire on purpose. Especially being your old room, it couldn't have been random."

He nodded. "We're not safe here, that's for certain. We still don't know anything about the Ptyraxite, other than that he likely stole that amulet from the temple. If we can't track him, we need to follow the lead we could have."

She looked toward the horizon where the first hints of dawn stretched pale across the sky. "Ravenglen, then."

He gave a quiet nod. "It's the best choice we have."

She met his gaze. "We have to leave before the sun's up."

"Agreed."

That was it. They decided without fanfare, just the quiet resolve of two people running out of safe places to turn. They packed in silence and, in the predawn light, led Tirin out onto the road heading east.

Chapter 26

Adinah

Three days passed.

The road to Ravenglen wound through low hills and patches of forest. Icy morning dew bloomed in the mornings and burned away under a pale sun. They moved quickly, too quickly to be truly comfortable, but it put them a half day ahead of schedule.

Adinah felt the tension in her shoulders lessen with every mile they put behind them. The air smelled clean again, the scent of smoke finally worn off her clothes and out of her lungs.

On the third night, they made camp on a rise overlooking a stream, surrounded by trees dense enough for cover. Stars had just begun to prick the sky when the attack came. The soft crack of a branch was all the warning she got.

Adinah rose in a low crouch, eyes narrowing toward the treeline. "Did you–?"

"Loud and clear," he said, already on his feet. He readied his hands. "We've got company."

Shapes emerged from the shadows like ghosts: seven masked figures, blades gleaming and steps silent. These were no regular bandits on the road. They were coordinated and experienced. In a second, Ezra and Adinah were surrounded.

"For coin or something worse?" Ezra asked her under his breath.

"Doesn't matter," she replied, drawing her blade. "They're not getting either."

The first attacker lunged, a short curved blade flashing toward her side. She pivoted, catching the strike on her blade, and answered with a brutal slash that opened the man's chest. Blood sprayed the grass as he dropped.

Another came from behind. She twisted, too slow to avoid the shallow cut across her thigh, but fast enough to elbow the attacker in the face and drive her blade through his gut.

140

"Left!" she shouted.

Ezra spun, catching the signal just in time. A bolt of flame burst from his palm, lighting up the dark and slamming into a cloaked figure mid-charge. The man crumpled, screaming. The air reeked of blood and smoke.

A fourth man rushed Ezra with a drawn axe, swinging low. Ezra leapt back, nimble despite the uneven ground, and swept his fingers across the air. He summoned a wall of force that slammed into the assailant like a battering ram, lifting him off his feet and snapping bone with a wet crack.

"They're working in tandem," he panted, eyes darting. "Flanking us."

"I noticed!" she growled. Her sword caught another blow, sending shock through her arm. She slammed the pommel into the attacker's jaw with a sickening crunch, then took open his abdomen with her blade.

A flash of movement at the edge of her vision pulled her focus. She turned just in time to parry a dagger strike meant for her throat. The wielder was fast, dodging her follow-up and dipping under her blade.

She saw Ezra out of the corner of her eye. He moved quickly, throwing out a fist to crush the nose of a bandit who'd gotten too close. Her heart caught for a second, pride swelling even amid the chaos.

Another figure emerged from behind him. She opened her mouth to shout, but it was too late. A blade slid deep into his side with a gristly, sickening sound. He cried out, stumbling forward and collapsing to one knee, his hand already slick with blood.

"No!" she screamed. She surged forward, rage searing through her veins. The attacker turned to strike again, but Adinah was faster. Her blade cleaved through the attacker's shoulder, nearly severing the arm, and he dropped with a gurgling scream. Another reached for her, and she kicked his knee before running him through with a brutal stab.

The last two bandits hesitated. She could see it in their stances, saw the fear in their eyes as they realized they'd misjudged this fight. She took a menacing step toward them, blood dripping from her sword, armor streaked with red and smoke curling in the air. When they ran, she didn't follow.

She winced as she turned back to Ezra. He was still upright, but hunched, pressing hard against the wound.

"I'm alright," he breathed. "Just–fuck, that hurts."

"No. You're not alright." She dropped beside him, her own arms trembling from exertion and pain. She felt the cut on her leg oozing and her shoulder throbbing, but none of it mattered. She placed her hands over his wound and closed her eyes.

The warmth of Ptyraxa's Dawn felt distant. Her connection to the divine was there, as always, but tonight it was buried beneath exhaustion and fear. It took everything she had to reach for it.

She focused on him. On the exact gold-flecked pattern in his hazel eyes and the shape of his smile when he wasn't smirking. On the way his fingers worked at the corner of the fabric at his waist when he thought intensely. On what it felt like to kiss him. On the crinkle of his eyes when he laughed.

A laugh I haven't heard enough.

Light bloomed beneath her palm, soft and warm. The wound began to mend. Flesh knit together slowly, as if even her magic didn't want to hurt him more. He hissed from the pain. She refused to open her eyes until she was sure the worst had passed.

"That's–That's good, Addi," he said, voice raw. "Time can take it from here." She lifted her hands, swaying uneasily when she moved. His robe was a bloody mess, but the skin beneath had completely closed, leaving only a dark bruise and a puckered, pink scar. She sighed, sitting back and breathing hard. Ezra stretched a bit, as if testing her handiwork. He retched once–mostly from pain, if her experience had taught her anything–but he would survive. That was enough.

Later, after clearing the site and dragging the bodies out of camp, they built a small fire. She insisted on lighting it with her flint and steel, not wanting him to push too far. He sat on a bedroll near the fire, pulling off his shirt to reveal the bruise in deep shades of black and purple.

"Let me see," she said gently, crouching beside him. He shifted, wincing, and she studied the area with narrowed eyes. It was clean and intact still, but clearly painful.

"Hold still," she instructed. Digging into her pack, she pulled out the small tin of balm he'd given her before, the scent of herbs strong. She got comfortable beside him, slowly dipped her fingers into the tin, and began to apply it. She gentled her hand as much as she could, her touches so light the balm barely spread. He hissed in a breath, wincing, but otherwise held still.

He was warm beneath her fingers. She tried not to think about it, about how solid he was and the way his smooth chest rose and fell with everything breath. She tried very hard not to notice the strength in his arms or the dusting of freckles across his cheeks. She swallowed.

Then, stupidly, her mind conjured up the image she'd tried not to think about since it had happened: the glimpse of him around the door, clearly having been in the middle of something very private. The memory hit like a physical blow. She turned her focus sharply to his skin, to the balm, to anything but the heat rising up her neck.

"You'll need to take it easy for a day," she said, her voice a little too steady.

"Easy," he muttered, "is relative." She helped him pull his shirt on, her fingers brushing his skin as she did. Their eyes met. Too close.

"I'll take first watch," she said quickly.

He nodded, settling back, and within minutes he was asleep. She pulled her cloak tighter around her shoulders and sat beside the fire, watching the stars above the treetops. They were soft tonight.

She glanced at him once more. He looked peaceful, mouth slightly open, a lock of hair falling over his brow. She watched over him in silence, vowing to keep watching him no matter how heavy the night.

A few hours before dawn, she roused him, having him take over watch. She would be dead tired on the road, but it would be worth it to let his body start healing. She fell asleep quickly, as if her body was desperate to claim every minute of rest it could before they continued the journey.

She woke again when the stars were just beginning to fade completely. She blinked the sleep from her eyes, the warmth of her bedroll making it harder than usual to rise. As she sat up and stretched, she caught sight of Ezra by the firepit, seated cross-legged with his elbows braced against his knees, staring into the flames like they might give him answers to questions she hadn't yet heard him ask. She rose quietly, rolling her bedroll and padding over with her boots in hand.

"I'm glad to see you're upright," she said, voice still husky from sleep.

He didn't look away from the fire. "I'll be fine. You mostly set me right last night."

She lowered herself onto the ground opposite him, boots forgotten at her side. "Something else wrong?" For a moment, she wasn't sure he'd answer. After a moment he reached to his side and picked up a small cloth bundle. It was tightly wrapped, tied with a leather cord.

"I was checking the bodies and found these."

She gave him a sour expression. "Trying to pick a dead man's pockets?"

"Trying to get answers," he corrected. "They were a bit too organized for my comfort." Adinah briefly wondered if there was a comfortable amount of organization for assailants.

He undid the wrapping and revealed five amulets. She inhaled sharply. Each was identical to the one they'd found in Elidane's tomb–an elegant flame-shaped pendant with a cold, black center. Even in the weak predawn light, the core seemed to drink in the light around it.

"Gods," she whispered. "They're following us."

"I think they're following commands from the amulets," he said. His voice was flat and distant. "I touched one of them. I didn't mean to. The cloth just slipped when I was wrapping them up."

Her chest tightened with dread. "Are you alright?"

He nodded slowly. "There was a voice. It was cold and harsh. It didn't speak words so much as put them into my mind. It knew my name, even said it could grant me power. It seemed to know me, promising I wouldn't be forgotten." She didn't speak, sensing he wasn't done.

"It knew things," he continued quietly. "Things I've never said aloud. It found the worst pieces of me and made them feel sharp, as if they were all that I was."

"Ezra..."

He looked up at her, jaw tight. "It made me feel like I'd already said yes to it. Like I already belonged to it."

She leaned forward, placing her hand on his. "You didn't, and you don't."

"I know," he groaned, but it came out more as a question than a statement. "It just felt real, like it saw me more clearly than I could ever see myself."

"That doesn't make it true. Evil's always good at lying, twisting what's already hard to carry." She tightened her grip. "You're still here, still yourself. That counts." He finally looked down at their joined hands. He nodded once, though it looked like he hated doing it.

"We should go to Caedmon," she said gently. "Maybe he'll know something about these things."

Ezra released a slow breath. "Yeah. That sounds right."

They re-wrapped the amulets, this time using a thicker cloth and leather before stowing them in a bag they both agreed would remain tightly closed. Ezra's face remained distant as they ate a quick breakfast, each chewing in silence, the mood heavy despite the soft gold creeping across the horizon.

The rest of their packing was already done, Ezra having nearly finished everything while she slept. He loaded Tirin quietly as she stood over the bodies of their attackers, arms folded. Ezra kept a respectful distance as she knelt, drawing a circle in the dirt around them with the tip of her finger, then touched her palm to the ground. She bowed her head.

"May your souls find morning," she began. "Not in the darkness you served, but in the light you once knew. Whatever you were, whoever you were, may the Morning Lord see it and grant you rest."

From a pouch, she drew out a pinch of fragrant herbs–lavender, thyme, and a sliver of sun-dried rose–and scattered them over the fallen. With a final silent prayer, she traced the symbol of Ptyraxa over her heart.

She could not ask forgiveness for them, only that the cycle of life and light take them. In doing so, she reminded herself to continue walking the path they turned from. When she rose, her face was somber, back straight.

"That's a new one," said Ezra.

She shrugged. "We should do it for any human life we take, technically," she said. "I admit that I'm not the best at taking the time for it, but with the type of darkness that held them, I think their souls could use some extra guidance onward." He was quiet, looking down at the bodies with a grim expression.

"Let's go," she said softly. "We've done what we can. It's already dawn." As they set off eastward, the autumn chill hung in the air, the colorful leaves shining in the morning light as if set aflame.

The next three days passed without incident, though Adinah could feel the tension in Ezra's shoulders and saw the way he occasionally pressed a hand to his ribs when he thought she wasn't looking. The injury he'd sustained was healing, though it was going more slowly than she'd like it to. She doubted the cold, damp mornings helped. Even Tirin seemed to sense the unease in the pair of them, keeping his gait steady and quiet.

They met a few travelers along the road, mostly merchants and small groups of tourists heading toward Ravenglen for the coming festival. Adinah and Ezra exchanged pleasantries with them, even sharing a few meals, but they never lingered long with the crowds. They were polite but guarded, unsure if one of them might hold another amulet.

On the sixth evening, Ravenglen came into view a few hours after sundown. It glittered like something from a dream. Nestled between wooded hills, the city shimmered and shone like a box of jewels. White stone towers rose high, lanterns casting gold and silver light along every winding street. Banners of crimson and gold fluttered from the rooftops. Music floated faintly from within the walls as the scent of roasted meat and sweet wine wafted toward them, even from such a distance.

Adinah's breath caught. "It's stunning."

"It's Ravenglen," Ezra said softly, a faint smile playing at his lips. "It always is."

They followed the main road to the city gates, which remained open to accommodate the stream of late travelers. Within, the streets buzzed with life, carriages rolling past performers and lantern vendors. Firelight danced off polished cobblestone.

Her head swiveled constantly, already overwhelmed. "I haven't the faintest idea where to begin looking for a place to stay."

He chuckled. "It's easy to get lost, but there's a place I've stayed a few times nearby." She followed him through winding streets to a three-story inn of polished mahogany and cream stone, ivy crawling up the sides. She caught a glimpse of the sign, bearing a rearing golden horse against a deep violet background. The Shining Mare. When they stepped through the door, a half-dwarf woman with salt and pepper braids waved to them.

"Allfather smite me! Is that you, Ezra?"

He nodded. "The very same." He smiled at her warmly. "How are you, Ressa?"

Ressa let out a humorless laugh. "Worked damn to the bone. This festival season has been particularly busy." She glanced at the two of them. "If the two of you are on my doorstep, I assume you're needing a room?"

"Yes," he said, motioning between Adinah and himself. "Two if you have it, but it looks like I'll be lucky to get one."

Ressa nodded. "You're lucky, yes, but not so lucky to get two." She turned, grabbing a key. "This is the last one I've got, and it might be the last room in the city at this rate. The festival fills every bed from here to the western watchtower."

Adinah glanced at Ezra. "We'll take it for ten days, if you've got room for that long."

The innkeeper nodded. "You're in luck again. It's a bit cramped for two, but it's cozy. Space in the stable, too, if your horse isn't too picky about his accommodations." They agreed, and Ressa passed over the key.

"Ten gold," she said, holding out her hand. Adinah nearly choked at the price, and even Ezra seemed a little stern faced.

"Here's my portion," Adinah said, pulling her last five gold coins from her pouch. *I'll need to stop at a Ptyraxite shrine and see about my stipend*, she thought. *Silver won't carry me too long at this rate.*

Ezra gave her a look, as if to protest her contribution, but the look she countered with offered no room for argument. Sighing, he dug out his own coin and passed it to Ressa, who dropped it into her pouch.

The room lived up to the warning. It was small, barely enough room for the bed that dominated the space, with a narrow nightstand on one side and a copper basin tucked beneath. Their bags took up most of the remaining floor space.

"Well," Ezra said, shifting his satchel to the corner. "We are once again in the conundrum of having a single bed."

She eyed it. "You should take it. Your wound—"

"Is fine," he interjected. "You're the one in armor all day, so I'd wager you would benefit from the comfort more than I would."

She crossed her arms. "We both paid. We both fought. We both need rest."

"Then I'll take the floor," he said simply.

"And let your ribs stiffen more?" She shook her head. "We share it, or I take the floor. Your choice."

Ezra's face turned red. "Addi—"

"I'm not taking no for an answer here. There's not even enough floor space for you to stretch out completely."

He groaned and ran a hand through his hair. "Fine. But I'm staying on my side."

"Good," she huffed.

They each stepped out in turn to allow the other to change. When he finally climbed into bed, he shifted as far to the left as possible, nearly hanging off the edge. She slid into bed beside him, making sure to keep as far to the right as she was able. Despite the space between them, she could feel the warmth of his body. The memory of his bare torso from the other night, of his quiet vulnerability that night by the fire, curled hot in her belly.

She wondered how it would feel to press her lips to that skin instead of pressing balm into it. Her cheeks flushed. She forced herself to close her eyes and lie still, hoping sleep would take her before temptation did. Sleep finally claimed her, but not before the image of Ezra–bare-chested, soft-eyed, smiling at her–lingered just a little too long in her thoughts.

Chapter 27

Ezra

Ezra lay on his side, his back to Adinah, though he could feel the tension in the air between them. The bed, though not particularly narrow, seemed to shrink beneath the awareness of her presence. Every breath she drew and soft rustle of linen when she shifted slightly sent a wave of energy through him. He stared at the wall in the dim light coming through the window, trying not to think too hard.

It was impossible not to. His thoughts dragged him backward to the night of the attack, to the warmth of her hands smoothing balm over his aching skin, the feel of her fingers brushing too softly. Desire coiled in him, but he didn't dare act on it. He cursed inwardly that he hadn't been able to relieve himself the other night.

Now, that same unfinished tension clung to him like smoke. He exhaled slowly, forcing his breath to deepen and steady. The scent of her, salt and worn leather mixed with steel polish and something faintly floral, lingered between them in the air. He hated how much it calmed him, how much it made him want to turn over and touch her. It wasn't even a lustful desire. He just wanted to be close to her, to wrap around her and savor the one sure thing in his world.

He closed his eyes, knowing he would eventually sleep.

He stood at the edge of a forest, the trees black and silver under the light of a moon too large to be real. Mist clung to the ground like breath, curling around his ankles. When he looked down, he wasn't wearing boots. He stood barefoot in soft, dewy grass. The world was quiet, but not empty. He could feel something pulling at him, a warm thread guiding him through the fog and around the trees.

The air changed as he walked. It became warmer and more familiar. The rustle of leaves became the sound of a hearth fire. The scent of rain and pine was overtaken by lavender oil and parchment. He blinked and the

148

forest was gone.

He was home. In his home. The walls of his private chambers in Surland rose around him like memory, softened in the glow of candlelight. The windows were open to a dark sky freckled with stars. The bed, wide and warm, was rumpled with sheets that still smelled like summer. She was already there, lying amongst the blankets.

Adinah. She wore no armor, carried no sword. Her hair was free from the usual pins that kept it behind her ears, tangled from sleep. She wore only a soft linen shirt, one of his, the neckline slipping just enough to reveal the curve of her collarbone and the strength in her arms. She looked up from the bed and smiled. It wasn't the hesitant one she gave when her guard was up, but something softer and genuine.

"You found me," she said, voice barely loud enough to carry across the chamber.

His chest ached at the tenderness there. "I never stopped looking."

He crossed the room like he was being drawn by gravity, and when he climbed onto the bed she met him without hesitation. Her hand found the back of his neck, drawing him close. His fingers wove into hers. Their mouths met with no urgency, just the aching care of two people who had waited too long to touch. It was languid and purposeful, the slow unfolding of something inevitable.

She laid him back on the bed and kissed him again, slower and deeper this time. The linen shirt brushed his bare chest as she moved over him, her knees on either side of his hips. She didn't rush or push, instead taking her time to look at him like he was a subject worth studying.

"You're always trying to carry the weight of things," she murmured against his throat. "Let me carry you, just this once."

He swallowed hard, moving his hands to rest on her waist. Her strength was something he'd always admired, but here it was what undid him: the steadiness of her hands, the way she moved like she was afraid of breaking him. A moan escaped him as her mouth brushed his jaw, his cheek, his temple.

"Addi," he breathed. He felt her face brush past his. She moved from his collarbone to his sternum, trailing soft kisses as she moved lower, pressing each one to his skin like a vow. Rather than lust, they burned with a calmer, more insistent desire. Holier, maybe, if such desires could ever be. His heart ached with how much he wanted to stay in each moment, to stall time so it didn't have to end.

"I've always seen you," she said, coming back up to press her forehead to his. Ezra closed his eyes, hands tightening on her hips. He wanted to tell her he loved her, that she made him want to be better, that she terrified him in the best and worst ways. His throat burned with the weight of it, but he

149

couldn't force out the sounds. He kissed her again instead, reverent and trembling like a prayer.

She kissed him back like she'd already forgiven him for everything.

His eyes blinked open in the faint glow of dawn, warmth pressed into his back. He went utterly still. Adinah's arm rested around his waist, her body curved against him. The sturdy strength of her frame was not something he could forget. She was solid and warm and grounding and, gods, he felt safe there.

He was just starting to drift again, lulled by the steady rhythm of her breathing, when she stirred. Her arm slid back carefully, the mattress shifting ever so slightly as she retreated to her side of the bed. He kept his eyes closed, feigning sleep to spare her any embarrassment.

Only once she was fully still again did he move, stretching with a slow groan as if just waking. He didn't dare look at her. She stretched beside him, slowly rolling out of bed to start the day before heading downstairs for breakfast.

The morning light filtered through the windows of The Shining Mare in hazy gold, catching on the motes of dust that danced in the air. The inn was humming now with the sound of travelers coming and going, the clatter of cutlery, and Ressa barking orders with her usual gruff cheer. Glancing over at Adinah, he noticed she looked a little more rested, though there were still faint shadows under her eyes. He knew they likely matched his own.

Behind the bar, Ressa waved as they approached. "Well, well. Good morning, Ezra," she said, her grin wide. "You never introduced me to your friend here."

"I did not," he said sheepishly. "Ressa, this is Adinah. Adinah, Ressa Truevein. A rare woman who can match me wit for wit and outdrink me by a scandalous margin."

Adinah chuckled. "I'm sure if it's only 'wit for wit,' she's been taking it easy on you." She turned to Ressa. "It's a lovely inn. We appreciate the room."

"That it is," Ressa said proudly. "My late father built it, but my sister and I made it golden."

"Not with literal gold," Ezra whispered to Adinah. "She just tells everyone that."

"Wouldn't be a bad idea." She slid a pastry for each of them across the counter, holding a hand up in protest when he moved to pay. "On the house this morning."

"Appreciated," he said. "I do need something from you this morning other than breakfast. I need directions to Caedmon's."

Ressa raised a brow, sly smile creeping to her lips. "Ezra, you silver tongued devil. I'm surprised you need directions. Thought you'd wear a rut in the road to Caedmon's estate back in the day. I'm surprised you haven't left a glowing line straight to his front door."

Adinah's eyebrows lifted a bit, but she said nothing. He flushed, and for a moment a memory flickered to life in his mind: pressed fingers and wine-warmed breath, the tempo of young and clumsy lovers marked by a summer storm behind shuttered windows. The vision passed as quickly as it came.

"We're hoping to see him today," he said, voice dipping as color rose to his cheeks. "We have something important to ask his insight on."

"I'm sure you do," Ressa said, eyes alight with mischief. "He'll definitely be home, probably busy preparing for the masquerade. You remember how over the top he likes to make things." Ezra chuckled.

Ressa grabbed a scrap of paper, scribbling down some shorthand directions. "Wrote them so your friend could find him, too, if needed," she said with a wink. Ezra blushed, thanking her as turned to leave the inn.

Outside, Ravenglen unfolded like a tapestry of opulence stitched across stone. Banners hung from balconies, swaying lazily in the autumn breeze. The cobblestones gleamed, newly swept, as festival vendors set to directing passing carts with trays of candied chestnuts and thick bread rolls drizzled with honey.

"I forgot how much this place thrives on showing off," Ezra muttered, drawing his cloak tighter against the chill. The sun was out, but it did little to soften the sharp kiss of autumn air.

Adinah arched a brow. "I take it you've been here often?"

He nodded. "I used to visit Caedmon frequently. His family has long ties here. He hosts rather legendary parties during the festival, as well as a few other events during the year."

She looked amused. "You attended parties? I figured you'd prefer your books."

He rolled his eyes. "You should see them," he said. "Masked revelry, music in every room, enchantments woven into the air itself. He turns the whole manor into a breathing thing." He paused, glancing sidelong at her. "Of course, I was here for far more than just parties."

She gave him a sly look. "Is that so?"

"Just studying," he said, lips twitching into a smile. "Well, maybe a few other visits."

Their path wound up a gentle incline toward the northern rise of Ravenglen, where the road narrowed and cobbles gave way to smoother stone and leafy trees that arched overhead. It was quieter up here, as wealthier districts usually were. Ivy clung to high walls, manicured gardens bloomed behind iron gates, and early festival decorations were being arranged by staff. They were meticulously placing silver ribbons, floating lanterns, and enchanted glass spheres that glimmered like starlight.

Caedmon's estate rose above the curve of the hill, commanding in its elegance but not gaudy. The manor's front gates were flanked by carved stone pillars etched with ancient glyphs and his family crest.

"Well," Adinah said, eyeing the structure, "he doesn't exactly live modestly."

"He was always a bit theatrical." Ezra raised a hand to the gate guard who had already taken notice of their approach. "He's trustworthy, though, and remarkably clever."

A familiar servant opened the gate for them without question, clearly recognizing Ezra. The man bowed stiffly and led them through the garden path where tall hedges hid secluded seating areas and white-gold roses bloomed even in the chill. The servant stopped just shy of the front doors, bowing.

"Please wait here, Master Moldravius. I will fetch Lord Thorneval." Ezra nodded and stood in the quiet, smoothing his sleeves unnecessarily. He could feel Adinah's eyes on him.

"You're nervous," she observed.

"No," he said too quickly, then sighed. "Maybe a bit. I haven't seen him in several years, and things were a bit complicated when I left." Adinah didn't press, but she didn't look away either. He was grateful for that.

The door opened, and Caedmon stepped out: tall, trim, well-dressed as usual in layered robes of midnight and silver. His dark hair was longer now, streaked with new grey at the temples, but his smile was as effortlessly charming as Ezra remembered. For a brief moment, warmth lit in his face like a flare.

"Ezra." Caedmon strode forward, arms open. "You look well."

"So do you," Ezra said, stepping into the brief, firm embrace. Caedmon still smelled of spiced ink and old tomes. When they separated, Caedmon's eyes moved to Adinah, who stood behind Ezra with her arms folded behind her back.

"This is Adinah Thorne," he said. "A good friend of mine." Caedmon's smile didn't fade, but Ezra didn't miss the slight shift in his expression. It was a brief flicker of surprise, or maybe disappointment. He nodded politely.

"Welcome to my estate, Paladin Thorne," he said with a slight bow. "Any friend of Ezra's is welcome in my home."

Adinah offered a respectful incline of her head. "Thank you for having

152

us."

Ezra stepped closer to Caedmon, dropping his voice to a whisper. "We're in need of discretion," he said, "and your expertise."

His brows lifted in interest. "Then come inside."

Chapter 28

Ezra

The manor was just as Ezra remembered it. The vaulted ceilings, marble floors, wide staircases, and stained glass windows that cast patterns across the floors in shifting hues reminded him of a time when things were less dire but somehow more complicated. The corridors still smelled faintly of aged wood, beeswax, and incense.

They were not led to the study most guests saw, but instead through a small hall tucked behind a bookcase in his office, triggered by a silent touch of magic. The hidden study was narrower but tall, filled with artifacts, sealed scrolls, and one entire wall of locked cases that shimmered with magical wards.

Ezra pulled the wrapped cloth bundle from his pack and laid it out carefully on a wide table. Caedmon eyed them hesitantly before putting on a pair of fine leather gloves. His expression changed as he unwrapped the amulets. They caught and seemed to absorb the light. He leaned over to inspect them closer, hands behind his back as if to avoid touching them even by accident.

"These are foul. There's a wrongness in the air, but it isn't infernal. They certainly don't appear to be old enough to bear connection to the dead gods, unless there's a new cult I've yet to read about."

"They belonged to a group that attacked us a few nights ago," Ezra said. "We found one in a broken Ptyraxite tomb before that. I should warn you: I made the mistake of touching one, and it spoke to me."

Caedmon's expression hardened. "A sentient enchantment?"

Ezra shook his head. "Something darker. It's cold and commanding, seems to look into you. It's too active to be a latent enchantment of any kind, or some silly parlor trick. This is active, powerful magic."

Adinah spoke up. "We don't pretend to understand the power that commands it, but we do need answers."

Caedmon studied them both, then nodded. "Leave one with me. Just one. I'll keep it warded and secured. You're right to be cautious." He moved to a desk near the back of the room, opening a heavy metal box with wards carved into the lid. He placed one amulet inside using a pair of tongs. He closed and locked it, sealing it with a string of arcane words that made Ezra's tattoo burn.

"I'll study it tonight. Return tomorrow at your convenience," Caedmon instructed. He looked at Ezra, and for a long moment, his expression softened. "It's good to see you again. Truly. You've grown back stronger."

Ezra hesitated, then smiled. "It's good to be back. For now, at least."

"No showing off your mask this visit?" Caedmon teased, stepping back toward the study door.

"Not this time," he said. "I'm here on other business, and by my recollection the masquerade is by invitation only."

Caedmon chuckled. "You never asked for an invitation, for what it's worth. I assumed you wouldn't have time anymore, since you've developed a habit of staying caught up in dangerous things."

He reached out briefly and clasped Ezra's arm, the gesture absent of any previous flirtation. "Be well," he said with a smile. "Both of you." Their gazes held a moment before he turned and walked with Adinah toward the courtyard.

The sun sat high but mellow in the sky, filtered gold through the crisp leaves of early autumn. Ezra stepped out of Caedmon's estate beside Adinah, the great double doors closing quietly behind them with a weighty thunk. His shoulders dropped an inch as they re-entered the city streets.

"That went... better than I expected," he said, adjusting the strap on his satchel.

Her gaze stayed forward, but he caught the faint lift of her brow. "You expected it to go badly?"

"No," he said, "I just expected more dramatic flair. You've never seen Caedmon host a wine tasting."

"Please don't ever make me."

They walked in silence for a few steps until she gave a sideways glance. "You know, I think if you'd sighed a little more longingly around him, I might've had to leave the room."

His head whipped toward her, eyes narrowing with exaggerated suspicion. "I did not sigh."

"Oh, you did," she said, savoring the words. "Right after he said your name in that very specific tone. You know the one."

He groaned, rubbing his hands over his face. "He's just dramatic. He always says my name like I'm about to get a sonnet written about me."

"And you didn't mind it one bit," she teased. "Do you always light up like that when a beautiful man opens a hidden door for you?"

He shot her a look. "I do not light up." *Did I light up?*

"You blushed."

"I did not!" His voice came out higher than he wanted.

She hummed, clearly unconvinced. "No shame in it. He's handsome. Polished. Excellent bone structure. Believe me, I get it."

"I hate you."

She laughed. "You absolutely don't."

He groaned again, but couldn't stop his own laugh from slipping out. "Fine. He's got good taste in coats and better taste in people. Can we let it die now?"

"Sure," she said breezily. "Unless he writes that sonnet. Then I'd like a copy."

They reached The Shining Mare still riding the high of easy banter, warmth settling between them like sunlight on stone. Ressa stood out front, now yelling at two delivery boys carrying bundles of velvet bunting. She waved them inside with a distracted grunt.

Inside, the common room was buzzing with a low murmur of early diners. A bard was tuning a lute by the hearth, the scent of roasted onions and herbs drifting from the kitchen. They sat at a corner table and ordered a late lunch. The food was simple but hearty: roast fowl with dark berry sauce, baked squash with butter and salt, and crusty bread still warm from the oven. Ressa brought over a tankard of cider for each of them without being asked.

As they ate, the conversation stayed light. Adinah told him about the time she tried to patch a chain shirt with prayer and stubbornness alone, and he shared a tale of Caedmon accidentally animating his own wardrobe during a party and blaming it on a jealous rival. There was no danger in the room or shadows in the corners, only the flickering firelight, the clinking of plates, and the rare and easy rhythm of shared peace.

When they returned to their room, the sun had just started its descent. The window caught the gold of it, filling the tiny space with a soft, honey-warm glow.

They moved around each other with a kind of familiar rhythm, Adinah unstrapping pieces of armor and folding her tabard as Ezra set aside his satchel and loosened his collar. They'd developed a carefully balanced routine, unspoken but solid.

When they settled into bed, him on the left and her on the right, they lay with a good foot between them, backs turned to each other. Outside, the city buzzed and glittered in anticipation of the festival. Somewhere, a song played faintly in the distance, laughter trailing after it.

Inside, in their cramped little room with its warm bedding and the faint scent of hearth smoke and beeswax, Ezra closed his eyes, trying to drive out the creeping dread twisting inside him. Memories of his brief conversation with the amulet haunted him, threatening to set the mundane life he'd spent years constructing ablaze.

Chapter 29

Caedmon

The house had gone still.

Candles burned low in the sconces, casting warm light across velvet drapes and the scattered clutter of books and alchemical tools. Caedmon entered the narrow room, the lock clicking into place behind him. He exhaled as the quiet of his hidden study folded over him. Here the world could not touch him.

He rolled back the sleeves of his robes and stepped to the arcane box on his desk. Despite its physical size, it seemed heavier with the weight of expectation. He paused before opening it, instead pouring himself a finger of plum brandy from the crystal decanter by the desk. It was tradition, in a way. He always thought better with something warm in his blood, and tonight he would need the heat.

He sipped, eyeing the box for a long moment before setting the glass aside. His fingers hesitated just a moment before undoing the latch and pulling back the lid. Within, cradled by velvet, lay the amulet Ezra and Adinah had entrusted to him.

It looked dark, elegant, and—somehow—hungry. The surface of the flame caught the candlelight and flickered as if alive. Its center seemed almost fluid, like staring into ink suspended in water. It was beautiful in the way some poisons were beautiful. He stared, unable to pull his gaze.

Curious, isn't it, he thought, *how the darkness glimmers?* He scowled at himself for the poetic thought. Then, almost involuntarily, he reached for the tongs beside the box and lifted the amulet into the air. Even at a distance, it felt closer than it should, as if his thoughts brushed something vast.

Ezra's warning came to him, sharp and sudden. *It's cold and commanding, seems to look into you,* he'd said. Caedmon swallowed. Then, foolishly, as if testing the edge of a blade, he reached out and pressed his fingers to the amulet's cold surface.

A voice slid into his mind like smoke into a locked room.

"Hello, Caedmon."

The breath went out of him. Not with fear, exactly, but recognition, the way a scholar knows when he's opened a page he shouldn't have.

"I see so much potential in you. Curiosity, ambition... a hunger that never quite fades. You know what it is to want, don't you?"

"Who are you?" Caedmon asked aloud, though his voice felt thin and distant. "You aren't one of the gods."

"No," the voice whispered, warm with promise, *"but I've spoken to them. Some listen. Some burn. You, though... You've always wanted to listen to the fire."*

He gritted his teeth, but something in the words thrummed inside his chest. A heartbeat too loud, a memory too sharp.

"You remember Ezra, of course. You were his first."

Caedmon's hand trembled around the amulet. He did remember: pale candlelight, ink, and the brush of Ezra's wrist against his.

"You marked him, connected him to something far older than you understood. It was a gift, yes, but also a wound. And when he burned brighter than you ever expected, didn't part of you hate him for it?"

"No," Caedmon whispered, but it rang false. He had loved Ezra. But yes, he'd envied the way the younger man had flourished, how he'd outpaced him. How easily he'd left. The voice smiled.

"He drew close to something forbidden, didn't he? Something he never should have reached. But you opened the door."

Caedmon wasn't sure what the voice referenced, but he took advantage of the moment of confusion. He wrenched his mind back, trying to wrestle his thoughts into a shield. "What are you?"

"A guide," it purred. *"A god to some. Power to others. I can give you what you gave him and more. No more doubt, no more wondering if you were left behind. Just say yes."*

It pressed on him like a storm tide. Caedmon jerked his hand back. The connection severed, but left his skin tingling and breath ragged. He dropped the amulet to the desk and grabbed the hammer from the wall. There was no hesitation.

With a shout, he brought it down. The amulet shattered with a sound like cracking ice, sending a sharp explosion of arcane energy outward. Candles guttered and dust danced. When the air stilled, he leaned over the shards.

The core was obsidian, cold and smooth. In its broken face was a network of sigils he didn't recognize, but the runes for telepathy and domination were unmistakable. The magic was clever, hidden around the edges of the amulet's inner ring where it touched the stone, rendering it invisible to a cursory inspection.

"Gods," he whispered. He carefully gathered the shards into the box, re-sealing the latch. As he did, one question lingered like smoke in his lungs: what exactly had Ezra done with the power granted to him?

Chapter 30

Adinah

Adinah stirred to the gentle weight of sunlight pressing against the shutters, the warmth filtering through the cracks just enough to paint soft lines over the cramped room. She lay still, the quiet rustle of sheets the only sound in the early morning hush. Ezra was asleep beside her, turned slightly toward the wall, his breath slow and even.

For a moment, she allowed to herself the indulgence of stillness, of simply looking at him. His dark hair was tousled, one lock curling just behind his ear. His brow, so often furrowed in thought or irritation, was smooth in sleep. In the warm light, he looked younger, peaceful in a way he rarely allowed himself to be.

She smiled softly, almost wistful. She basked in the quiet warmth that came from long nights, from battles fought shoulder to shoulder, and from watching someone bleed and stand again. It was warmth born from trust, from knowing him and letting herself be known.

She slipped carefully from the bed, dressing in silence so as not to wake him. When she stepped downstairs, she found Ressa already bustling behind the bar, polishing mugs and humming a lilting tune.

"Morning, Paladin," Ressa said, not looking up. "Your boy still asleep?"

Adinah laughed softly. "He's not my–" She stopped, shaking her head. "Yes, I left him to it."

Ressa grinned, humor not meeting her eyes. "We're between pastry trays, but there's a bakery three streets down, right off the square. Best tarts in the region. I'll tell Ezra where you've gone off to."

Adinah perked up. "That sounds perfect, actually."

She left with a grateful nod and stepped into the morning bustle. The streets were already growing busy, final festival preparations in full swing. Silk streamers fluttered from balconies, merchants called to one another as they unloaded crates of spices and fabric, and the air smelled faintly of honeyed nuts and woodsmoke.

The bakery was exactly where Ressa had said. It was a squat stone building painted pale yellow, the windows fogged with warmth. Bells chimed overhead as she stepped in. Standing at the corner of the counter in a crisp, slate-blue tunic that set off his lightly tanned skin and burnished hair, was Dolran.

He turned at the sound, smiling when he saw her. "Paladin Thorne," he said warmly. "I hoped we'd cross paths again."

She faltered. He looked good. There was no denying he wore the clothes well, the tailored lines emphasizing broad shoulders and a narrow waist. He looked less like a battle-worn knight and more like a courtier fresh from a noble hall. Not soft, though. He still moved like a swordsman, carrying himself with the grace of someone who could kill you before you finished blinking.

"Dolran," she said, stepping further in, trying to keep her voice even. "You clean up nicely."

He chuckled. "And you are as radiant as always."

She snorted. "I'm wearing half-dusted armor and my hair is an unkempt mess."

"All the more impressive that you're so dashing, then."

They approached the counter side by side, browsing the rows of warm pastries. Dolran asked for a cranberry-walnut roll, and she chose an apple tart, still slightly steaming. He paid for both before she could reach for her coin purse. He didn't move to leave.

"I was hoping I might see you again," he said after a moment. "And since the gods are kind for once, I'd like to extend an invitation."

She blinked. "An invitation?"

"To the Amber Masquerade." His tone was smooth but not presumptive. "Four days from now, at the Thorneval estate. I'm told it's quite the spectacle, and the kind of thing one doesn't attend alone, if they can help it."

The tart felt suddenly heavier in her hand. "You want me to go with you."

"I do," he said simply. "You'd enjoy it, I think. And I'd enjoy your company."

Her mouth felt a little dry. Something about the way he said it, like the invitation was an offer and a challenge all wrapped in velvet. She wasn't oblivious to how he looked at her, either. It wasn't lewd or aggressive, but there was a definite heat to it. It had been a while, and her body remembered faster than her head.

"I–Dolran, I'm flattered. Really. But I need some time to think about it."

162

His smile never faltered. "Then take it. I'd never presume."

She nodded, fingers tightening slightly around the small paper bundle that held her pastry. "Where should I bring my answer?"

"There's an inn across the canal called The Hollow Briar. The innkeeper, Rivel, is a friend. Tell him you have a message for me, and he'll see it's delivered."

"Hollow Briar," she echoed. "Got it."

Dolran stepped back, offering a bow so low it might've been mocking if it weren't so damned graceful. "Until then, Paladin Thorne."

With that, he was gone, vanishing into the throng outside like a particularly smug daydream. She stood there a moment longer, warm tart in her hand. *I'm in trouble,* she thought, pushing down the heat pooling in her stomach.

She took a while to wander the streets nearby. Still faintly flushed, she took small bites of her tart, letting the cool air help her settle. Festival preparations swirled around her. Music mixed with the scent of sugar and cedar, the constant hum of the city providing a steady undercurrent. Ravenglen was coming alive, and it felt good to get lost in it for a while.

By the time she returned to The Shining Mare, Ezra was seated at the back of the common room, nursing a mug of something dark and bitter.

"You missed a surprisingly eventful bakery run," she said as she dropped into the seat beside him.

He lifted an eyebrow. "Eventful?" She bit into the last of her tart and didn't answer.

A few hours later, when the sun began its descent, they set out again for Caedmon's. The estate looked much the same in the afternoon light: elegant, old, and alive with the hum of magic and wealth. Caedmon greeted them at the gate, having been sitting in his garden. He invited them in, guiding them through the manor and ushering them into the study with a practiced gesture.

The amulet was already out on the table, smashed, the core fractured into black shards. A dull sheen clung to the edges, as though it were still leaking some foul, arcane residue.

"I had a closer look," Caedmon said without preamble. "You were right to be cautious. I've never seen anything quite like it."

Adinah leaned in, brow furrowed. "Did you find anything useful?"

"Obsidian core," he said, tapping a shard with his tongs. "It had inscriptions between the metal and the stone, hidden until broken. They suggested a communication spell of some kind. Whoever crafted this wanted direct, sustained contact with the bearer. Beyond those few runes, there aren't any sigils I recognize." Ezra's expression hardened, but he didn't speak.

163

After a pause, Caedmon turned to him. "Ezra. A word?"

Adinah blinked as the two men stepped into the adjacent room, the door closing quietly behind them. She stood there, not quite sure what to do with her hands, and listened to the faint hum of silence on the other side. When Ezra returned, his expression unreadable, she didn't press. He only gave her a nod, and together, they stepped out into the cool late afternoon.

The walk back to The Shining Mare was quiet, save for the cheerful hum of Ravenglen's festival preparation. It was a beautiful day, sun warmed and golden, but she couldn't quite enjoy it, especially with the way Ezra kept glancing sidelong at her like he had something to say.

He finally cleared his throat. "I, ah, need to stop by a tailor."

She arched a brow. "A tailor? Why? Picking up Caedmon's newest coat?"

He rubbed the back of his neck, ears tinging red. "Caedmon asked me to attend the Amber Masquerade. As his guest."

The words hit her, sharp and unexpected as a slap. "Oh."

Ezra winced. "It's not a thing. I mean, he said it would be a good opportunity to talk more about the amulets, to meet other arcanists who might know something. The setting would allow for additional discretion. I didn't think–"

"You didn't think to mention it?" she snapped before she could stop herself.

He blinked at her, wounded. "I was going to, I just–"

"That's a coincidence," she said, voice too breezy to be real. "I'm going with someone too." That shut him up.

He stared at her, lips barely moving to form the words, "You are?"

"Mhm," she said. "An old friend of mine invited me." She met his gaze squarely, daring him to react. "Apparently I clean up nicely enough to be seen in polite company."

Ezra looked like she'd punched him in the gut. "Oh." The look on his face hurt her more than his going with Caedmon, but pride wouldn't let her take it back. They continued their walk in silence.

When they reached the square, she said, "You go to your tailor. I'll find another."

"Addi–"

"I'll meet you back at the Mare," she said tightly, turning on her heel before he could answer or see the tears beginning to sting her eyes.

The temple of Ptyraxa was a cool, white stone sanctuary tucked at the edge of the merchant quarter, framed by climbing roses and a statue of the Morning Lord with sunbeams radiating from His back. Inside, it smelled of incense and beeswax. The attending priest, a fresh-faced acolyte, offered her the standard stipend for visiting paladins. It wasn't much, but it was a few nights' lodging and a modest outfit. Adinah thanked him as she left, heading straight to the nearest tailor.

It wasn't modesty she was after. No, if Dolran wanted her at his side while Ezra wanted to play dress-up with his former lover, she was going to make a statement.

The shop was luxurious, lined with velvet bolts of fabric and shelves stacked with gowns too fine for any practical use. The tailor, an older woman with silver-threaded braids and shrewd eyes, looked her up and down and smiled.

"You've got a fighters' frame," she said appraisingly. "A bit bulky, but I can work with this. Let's make you something to look at." The tailor set to work with a speed Adinah was convinced must be divinely assisted. When she turned around to face a mirror at the end, her mouth fell open.

What the tailor produced was breathtaking. The gown was scarlet, deep and decadent as a rich wine. It shimmered subtly when it caught the light, glowed like embers beneath silk. The bodice hugged her curves with commanding precision, shaped with a neckline that showcased the strength of her shoulders and the curve of her collarbone. The sleeves were sheer and dramatic, draping off the shoulder with crimson embroidery that whispered of roses and blood. The skirts flowed like cascading fire, layered and long, brushing the floor with every step. The back dipped low, revealing the strong planes of her back. She looked like a woman born of battle and beauty, made to wield a sword in one hand and command adoration with the other.

For a moment, it wasn't about Dolran. It wasn't even about Ezra. It was about *her*, reclaiming her strength and body and desire. If she looked heartbreakingly beautiful doing it? All the better.

She paid the full price in coin and a smile, arranging to pick it up the day before the festival. She had one last stop to make before heading back to the inn.

It took a bit of asking around, but before long she found herself walking into The Hollow Briar. It was a nice enough establishment, though not half so warm-feeling as The Shining Mare, with a few intoxicated patrons at the bar singing along to a particularly rousing song played by a few musicians in the common room.

A man stood behind the bar cleaning a glass, taking the order of a patron. Adinah walked up to the counter, patiently waiting till she caught the attention of the innkeeper.

"Rivel?" she asked. He nodded once, eyebrow raising. "I have a message for Dolran Brightwater," she said. "Can you help me get it to him?"

"Dolran, eh?" He eyed her with a devious grin, giving her a once-over that made her skin crawl. "Of course. Dolran and I are good friends. What's the message?"

"Tell him Paladin Adinah Thorne would like to accept his invitation and will meet him in the common room of The Shining Mare an hour and a half before the event."

Rivel looked surprised. "So you're the woman he talked about taking." She felt her cheeks grow hot. "His taste in wine may be shit, but it's good to see his taste in women isn't." She laughed nervously, quick to wave and slip back out into the streets.

Her stomach twisted, the taste of bile burning at the back of her throat. For every ounce of jealousy she'd felt earlier, she now felt a pound of guilt. *I was certain if I'd gone to something like this, it would be with Ezra.* The image of him filled her mind, his expression twisted by hurt and betrayal. She felt physically ill the entire walk back to the Mare.

When she arrived, Ezra was clearly a few drinks into the evening, expression sour as he stared at the bar top as if he could see through it. Ressa hovered close by as if keeping watch on him. When Adinah approached, Ressa wordlessly slipped her a plate of food with a scrutinizing expression.

The message was received loud and clear. *Leave Ezra alone.* She took her food to a small table furthest from the bar, picking at it in silence. She left it, deciding it was better to turn in early than to sit in awkward silence. She went upstairs alone to their small room, changed, and crawled into bed. Lying there, vulnerable beneath the covers, she let the tears come, gentle sobs shaking her frame till she drifted to sleep.

Chapter 31

Ezra

The fire in the hearth had long gone out, but Ezra still sat before it, nursing the last inch of amber liquor in his glass. The inn was quiet now– Adinah had gone to bed hours ago, her silence like a slammed door. He couldn't blame her. The drink was sharp, but it dulled nothing.

Memories burned to the surface.

Caedmon's mouth tasted like firewine and forbidden things. Their argument had come mid-kiss, as many of their best ones did.

"You push too hard," Caedmon murmured, his breath hot against Ezra's throat. "You want divinity to bow to your will like it's just another spell you've mastered."

"And you don't?" Ezra pulled back, eyes alight, daring him. "Don't pretend you aren't just as desperate to touch something bigger. You're the one who found the key."

Caedmon went still before, with maddening calm, he whispered, "I found a way to tap into it. Not just magic. Her. Xernaea. Her divinity."

Ezra stared at him, breathless.

"She can't ignore us anymore," Caedmon said. "Not after what happened. Not after what they did."

He was referring to the Inquisitions. Ezra had heard the stories growing up as he struggled to find teachers.

The paladins had arrived in crimson and gold, with sunbursts on their breastplates and holy conviction in their eyes. The elder mages who'd survived swore they could still hear the screams, their stares hollow and distant.

The Inquisitions were still in living memory. The way the paladins had burned the colleges and torn spellbooks from students' hands only to throw them into pyres. Mages strung up on gallows, crucified outside guild halls, buried in mass graves marked only by melted candle wax and ash.

Ptyraxites. He grew up hearing their name spat like poison. They'd claimed purity, said they were purging the corruption of unbridled magic, and where had Xernaea been?

Silent.

Her statues had crumbled in destroyed academy halls, silence echoing in the prayer rooms. The more he learned of what happened only a few decades prior, the more a bitter taste crept into every spell he dared cast, knowing he did so alone.

He'd worked with Caedmon, having him carve the sigil into his own skin. It was burned there with magic, a scar that would never entirely heal, an anchor to Xernaea's font. It allowed him to bypass Her blessing, to force Her to see him.

It worked. For a while, he'd done miracles.

He'd split the sky open above a poor, plague-ridden village and called down starlight to heal the dying, the ones Rhuvena's healers turned away. He'd halted a river's flood with a word. He'd burned a pack of infernal wraiths away with a wave of his hand.

She noticed, and She came to him. Xernaea Herself, all starlight and solemn beauty. She wasn't cruel, just cautious, like a mother watching Her child play with knives.

He told Her the truth of his ambition. He asked why She abandoned them, why She let Her faithful die while others butchered them in the name of righteousness. She said he didn't understand, that the paladins and clerics saw the balance between divine and arcane as fragile. She said they were only doing what they thought was right.

He accused Her of cowardice. He raised his hand against Her, probably nearly killed Her. She never moved to stop him. In the moment before striking the final blow, he'd gazed upon Her, pity rising in him. He stayed his hand.

Still–*still*–She showed mercy. With tears in Her eyes, She severed the tether he forged, the snap of it rattling his bones.

"You were never meant to be mine forever," She said sorrowfully. "You were always good. I had hoped you would be great."

He fell. The crack of it had echoed across the planes. His magic was gone. He remembered the panic of the moment, the raw, awful emptiness where wonder once lived. He stumbled through the mortal realm like a ghost of himself, the arcane whisper no longer in his blood. He'd gone to Caedmon, desperate and broken, and was met with coldness rather than comfort.

"You made your choice," Caedmon said, his eyes unreadable. "You wanted to burn brighter than the rest of us. And you did."

And then he, too, had turned away.

The years after blurred into grey days and blacker nights. Slowly, slivers of magic returned. He wasn't sure if he believed they were from Her or from himself, pieced together from memory, grit, and defiance. Hard-won.

Then he remembered Adinah. Her light. Her strength. Her faith.

He remembered her eyes when he told her about Caedmon's invitation, the hurt he'd seen there. It was the same Xernaea gave him moments before She let him fall.

He finished the last of the liquor and set the glass down with care, as though being gentle with it might somehow absolve him of anything. The stairs creaked under his feet as he made his way to their room. She was already asleep when he slipped in.

Sort of. She lay curled on her side, her face turned toward the wall, but he could see the streaks on her cheeks, the faint pink rim around her eyes. Guilt twisted in him like a knife.

He laid down on his side of the mattress, watching her for a moment. The rise and fall of her breath. The soft furrow still between her brows. He reached out, slowly, gently, and brushed a knuckle along her cheek.

Her lashes fluttered. A little sound escaped her–half sigh, half sob– and she rolled toward him, burying her face against his chest. Her fingers gripped the fabric of his shirt like she needed something, someone, solid. He hesitated, waiting to be thrown off the bed, but she was still asleep, her breaths still slow and steady.

He didn't hold her back. He couldn't. She deserved someone unbroken, untouched by divine disappointment and the ache of their own ambition. He let her cling to him as he lay there, hand useless at his side, and cried as quietly as he could.

He cried for the gods, for Caedmon, for what he lost, and for what he ruined. For the beautiful, holy thing curled against his chest. The thing he didn't deserve.

Eventually, his sobs faded into silence and sleep claimed him like the tide.

Chapter 32

Adinah

Adinah wasn't particularly interested in the first day of the festival.

While the city of Ravenglen thrummed with life, music, and glittering decor, she spent the better part of the day perched in the window of their room at The Shining Mare, leafing through her holy text and silently polishing each piece of her armor. Ezra came and went, offering only surface-level pleasantries when they crossed paths in the common room or by the stairs. She didn't press him. She didn't have it in herself to try.

The common room below was a madhouse. Musicians, jugglers, and bards rotated in and out, the crowd loud with laughter and clinking glasses. From time to time, she allowed herself to simply listen, but she never joined them.

On the second day, she left to pick up her gown. The seamstress, an older woman named Wren who smelled faintly of lavender and chalk, hummed around her as she worked the final fittings. For all her strength, all her skill with a blade and shield, she looked beautiful. Devastatingly so.

Still, she didn't see Dolran that day, and Ezra slipped off again sometime around dusk. She didn't ask where he went. She didn't want to know.

And then, the third day arrived. The Masquerade.

The morning passed in a blur of restless pacing and half-hearted page turning. By midday, Ezra appeared, dressed in a neat, if unremarkable, ensemble, a small wooden box in his hands.

He didn't say much, only offering the box with a quiet, "Open it after everything else is done, before you leave."

She took it wordlessly. His eyes lingered on her for a moment, something wounded and soft in them, before he turned and disappeared down the stairs, off to Caedmon's estate. To help him get ready, she figured. To stand at his side. Jealousy raked at her insides. She stared at the box for a long while before setting it aside.

Later that afternoon, Ressa shooed her upstairs and handed the inn over to her younger sister, Aliave. "You're not leaving this room until you look like a goddess of war decided to go dancing," Ressa declared.

Getting into the gown was a battle unto itself, and she was grateful for Ressa's expert hands tugging and cinching and straightening with confident grace.

When they finally stood back, Ressa clapped her hands and grinned. "Look at you! If Ezra doesn't weep, I'll eat my apron."

Adinah turned to the mirror and found herself momentarily breathless. She didn't often indulge her vanity. Tonight, however, she let herself feel it. Just a little.

"You're quiet," Ressa noted, pulling pins from between her teeth as she started on Adinah's hair, standing on a stool to reach.

"I'm just…" Adinah hesitated. "He didn't invite me."

Ressa hummed. "He's a fool when he's scared, and Ezra's scared more often than he lets on."

Adinah gave a weak laugh. "He's charming and brilliant. He has the world at his feet."

Ressa pinned a twist of hair behind Adinah's ear. "He's also lonely. Guarded. Always chasing something–recognition, maybe. Safety? I don't know. But I've known him a long time, and I've never seen him look at someone the way he looks at you." Adinah swallowed, her heart doing something unpleasant in her chest.

Ressa smiled. "Even when he was young and reckless with Caedmon– gods, young love is intense, isn't it?–it was never like this."

Adinah scoffed lightly. "He probably looks at everyone like that."

"He doesn't," Ressa said firmly. "He admired you. He still does." They were nearly finished when Ressa retrieved the box.

"Now," she said, the mischief back in her tone. "Open it."

Inside was a hairpiece, delicate and glimmering: silver and gold winding together like the first light of dawn, forming interlocking sunbursts. It shimmered with a soft, warm light, faintly enchanted. Adinah touched it reverently, instantly sensing it wasn't Ptyraxite in make or enchantment, but powerful nonetheless.

"He's been working on it the last two days," Ressa said through a smirk. "He found the piece in the market and talked Caedmon into helping him enchant it. I don't know what it does, exactly, but he poured a lot of thought into it."

Adinah couldn't speak. Ressa let the silence hang as she tied on Adinah's mask, a half-face one of warm-toned gold filigree with its own curling sunburst motifs and small red gems. The innkeeper tied the deep red silk ribbons, careful to ensure it would hold through the evening, and

171

helped her position the hairpiece.

"You're not going together," Ressa said. "I know. But maybe save him a dance." A knock at the door interrupted them.

Aliave's voice called through. "Paladin Thorne? A gentleman's waiting downstairs for you." Adinah took a final breath, straightened, and went downstairs.

Dolran was waiting by the hearth. Gone was the soot-stained, blood-worn paladin from their past. In his place stood a vision of poise and clean-cut elegance. He wore a dark wine-red doublet with gold thread along the seams, the high collar emphasizing the line of his jaw. A gold half-mask shaped like a hawk's wing framed his face, leaving his sharp eyes and mouth exposed. His boots were polished to a mirror shine. A rapier with a decorative hilt, likely just ceremonial, rested at his hip. His eyes widened when he saw her.

"By the gods." He moved toward her slowly, offering his hand like he was receiving a blessing. "You're radiant, Adinah."

She took his hand, cheeks warming. He tucked it into the crook of his arm like a court-trained gentleman and led her into the dusk.

The Thorneval estate was already alive with activity by the time they arrived, with torchlight glittering across the manor and music spilling from open doors and windows. Lanterns hung like constellations above the lawn, and finely dressed nobles and visitors milled about with masks in every shape and color.

Adinah turned heads as they entered. Dolran seemed to enjoy that. He guided her easily to the dance floor, his steps confident as a soft, sweeping song began. She followed him through the dance, surprised at how well they still moved together.

"You really do clean up," he murmured close to her ear with a soft grin.

"You aren't so bad yourself."

He gave a low chuckle. "If I didn't know better, I'd say you're enjoying this."

"I'm reserving judgement."

The music paused. A herald announced the guest of honor and his chosen escort.

Caedmon stepped into the ballroom first, dressed in a long, emerald velvet coat with silver stitching, elegant and stately. Ezra followed and Adinah forgot how to breathe.

He wore midnight blue layered in silver threads, a jacket tailored within an inch of perfection, embroidered with arcane sigils and constellations so fine they shimmered as he moved. His white shirt beneath was open just enough at the throat to be devastating. A half-mask of deep onyx curled like a raven's wing around his left eye. He was regal, radiant. Unattainable.

Dolran's gaze cut to her. "Ah," he said softly. "I see I misjudged your relationship."

She couldn't respond as guilt twisted in her chest. She felt naked despite her finery, like Ezra could see right through her. Dolran politely excused himself, possibly to greet a contact. She barely heard him. She was left by a refreshment table, cheeks warm, fingers tangled nervously in her skirt. She locked eyes with Ezra as he swept into the ballroom. His ears turned red and he stumbled, as if seeing her there sent an arcane pulse to trip him. For a brief, fragile second, they stared at each other across the golden-lit ballroom, two people dressed in masks but exposed anyway.

Chapter 33

Ezra

His breath caught in his throat like a snare trap springing shut.

The mask did little to hide her from him. From the elegant arch of her cheekbone to the dark gleam of her eyes, he recognized her. She might've been wrapped in red and gold and the glow of ten thousand lanterns, but it was her. It was the woman he had fought beside, bled beside, and possibly fallen in love with in silence.

His heart thundered so hard he thought the whole ballroom might hear it. Gods, she was beautiful. Every movement was fluid strength cloaked in grace, the sway of her scarlet skirts making his mouth go dry. Something inside him twisted. It was sharper than longing, almost sickening, curling like bile in the back of his throat.

She was someone else's tonight.

"Ezra."

Caedmon's voice reached through the haze, a warm hand settling lightly on Ezra's arm. "Come. I want to introduce you to someone from Silverton."

Ezra blinked, dazed, and tore his eyes away. "Yes. Of course." He forced a smile. Following Caedmon, he allowed himself to be guided like a boat dragged downstream.

They stopped near the edge of the ballroom, where Caedmon exchanged pleasantries with a regal-looking mage draped in robes of dark starlight. Ezra bowed and murmured something polite, but none of it landed in his mind. The moment their hands parted, his eyes slipped away, drawn to the far corner of the room near a set of arched double doors.

There, near the shadowed curve of the wall, speaking with a server, was the false Ptyraxite. He was the same man from The Gilded Vial, likely the one who'd ransacked the room to steal the amulet and walked away without a trace.

Ezra ground his teeth. The man's hair was styled differently now, his

174

bearing more noble, but Ezra's gut clenched all the same.

"Excuse me," he said softly, already slipping out of the conversation. Caedmon looked surprised, but said nothing.

Ezra moved fast, pressing through the swell of silk and laughter and movement. The music lifted, a fast-paced reel that churned the crowd like a river current. Every time he thought he caught a glimpse of that honey-gold hair or the sharp set of those shoulders, he lost them again behind whirling dancers or masked nobles fanning themselves dramatically.

He cursed under his breath. The man was gone. So was Adinah.

The rest of the evening passed in a frustrating blur of forced smiles and polite co-hosting. Nobles drifted up to him like petals on a breeze, congratulating him on his magical contributions, asking questions about Ravenglen's wards, offering him wine and praise. He nodded, even laughed. All while his eyes flicked constantly to the corners of the room.

The masked paladin appeared again, fleetingly. He was seen near a vendor table, then beside the musicians. He was never still, never quite close enough. Every time Ezra tried to follow, someone intercepted him, smiling and oblivious.

By the time he slipped up to the second floor balcony overlooking the ballroom, his jaw ached from grinding his teeth. He leaned against the carved railing, fingers curled tight around the wood. Below him, the ballroom glowed like a dream, gilded and full of color, a sea of movement and candlelight.

Then he saw them: Adinah dancing with the false paladin. It wasn't just a dance, though. The masked man's hand rested possessively at her waist. Their faces were close. She said something and he laughed, lifting her effortlessly into a turn. Her gown flared in the lamplight like flame. When they settled, their bodies remained too close, too familiar. She looked up at him, her expression soft and vulnerable. Trusting.

Ezra's blood ran cold. He saw it like a spell unraveling before his eyes. This was not a stranger's dance. They knew each other. Something in him broke, a deep, wrenching wrongness twisting through his ribs. He couldn't let this go on. He had to reach her before something happened he couldn't take back.

Chapter 34

Adinah

The music swelled around her, lilting and graceful, and Adinah moved with it. Her feet were light on the polished floor, guided easily by Dolran's practiced steps. He was an elegant dancer, there was no denying that. His hand at her waist never strayed, his grip on hers always firm but never controlling. He complimented her with every turn, in word and gesture, and it was pleasant, even if her mind wasn't fully present.

Her thoughts kept flickering, annoyingly, to Ezra. Here wasn't the Ezra who disappeared for hours at a time the past few days, or the one who infuriated her with knowing smiles and frustrating conversation, but the Ezra who gave her the hairpiece. He was the one who looked at her in that moment like she was the sunrise.

Dolran dipped her slightly, bringing her closer as he said, "You look beautiful tonight."

She blinked, offering a half-smile as they twirled again. "Thank you."

It should have meant more, should've stirred something in her chest, but instead she kept wondering what Ezra would think of her. Had he noticed how carefully her hair was styled, how the scarlet silk caught the light just so? She didn't have time to find the answer. The song slowed, nearing its final bars, and Dolran stepped back just a touch to offer a slight bow.

"Would you–"

"I'm cutting in," came a voice behind her, sharp and unmistakable, like flint striking steel. Adinah turned as Ezra stepped forward, his dark eyes locked on her with an intensity that nearly stopped her breath.

"Ezra–"

He didn't wait for permission. He took her hand in his and placed the other lightly on her waist, sweeping her into the next dance as if he had every right to. She stumbled for half a step, not because of the movement, but because of the electricity in his touch.

She tried to refocus. Quick steps that cut to a promenade, then to a rock step and turn. She had just enough experience in courtly dances to follow and just enough to know she was outmatched. Despite her inexperience, Ezra led with such skill she was pulled along, passing even the most skilled of nobles. During one particularly tight turn, she was so close to Ezra that her breath caught and her mind went fuzzy. His sandalwood and parchment scent tugged at her very sanity, threatening to drag her under.

When he finally spoke, his voice was taut with emotion. "Do you know who you were just dancing with?"

Her brows knit. "Excuse me?"

"That man," Ezra said, voice low, close to her ear, "is not who he says he is."

Adinah's stomach turned. "You don't know that."

"I do. I've seen him before, in the potion shop. I can almost guarantee you he's the one who stole the amulet."

Her heart thudded. "You're wrong."

"I'm not." Ezra's fingers tightened slightly on hers, just enough to anchor her. "You don't know what he is, Addi."

"Oh, and you do?" she snapped, eyes narrowing. "I'm here with an old friend after you decided to spend an evening with Caedmon, and you show up just in time to ruin it?"

His eyes burned into hers. "You think this is jealousy?"

"You're jealous of Dolran. That's all this is." She hated how much it hurt to say it, how much the idea that Ezra could be jealous of Dolran made her feel strange. She felt exposed and wanted.

The dance spiraled, their steps just a hair too clipped and sharp. They moved in time to the music, but there was nothing graceful about it anymore. They were thrown in a tempest of emotion, all sharp edges and hurt feelings.

"This isn't about him," Ezra growled. "It's about you. Your safety. I'm trying to protect you–"

"I don't need you to protect me," she bit back.

"Then stop dancing with mistakes and proving you do." That stunned her for a beat, just long enough that the music faded and a new song began.

"Adinah," came Dolran's silken voice, a bit too warm and sweet. He stared daggers into Ezra. "You seem to have stolen my date."

She turned, breath still shallow, to see him smiling. It was a thin veil for his temper, too white and perfect to be genuine. It didn't reach his eyes.

"Apologies," Ezra said coldly. "I wasn't aware you'd claimed her."

Dolran didn't respond, not directly.

He looked at her, cocking his head slightly. "Everything alright?"

"I'm fine," she said too quickly. She pulled in a slow breath, smoothing the front of her dress with one hand. "I think I've danced enough for now."

"Of course," Dolran said, offering his arm. "Come. Let's get something to drink."

She hesitated for half a second, just long enough to glance at Ezra, whose eyes were locked on her with an expression she couldn't put her finger on. Anger, yes, but pain, too. Beneath it was something softer, something she couldn't bear to look at too long without unraveling.

Still, she placed her hand on Dolran's arm and walked away.

Chapter 35

Ezra

Ezra moved like a shadow through the crowd, keeping his distance but never letting Adinah or the false paladin slip from view. The music swelled behind him but his heartbeat thudded to a different rhythm entirely: tight, fast, and full of dread.

They stopped at the refreshments table. It was an enchanted monstrosity of luxury and excess, a crystalline fountain of golden wine cascading in streams from floating decanters suspended midair by unseen sigils. Goblets glided beneath the flowing streams, filling themselves before rotating along a lazy, magical arc to be plucked by partygoers. It was arcane indulgence at its most grotesque.

Dolran moved with ease, selecting two goblets from the slow spin. Ezra saw the shift in his shoulder first, the way his hand curled unnaturally close over one glass, shielding it from view. He saw the flick of a finger, barely perceptible, sending a pinch of powder into the wine. It dissolved instantly, vanishing into the deep amber liquid like it had never been there at all.

The rage was cold and crystalline. It wasn't burning and loud, just there, heavy and solid beneath the surface.

He didn't waste a moment. As Dolran turned slightly toward Adinah, Ezra slipped through the crowd, every motion casual and calculated. He snagged a half-full goblet from a passing guest's hand with a muttered "Apologies," not even breaking stride. He timed it perfectly: two steps, a breath, then he stumbled.

It looked real. It felt real. He collided into Dolran's back, just hard enough to jostle him.

"Gods, I'm–" His hand swept in low and fast, knocking one goblet just slightly off-kilter while he palmed the other. The tainted one. His fingers moved with practiced ease, sleight of hand born of youthful cons and high stakes games, switching the glasses mid-motion. In a flash, he exchanged

179

doom for borrowed wine. He righted himself with an apologetic grimace, now holding the tainted goblet.

"Clumsy of me," he muttered, offering the replacement goblet to Dolran without meeting his eyes. Before Dolran could protest, Ezra turned and pressed the tainted wine into the hand of a laughing noble nearby, a woman in a green mask with a ridiculous train of silk feathers. She accepted it with a gracious nod, raised it in a toast, and drank.

He turned to see Adinah staring at him. She'd seen the switch. Her lips parted, clearly about to demand an explanation. He heard the woman behind him clear her throat and turned to see her blinking rapidly.

She swayed, just a little at first, nothing more than a curious flutter of lashes. Her wine glass slipped from her fingers and shattered on the floor. She staggered backward, catching herself on the edge of the table.

"Is— is it warm in here?" she mumbled. Her voice was faint, as though she was out of breath. Her knees gave out. She slumped, unconscious before she landed in another guest's arms.

Gasps rose around them. The music faltered. A server rushed forward with a damp cloth, calling for help as the woman was eased to the ground.

He looked back to Adinah, her eyes wide, uncertain and accusing. His eyes didn't linger on her, though. He focused on Dolran and saw it again. That flicker. It wasn't shock or concern, just that faint, too-tight smile.

Ezra's pulse roared in his ears as the tide of fury rose within him.

180

Chapter 36

Adinah

Gasps gave way to silence, broken by a few people joining in a servant's shouting for a healer. All she could focus on was the pounding of her heart and the soft echo of the broken glass skittering across the floor.

She had seen it. Ezra's switch, fluid and practiced, his passing the glass originally intended for her to the noblewoman. Her stomach flipped, blood turning to ice. *Oh gods. Oh gods, I was almost–*

Dolran reached for her gently as if nothing had happened, as if the world hadn't just come apart at the seams.

"Adinah," he said, voice full of calm, "we should get out of here. It isn't safe."

She recoiled. His hand hovered in the air where her wrist had been. Her feet shifted back instinctively, her gown whispering against the floor. Her face twisted, not in fear but in disgust. It rolled up her throat like bile, thick and choking.

"You were going to–" Her voice caught. She couldn't finish.

Her mind sparked in fragments. The memory of the way she'd once loved him, when he was kind and bright-eyed and full of faith. They'd talked for hours about duty and justice and the gods. He'd kissed her hand with reverence, not deception.

He's not that man anymore. He might never have been.

Dolran stepped forward, a flicker of something dark behind his eyes. "Adinah–"

Ezra's arrival interrupted him. The punch came so fast she barely saw it. A flash of movement gave way to the crack of bone splitting. Dolran reeled back, blood spilling from his nose, crimson trailing down to his doublet. For a second, the entire ballroom held its breath. Then chaos broke loose.

Voices turned to shrieks. Guests surged in every direction, stumbling and pushing past others as they fled. A pair of nobles shouted that Ezra was attacking a guest. Others called for guards. Dolran staggered back, cupping his face with a glowing hand, teeth bared with shock and fury. Ezra's hand seized hers.

"We have to go," he hissed, tugging her after him. She didn't think, just followed, dodging through the crush of silk and feathers and screaming guests. She caught a glimpse of Caedmon fighting his way toward them, emerald-cloaked and wild-eyed. His voice cut through the noise.

"This way!" he called. They ducked into a side hall. A tapestry was pulled back to reveal a hidden door, which Caedmon wrenched open before ushering them through. Dim lanterns lit a narrow stone corridor. They ran, footsteps echoing off damp walls, twisting through passages she couldn't possibly remember.

Finally, after what felt like forever, they emerged into the open air. Rain came down in sheets, soaking them through. In the distance, the shouts of the town guard rose in tandem with the storm. Men descended upon the Thorneval estate like crows upon carrion.

Adinah and Ezra ran, the gravel path slick beneath their feet. They took alleys and side streets, dodging through drenched festival crowds who had no idea what had just happened. By the time they reached The Shining Mare, her breath came in shallow bursts and her curls clung to her face, now free of their pinned elegance. Ressa met them at the door, eyes wide and frightened.

"You don't know we're here," he said, voice rough with urgency. Ressa nodded and sent her sister for the guard, locking the door behind them.

Upstairs, the room was dark. They didn't speak as they packed, throwing things into their bags with frantic energy. Her hands shook as she gathered her armor, wondering if she had time to put it on. Her eyes stung, tears threatening to spring free.

"I can't believe it, after all these years," she started, finally breaking. "To think he tried– I could have died!"

He turned toward her, wet hair plastered to his face, eyes wild and wet. "You were with him, Adinah. I couldn't believe it when I saw it. I don't know what I would have done if I hadn't trailed the two of you." The ensuing silence was thick until, like fire to dry tinder, they collided.

The kiss was messy, desperate, full of all the things they hadn't said. His hands moved from her face, to her shoulders, to her back. She grabbed his coat with trembling fingers. It was like breathing for the first time after nearly drowning.

A knock broke the spell. Caedmon stood on the other side of the door, flanked by two guards, his hair wet but composed as ever.

"Contrary to what the gossips will say, Ezra, I'm fairly certain you and Paladin Thorne were the targets of an attack tonight," he said. "Not the other way around. I don't suppose either of you want to stay here and find out if they know where you two are staying." Her blood ran cold. *Dolran knows exactly where to find us.*

It didn't take convincing to drag them out of the inn, bags in tow. Within minutes, they were bundled into a covered wagon bearing the sigil of Ravenglen's guard, their things tossed in after them. Tirin was hitched alongside it, his hooves clattering through puddles as they made their way back through the drenched city.

The Thorneval estate was a mess, the floor littered with smashed glass, half-melted candles, and masks abandoned like corpses. Whatever splendor once existed was now drowned in spilled wine and fear. Caedmon ushered them through the halls quickly, bypassing servants and the few remaining shaken guests. When they reached the hidden study, they found it quiet, dry, and safe.

Caedmon left them alone in the study with directions to rouse him if needed and explanations of the various protective measures. The study was narrow and cozy, lined with old tomes and spellbooks. The furniture had been pushed to the perimeter, opening up as much floor space as possible. In one corner, blankets and pillows were piled for them. Both bedrolls were spread out, side by side, barely a hand's breadth apart in the small room.

Then came the matter of their soaking clothes. Adinah, after the waves of adrenaline, was increasingly aware of the chill setting into her bones. She shivered, teeth chattering, fingers and toes left feeling thick and numb. Retrieving fresh clothes from her bag, she realized she would be changing in front of Ezra. A wave of heat rolled over her. She heard rustling behind her, realizing he was likely already in the middle of changing while her back was turned. She reached behind her, fumbling with the laces of her bodice a bit before giving up.

"Ezra," she started, voice as weak as she felt. She felt him behind her, the heat of him scorching her skin. "Can you–?"

She felt his own hands shake as he handled the lacing. She felt the brush of his fingers against her spine, a gentle touch that sent sparks through her. Her breath caught as the damp fabric loosened. Suddenly, he was just there, close, standing against her back, steady and warm. He held her and she let herself lean back, for once succumbing to temptation and surrendering to comfort.

Chapter 37

Ezra

Her skin was damp beneath his fingers, warm despite the cold, soaked fabric. Ezra's breath caught as he stood behind her, his chest just barely brushing her back. He could feel her, really feel her, and it was like some impossible tether had drawn taut again, like the whole world had narrowed to the rhythm of her breathing.

She looked like something from the most beautiful dream: curls gone wild and dripping, her gown beginning to sag from the weight of rain and exhaustion, yet still radiant in a way that made his throat ache. Careful not to hurt her, he freed her hair of the glowing ornament, gently setting it on one of her packs. Standing again, he kissed the crown of her head. A soft moan slipped from her, something between a sigh and a hum, and it made his pulse stutter.

His hands hesitated at her sides, unsure until she leaned, just barely, back against him. It wasn't much, but it was enough to let him know. It made his restraint unravel.

His lips pressed to her temple first, then lower to her ear, his breath brushing the shell of it before his mouth found her neck. She gasped, sharp and quiet, her chest rising so fast he could feel it against him. Her breath was ragged, and he was already trembling.

"Is this okay?" he whispered.

"Yes," she breathed, gritty and almost choked with want.

He kissed down the curve of her throat, then over to her shoulder. Her hand lifted, fingers tangling in his hair, anchoring him there as if she could not bear to let him go. Her skin tasted of rain and silk and salt. His own hands found the stubborn lacing of her bodice and, with great care, began to free her completely from it.

When it finally slipped from her shoulders and fell with a wet sigh to the stone floor, she shivered. His hands roamed across her now-bare torso, slow and intentional. His fingertips trailed from her ribs to her stomach, then up again, taking in the curves of her. He didn't rush. He would never rush her. Every inch of her was a miracle he didn't deserve.

His forehead rested against her shoulder as he sucked in a shaking breath. "I want you," he said. "Desperately. But not tonight, not like this, so close to everything going to the hells. I want any first time between us to be something you choose–really choose. Not something we fall into because we're scared."

Adinah turned in his arms and looked up at him with that same fierce light in her eyes that had undone him since the beginning. She didn't argue, just nodded once. Mustering all of his willpower, he handed her a dry shirt, which she accepted. He helped her dress, fingers gentler than they'd ever been in his life, before stripping off the last of his own wet finery and donning something dry. When they finally lay down, the bedrolls touching, their bodies found each other without hesitation.

She curled into him, one leg tangled between his, face tucked against his throat. He wrapped his arms around her, pulling her as close as he could. They kissed slowly, lingeringly. Her hand trailed under his shirt, resting over his heart. His hand slipped under the hem of hers, fingers grazing the bare skin at her waist.

There was no urgency in it anymore, just the quiet ache of two people finally letting themselves have this. Eventually, the weight of everything caught up with them. They drifted off together, held tight in each other's arms.

It was the soft knock at the study door that stirred them. Ezra blinked awake to find Adinah still curled against him, one of her hands sprawled across his chest, her fingers twitching faintly in sleep. He didn't want to move. He never wanted to move again.

Caedmon's servant called from the other side of the door. "My Lord Caedmon says he may have something. It's urgent." With a frustrated sigh, he gently roused her, pressing a soft kiss to the top of her head as she woke. They dressed quickly, still a bit stiff from last night's cold. He watched as Adinah pulled on her armor and tabard, clearly bracing for the worst. When Caedmon entered a few minutes later, he looked pale and grave.

"I've been working on a new method of divination," he said without preamble. "It's experimental, and maybe a bit dangerous, but potent. With the amulet you brought me, I think I can trace its resonance. It's not just cursed; it's linked to its master, a type of entity I don't recognize."

He set out a mirrored bowl, pouring silver-threaded water into it. Runes lit up on the rim as he whispered incantations. The image in the water warped, shimmered, then coalesced into the jagged silhouette of a ruined stone temple, almost swallowed by shallow cliffs and mist.

"I know that place," Caedmon murmured. "Or what it was, at least. In the time of the Cataclysm, it was a temple dedicated to Varkhal, the god of conquest. Dead now, or as close to dead as a god can be."

Adinah and Ezra exchanged a look. "Why is it always ruins?" he groaned.

"You'll want to prepare if you plan to see this through," Caedmon said as the image in the bowl disappeared. He was sweating, color drained from his face. "I recommend leaving after you rest up. You'll need it."

Chapter 38

Adinah

The name tasted bitter on Adinah's tongue. "Varkhal," she said slowly, pacing the room. "I've heard that name before somewhere."

Caedmon nodded, arms folded. "He was known as The Iron Wyrm, a god of conquest, war, and dominance. Before the Cataclysm, He fueled empires. Legion after legion swore fealty to Him. His priests bathed in blood and fire, claiming glory in His name."

"And after?" Ezra asked, moving to stand beside her, expression tight.

"After the Cataclysm," Caedmon continued, "His temples were razed, His worshippers scattered. There are whispers He died with them, but others say He still exists, diminished, buried under centuries of silence and dust." He frowned toward the basin. "That ruin is about a day and a half's ride to Kaevryn's Teeth, the old wood to the southeast. It should be just before the foothills."

Adinah let the information settle, dread churning low in her gut. "We'll need to ride fast."

Caedmon raised a brow. "Then you'll each need a horse. I assume Tirin is a non-negotiable?" Adinah and Ezra opened their mouths at the same time, and Caedmon gave a long-suffering sigh.

"Fine. You'll take Tirin." He turned to Ezra. "I'll lend you another from my personal stables, just as fast and surefooted. Not as sweet tempered, mind, but amicable enough for the trip." They both nodded.

Adinah dipped her head sincerely. "You've helped us more than we can repay. I am eternally in your debt."

"I'll hold you to that in the future, should I ever be in need," Caedmon said, already turning toward the door.

They gathered their things quickly, slipping out the back entrance of the manor. The cobbled lanes gleamed with morning rain. As they approached The Shining Mare, Adinah's thoughts turned to Ressa. The innkeeper had taken them in without question, and after last night, she deserved more than silence.

The bell over the door hadn't finished chiming before Ressa was on them.

"Don't you ever scare me like that again!" she chastised, throwing her arms around them both, tight enough to knock the wind out of Adinah.

She let out a surprised breath, hugging her back. "We're so sorry. For making you worry, for tracking water everywhere last night, for putting you at risk, for–"

"Don't be ridiculous." Ressa stepped back, hands on her hips. "You did what you had to. I'm just glad you're alive." Her gaze softened. "I won't lie; staying here probably isn't safe, if the rumors I heard about last night's spectacle are true. But…"

She paused, then smiled slyly. "I hope you both find what you're really looking for."

Adinah blinked. "What we're–?" Ezra cleared his throat, blushing to the tips of his ears. Ressa only grinned wider.

They said their farewells with warm embraces and heartfelt thanks, promising to repay her kindness if they survived the next leg of their journey. As they stepped outside again, the wind biting colder now, Adinah felt a strange mix of peace and urgency.

"We need a place to sleep tonight," she said.

"I'd sleep in a field if I had to," Ezra sighed. "But I'd rather not, if I'm being honest. I just don't know if any of the inns can be trusted."

She smiled. "I know a place." Taking his hand, she led him through town.

The temple of Ptyraxa stood near the canal's edge, pale stone gleaming faintly in the wan light. Her boots echoed through the main hall as she pushed open the door and stepped inside. She straightened her tabard and drew herself to full height, as if the crimson didn't mark her as one of Ptyraxa's highest chosen.

The acolyte who approached was the same from a few days ago, his steps quick and his eyes wide. It was clear he hadn't known who she was, much less her rank, when she'd come to collect her stipend.

She didn't wait for him to speak. "I am Paladin Adinah Thorne, Dawnshield of Ptyraxa, here on a holy mission in the name of the Morning Lord. I require quarters for the night."

His mouth opened and closed a few times before he finally said, "Of course, Paladin Thorne." He hesitated, glancing at Ezra. "And he…?"

"This is my partner," she said firmly. "He will be staying with me." She didn't elaborate. She didn't need to. The boy nodded, clearly a bit flustered, and didn't press. At her side, Ezra didn't say a word, but she caught the faint blush rising to his cheeks and the way he squared his shoulders like he was proud to be claimed.

They were given directions to a modest room, bare but warm and dry. She exhaled slowly as they stepped inside, the scent of beeswax and linen grounding her. As she set down her pack, she glanced at Ezra, who was eyeing the small cot, clearly intended for one, with amused skepticism.

"Could be worse," he said.

She offered a small, tired smile. "We've definitely had worse."

They began unpacking in silence, the weight of the coming journey settling heavy around them again. Even with that, they were together, and she realized that was enough.

Chapter 39

Dolran

Dolran ran through the forest like a man with no body, only a haunted mind. Branches whipped at his face, catching in the torn remains of his mask and fine clothes, but he didn't slow. The mud sucked at his boots. His breath came ragged and harsh, white clouds in the morning dark.

She was supposed to be mine by now.

The words circled like vultures in his head. They'd spiraled ever since he slipped through one of the many secret passages at the Thorneval estate, ever since his hands stopped shaking, ever since he'd felt the mark of Veylan thrum against his chest again. It reeled him home like a hook in his ribs.

She looked so beautiful that night.

He saw her still: hair pinned back, mask and hairpiece glittering in the firelight, gown the rich crimson of a Dawnshield. There was a light in her eyes he hadn't seen before since their old days, those quiet sunrise mornings sparring near the monastery gate.

He had loved her.

He loved her still.

He'd meant for her to sleep through the worst part of travel. Just a sip of the drink, then he'd carry her out like a ghost in the dark. She wouldn't have known, not until after, when they were already before Veylan.

He remembered how she'd looked at him, absent of any previous admiration. She didn't even look at him like a stranger. Instead, she eyed him like a monster, something terrible and dangerous. How wounded she'd looked. He couldn't get away from the memory of her eyes, wide and betrayed, searching for a truth that didn't exist. His heart twisted in his chest.

He'd done it for her. All of it.

But Ezra had been there. He was always there, like a damn shadow stitched to her heels.

190

Dolran tripped, slamming a shoulder into a tree trunk, and cursed under his breath before pushing forward again. The temple wasn't far.

He remembered Veylan's voice, like velvet over a blade, as he'd first spoken to him in the crypts so long ago.

"I trust your judgement is sound, Dolran. She will will be the key to our goals." It hadn't made sense then, but it was all coming together. Adinah, a last daughter of the Light, the final bearer of the flame, and his personal dawn. He'd been right to suggest her recruitment to Veylan. Of course she was the key, the perfect person to recreate the divine order of things.

But Elidane… That had been a horror.

That holy monstrosity had nearly flayed him open. He still bore the scar on his ribs where her wrath had torn magic through him like wild lightning. She had what he needed, though: a runestone key to the wards surrounding the Heart. He'd wrested it from her tomb only moments before her spirit had risen, shrieking, coming at him with divine wrath.

It had all been worth it.

Even convincing that simpering innkeeper from The Amber Hearth to drop word of the Masquerade to the right ears. Even planting the powder in his ring, precise and hidden. He'd placed a trail of "accidental" clues for her to find.

She had come. She had always come when he called, and now she'd come again.

The trees fell away ahead of him, revealing a narrow ravine choked with roots and ash and stone. Rising at its heart, carved into the short cliffs like a wound in the world, loomed the shattered ruin of the temple.

It hadn't always been a ruin. Once, before the Cataclysm, it had been the crown jewel of Varkhal, an altar of conquest and dominion. Now, the stone was blackened, scorched with ancient flame. Rusted chains hung like vines, reaching out from the bones buried in the roots. He eased himself down the broken staircases and ladders to the deepest parts of the ruin. Deep within, where the sun could never reach, Veylan waited.

Dolran slowed. His breath hitched. The wards pulled at his skin, faint and cold. The amulet around his neck burned with answering heat. The moment he stepped through a cracked threshold, the air shifted. It was heavy, rotten with the scent of old power. There, beyond the altar, amid crumbling pillars and shattered icons, stood the Twice-Born.

He looked nothing like the man Dolran had read about in Elidane's journals. Veylan's body was a mockery of life: tall, robed in dark silks embroidered with his sigil, a long mantle of scorched velvet trailing behind him. His skin, where visible, was pale as ivory, and cracked in places like fine porcelain fractured by heat. In his eyes burned twin embers of molten gold, too bright, too hungry. His smile was gentle, his hands gloved in shadows. His voice, when it came, was full of poison and promise.

"You're late."

Dolran dropped to one knee, breathless. "I–I feared…"

"That I would destroy you?" Veylan chuckled. *"No. You did not fail me, child."*

Dolran looked up, throat tight. "I didn't?"

"You merely prolonged the inevitable." Veylan glided forward, robes whispering. *"Adinah will come. You saw it in her eyes, didn't you? The love still held there."*

"I–I think so." Dolran swallowed. "Yes."

"Then she'll come." Veylan knelt beside him, lifting his chin with one finger. *"Perhaps with the wizard, yes, but that only gives you the chance to permanently correct what was taken from you."*

Dolran's breath shook. Fury sparked behind his ribs, his eyes flaming with white light. Ezra's face returned to him, furious, possessive, daring to protect her like she was his. Dolran would burn that smug look from Ezra's face, and burn every memory of him from Adinah's mind.

Veylan rose again. *"Once the Dawnfire Heart is awakened, everything changes. No more death, no more rejection. No more gods to turn you away. To turn her away. You and Adinah will have eternity."*

Dolran let the words settle like balm on his frayed soul. He imagined it: just the two of them, no more pain or uncertainty. She wouldn't have to choose between him and her god. She wouldn't be able to.

Veylan's power would make that choice for her. All Dolran had to do was wait. This time, he wouldn't fail.

Chapter 40

Ezra

Night settled gently over the temple, casting long shadows beneath the pale stone arches. The air had quieted with evening prayer, save for the soft echo of footsteps and the hush of candlelight. Ezra and Adinah were grateful to eat at the temple's modest refectory, enjoying simple, warm fare that soothed the day's weariness.

When they returned to their room after dinner, after a brief exchange of glances, they spread their bedrolls across the floor side by side in wordless agreement. He stood by the lantern, fingers brushing the flame lower. Shadows deepened around them, soft and golden. He turned and found Adinah watching him. There was something different in her eyes. It wasn't just warmth or affection anymore; something charged had crept in. It was a crackling tension like lightning behind the clouds.

She stepped toward him slowly, bare feet silent on the floor. She wore a simple tunic and leggings, no armors or sigils of rank. For once, she was just Adinah, his Addi, stripped of duty and ceremony.

"Last night," she started, "you said you wanted to, but that it had to be my choice, and not one I made while we were in danger." She shifted her weight nervously. "We aren't in danger here, and I've made my choice. I wanted to ask: is this–am I–still what you want?"

The words struck him, driving the air from his lungs. His mouth went dry. He swallowed.

"More than anything," he said, voice rough. "But only if you do."

"I want you," she said, voice heady with desire. He froze. There was no hesitation in her gaze now, only the fierce, quiet truth of it.

They reached for each other in the same instant, both beyond words. The moment their mouths met, the tension unraveled like ribbon unwinding from a spool. Her lips parted under his, warm and pliant, and he cradled her face like she was made of something holy.

They undressed each other slowly. It was clumsy in places: she

193

laughed quietly when his tunic got stuck, his breath caught when her shirt slipped over her head. She wasn't adorned, but to him, she was radiant. Every freckle and scar, every place he'd imagined and never dared to touch, was laid bare before him.

They sank down together, knees brushing and breaths mingling. He kissed her collarbone, nipped her shoulder, moaned into the hollow of her throat. She sighed, arching into him, fingers threading into his hair. When he hesitated, she guided his hand to the hem of her leggings, helping him peel them away. The bare heat of her sent sparks running through him.

"You're..." he whispered, trailing off as he shook his head. "There aren't words."

She smiled, eyes glassy. "Try anyway. You always do."

"You're like hearing a favorite song the first time, like the sun before it breaks on the horizon." She kissed him hard enough to steal his breath. He returned it tenfold.

When she pulled him close again, murmuring a soft "please," he settled between her thighs. Their skin met, warm and alive, and he braced himself on trembling arms.

"I need to hear you say it," he whispered. "That you want this. I need to know you want me."

"I do," she said breathlessly. "I want you, Ezra. All of you."

The words undid him. Suddenly, there was no teasing, no distance, just the heat of skin on skin and the ragged edge of breathless desire. His body trembled with need and the weight of being wanted. Her fingers curled against his back as he pressed inside her, and he didn't know if it was his groan or hers that came first.

She wrapped around him like she was made for it, guiding him with insistent, breathy words and firm hands. He followed instinct more than thought, catching her mouth with his and moving with her as she set a rhythm that felt inevitable. He gasped her name once, voice breaking, and she kissed the sound from his lips.

Every stroke of their bodies together unraveled another layer of fear, every sigh from her pulling him deeper under. It wasn't frantic. It was consuming, slow and steady, until the only thing left in this world was the feeling of her around him, beneath him, holding him like he was something worth keeping.

After, they lay tangled in the blankets, breath cooling, hearts still wild. Her fingers drew slow, lazy patterns across his chest. He kissed the crown of her head, the curve of her brow, and the scar on her shoulder.

"You know," he murmured, "I've read about love a thousand times. Poets have tried to explain it. Scholars have tried to bottle it. None of them ever came close."

"No?" she asked sleepily.

"No. Because this… This is what they were all trying to name. You make me want to stay. To live." He tilted her chin up with his hand, kissing her gently.

When he pulled back, he rested his forehead against hers. "I love you." The words were as close to a prayer as he dared. "I am so terribly sorry for taking this long to tell you."

"I love you, too," she said, gently pulling him in for another kiss. "You're very good at saying things I never knew I needed to hear."

"I'll say them for the rest of my life, if you'll let me," he said, pulling her close to him.

She pulled the blanket higher, curling into him. "Then don't stop."

He didn't. He whispered words into her skin, her hair, and hollow between her collarbone and neck. They were soft, fervent things: how she made him brave, made him whole. Slowly, her breathing slowed.

"Oh, Ezra," she sighed, drifting off. "You've always been those things." He stayed awake a little longer, holding her in his arms, head tilted toward the ceiling.

Thank you, he thought, not knowing if he meant it for Xernaea, or Ptyraxa, or the stars. *Let this last.*

He drifted, too, wrapped around her like a shield, heart full for the first time in a long while.

Morning broke soft and gold through narrow window slats. Ezra awoke with her breath on his shoulder, her hand on his chest. A stray sunbeam played across her cheek, and for a brief moment, he wondered if he could convince Xernaea to let him stop time, or if he had a chance of bargaining with Khoravae. After a moment, Adinah stirred and sat up, blinking sleep from her eyes.

"I really should attend morning service before we set off," she said, voice low with sleep.

"I'll come," he offered. Her brows lifted in mild surprise, but she nodded.

He didn't know what he believed anymore. To him, Ptyraxa was a demanding god, radiant and cruel by turns, giving just enough to keep those like Adinah tethered but never enough to give them peace. Xernaea, for Her part, had always been generous with Her gifts, but she was absent. Watching, perhaps, but distant.

As they sat in the back row of the temple hall, voices lifted in quiet prayer, Ezra bowed his head. He didn't pray often, but now, silently, he asked one thing: *Just once, let the scales tip in our favor.*

They packed after breakfast. He helped her fasten the clasps of

195

her armor and she smoothed the front of his robes. The awkwardness between them had burned away, leaving a closeness that no words could touch. They stepped out into the sun-drenched courtyard, heading toward Caedmon's estate and the ruin that waited beyond. They walked side by side, and for once, Ezra didn't look back.

Chapter 41

Adinah

They departed for Caedmon's manor, stopping only to gather provisions for the journey. The estate was quiet when they arrived, even the birdsong seeming cautious. Caedmon had stored some of their larger equipment while they'd gone back into town and had it organized in tidy stacks on their return. He ordered servants to carry it out to the stables, walking with them in tense quiet.

Tirin stood in the stable, tossing his head expectantly when Adinah approached.

"Yes, dear," she murmured, pressing her forehead to his. "Time to work again." In the next stall over, a stallion shifted and nickered softly.

"This is Halberd," Caedmon said from behind them. The tall, tan stallion flicked his ear at his name. "He's fast and stubborn. Favors high ground and doesn't like mud. He hates goats, too, so avoid those."

Ezra arched a brow. "Avoiding goats. Noted."

Caedmon looked between them as they saddled their mounts. His gaze lingered, not intrusively, just long enough to catch Adinah's attention. She met his eyes and saw the flicker of a knowing smile beneath the tension in his brow. He didn't comment or tease.

Looking between them, he simply said, "Come back alive."

Adinah and Ezra left Ravenglen by the south road and reached the woods of Kaevryn's Teeth by early evening. The change was immediate when they reached the forest. Trees leaned too close together, bathing the path in cold shadow. What should have been quiet woodland felt watchful. The breeze was too still, the birds too silent. Her hand drifted to the hilt of her sword more than once.

By nightfall, the fog began to roll in, low and clinging. Shapes danced at the edges of it, flickering like hazy memories. They made camp cautiously in a shallow glade off the trail, lighting no fire.

While Ezra worked on setting wards, she stepped away to check the perimeter of their camp. She hadn't gone more than ten paces when something lurched out of the mist: a low, crawling thing, not quite dead or alive. It wore the bones of a deer like armor, twisted flesh stitched with shadows, its jaw split down the middle as if screaming eternally.

She struck fast, sword flashing in the dark. It was easily killed, but it was wrong, unclean in a way that chilled her deeper than any winter. It crumbled in a hiss of ash and fog, and she returned to camp with her jaw tight.

Ezra glanced up. "Everything alright?"

She nodded. "Just a weak, twisted creature. It was solitary, but it felt like the wolf... *things* we saw on our way to Chembrus."

He swore and returned to setting the tents. When he unrolled his own, the fabric tore, an angry, jagged split right down the spine of the canvas.

She frowned. "I don't remember it being torn."

He sighed, scrubbing a hand over his face. "It wasn't, but I can't say I'm surprised. I've had this thing for years. Just my luck it'd wear out now, though."

She looked to her own tent, mist curling at the edges. "We can share mine. Not the first time we've done so."

He chuckled as they ducked inside. As she entered, she paused. The inside was warm and dry, almost comfortable. She reached a hand to the canvas wall near the ground.

"It's not wet."

He sat his satchel by the bedroll. "I stitched a ward into the seam before we left the ruins," he said casually. "It's nothing fancy, just keeps water out and warmth in as long as the threading holds."

Her throat tightened. "You did that for me?"

"Of course," he said gently. "I figured you'd want at least one place where you didn't wake up shivering." She stared at him for a moment, heart aching, before she pressed a kiss to his cheek.

"Thank you." They curled into the blankets together, bodies finding each other easily now, his arm snaking around her waist as her hand came to rest over his heart. She felt sleep tugging at her, soft and heavy. Ezra murmured something into her hair she didn't catch.

Then the world shifted.

She stood in a field of gold. The grass was tall and gentle beneath her boots, the breeze carrying the scent of morning. The sun hung low on the horizon, never fully rising nor setting, casting the sky in endless coral and rose. Ptyraxa waited a short distance away, barefoot, clad in radiant robes that seemed woven from the dawn itself. The light of Him burned gently, like warmth from a hearth.

"You are standing taller than before," He said, smiling. His smirk was subtle, knowing, as though He saw something she had yet to grasp.

Her breath caught in her throat. "My Lord–" she began. He lifted His hand slightly, an easy gesture.

"You carry yourself differently than you once did," He observed as he closed the distance, His presence warm but weightless, like standing in a sunbeam. "There is something new in you. A certainty, a devotion that was once a question, but now an answer."

She furrowed her brow. "If I have changed, I do not know how."

Ptyraxa's golden haze held hers, amusement flickering at the edges. "Do you not?"

Suddenly, she felt it, a shift deep within her. She felt the awareness of the strength she gained, the faith she reforged. It wasn't just faith in herself or the ideals she fought for, but in something, or someone, else.

A memory stirred: the night Ezra was stabbed, when she vowed to watch over him, no matter how dark the night. She'd sat, heart open, no longer fighting just for duty, but for something more. For him. Her stomach tightened, the realization almost terrifying.

Ptyraxa smirked. "You walk, strengthened now by two vows. One you took in a sacred temple hall, and one you took even more earnestly. It makes you strong enough for the path ahead."

She blushed, bowing her head. "You've been gone. I have tried to walk in Your light. I have prayed desperately, but You have remained silent."

"I had to be," He admitted. "Every time I answer the call of my faithful, every bit of power I exert, he sees. You are fortunate I intervened with Elidane. My light serves as a beacon for both my faithful and my enemy."

Her breath caught. "Veylan?" she asked, part of her already knowing the answer.

"He has bound himself to a piece of my divinity using ancient and terrible magic. He clings to it, watching me, drawing my power by force to achieve his wicked ends. I could not risk drawing his eye when you were not ready. This new oath gives you power where I cannot."

"It's different," she insisted, heat rising in her cheeks.

"Is it?" Ptyraxa asked softly. "You are a paladin. Words carry power; promises bind. You gave him a promise."

She swallowed. "Is it really an oath if no one witnessed it?"

He stepped forward, reached out, and laid two fingers gently over her heart. "I witnessed it."

She felt faint under the weight of a vow she hadn't even known she was keeping. Even though she'd kept it unaware, the truth of it rang in her bones.

"Ask him," Ptyraxa commanded as the dream began to fade. "Ask the wizard what it means to be bound to divinity."

She reached for Him desperately, even as He faded. "I don't understand—"

She woke with a gasp, sitting bolt upright in the tent. Ezra stirred beside her, hand reaching.

"Addi?"

She turned toward him, heart pounding. "What do you know?" she demanded, whispering. "What does it mean to be bound to divinity?"

His eyes opened fully then, awake and alert. Her stomach dropped as she realized he likely already knew what she was asking.

Chapter 42

Ezra

The question lingered in the air between them. *"What does it mean to be bound to divinity?"* Ezra stared at her, bleary from sleep but now unmistakably awake. He could almost feel the mist outside pressing against the tent like a held breath.

He swallowed. "It isn't completely bright out yet, you should sleep," he said, voice hoarse.

Adinah didn't move. "Please. I need to understand."

Of course she did. She'd never been one to leave a question hanging. She met danger head-on, even the kind that wasn't shaped like a sword. He exhaled, running a hand through his hair.

"It started with Caedmon," he said softly. "Years ago. He'd discovered a method to contact gods directly through sigils. A sort of arcane shorthand, if you will, linking the written form to their divine echoes. There was no wondering if they'd heard our pleas." She leaned in, listening intently.

"At first it was harmless," he went on. "Incense, runes, candlelight. But something changed. I don't remember what triggered it. He'd been experimenting, but something went wrong with one of the patterns. Suddenly, he wasn't just reaching out, he was tapping in. Into their divinity, their source. He'd nearly set his whole study ablaze in arcane fire with the eruption of power."

Adinah's eyes widened slightly, but she said nothing. He looked down at his hand, at the faint, intricate lines etched like silver beneath the skin. The sigil was still as beautiful as it was painful.

"I asked him to do it to me," he said. "To burn a link into my hand, to make me a vessel for that same power. I didn't want to use it for worship or guidance, though. I wanted to be strong enough to confront Xernaea Herself."

He closed his eyes for a moment, remembering the fire, the searing agony and the way it laced into bone. He could still feel the way it thrummed when he called on it. The scar glowed a bit as his emotions rose.

"I was angry. Furious, really. I'd been reading more about what the Inquisitors did to mages. It was only a few decades past. I saw the records, the burnings, the forced executions. I wanted answers from the goddess who gave us magic and stood silent while we were slaughtered."

His voice caught. "I told myself it was justice. But really, it was rage. I became powerful: far too powerful far too quickly. I forced an audience with Her. Do you know how many mages have tried to do that? How many have failed?" She just stared at him, tearing up.

"I almost killed Her." His voice broke. "I was ready to rip the magic from Her. I wanted Her begging for mercy. I told Her I'd spread Her power across the world, let every arcanist wield it without limit when threatened. I would take away Her control."

A bitter, broken laugh escaped him. "I thought I was better than the gods. I thought I could make them answer." Adinah reached out, brushing her fingers over the back of his hand.

"She got through to me," he continued. "Somehow, in that moment, She didn't plead or threaten. She asked if I could bear the weight of it. All of it, every soul who would twist that gift. Every loss, every war." His shoulders hunched. The tears came fast now, hot and silent.

"I let Her go. I chose mercy. And that was when She took it from me. She didn't do it out of cruelty. I think I wasn't meant to hold that kind of power. Maybe I was just too close to becoming a Veylan."

He sobbed then, voice cracking under the weight of the shame he had wrapped around himself for years. It unspooled in a breathless rush, raw and unguarded.

"I am so sorry," he choked. "For what I did. For what I almost became."

Adinah pulled him in without a word. She wrapped her arms tightly around his shoulders, one hand cradling the back of his head as she rocked him gently, trying to calm the storm.

"You're not him," she whispered. "You know what that darkness feels like, and you turned from it. That's what makes you different." She stroked his hair gently. "I need you. The world needs you." He clung to her like she was his anchor to the present, as if clinging to her would keep him from falling the way he had before.

"You didn't lose yourself," she murmured. "You chose mercy. You didn't let the rage devour you, and that choice means everything."

When the sobs finally slowed, he held her tighter, burying his face in her neck. Her scent was warm, like smoke, softened by that of the forest.

Her presence held back the tide of despair rising in him.

He kissed her softly. She kissed him back like she'd already forgiven him for everything. They stayed like that, caught in each other's arms, until dawn crept over the mist's edge, barely breaking through the trees to rest on the roof of the tent.

The travel was quieter after that, contemplative. Adinah rode ahead, eyes sharp on the horizon. Ezra followed, cloak pulled close to keep out the chill, Halberd's reins steady in his hands.

The deeper they rode into Kaevryn's Teeth, the less the forest resembled the world they'd known. The trees grew denser, gnarled in unnatural ways, their branches twisted like clutching fingers. The bark was blackened in places, veins of deep red pulsing beneath the surface. No birds sang. Even the insects had fallen silent. Even the light felt wrong. Mist hugged the ground, thick and metallic in scent. The sun barely reached through the canopy, casting everything in a leaden grey.

By late afternoon, they found the ruin of Varkhal's temple in a narrow ravine. The stone was cracked and half-sunken into the forest floor, the columns overgrown with strangling ivy that seemed to shrink away from touch. The entrance was built into a short cliffside, a yawning entrance that stood like a mouth into the deep. The place reeked of old power, of something forgotten on purpose.

He looked at Adinah, the woman who had called him back from the brink. She met his gaze, nodding once, as she dismounted Tirin. She took only the essentials, leaving Tirin untethered. He did the same with Halberd, taking her hand as they stepped forward into the dark.

Chapter 43

Adinah

The entrance to the ruin was gaping and insidious, an open wound in the earth where the foothills began. A massive archway loomed before them, carved into the wall of the ravine. A cracked lintel above bore an inscription in a language long dead. The metal-bound doors were missing, flung inward into darkness. She stepped forward and gasped.

The moment she crossed the threshold, something passed through her like a ripple in her skin. Her stomach lurched and her torch flickered violently, almost going out. Ezra hissed behind her, staggering.

"Did you–?"

"I felt it," she said quickly. "Keep moving."

The temple's upper level had collapsed long ago, the stone torn about by some violent upheaval. Now the only way forward was down. They navigated the massive chasm that opened within the sanctum, using broken beams and makeshift bridges to reach a spiral stair descending deep into the earth.

The smell of ash grew stronger. The walls began to glow with faint red veins of old magic, dying embers of something once divine. Varkhal's power lingered like coals in a ruined hearth, flickering with wrath and ruin. Still, there was something else, a subtler second presence, watching.

The floor leveled at last, opening into a vast subterranean corridor. Ahead, blackened columns rose like the ribs of a long-dead beast. Crumbling frescoes flickered with ghostly light. Remnants of statues lined the path: paladins, clerics, kings. All were headless; all were shattered.

Adinah drew her sword, its faint glow flaring a warning. She turned to Ezra. He was pale, sweat clinging to his temple, tattoo on his hand glowing.

He nodded. "We're close," he said through gritted teeth.

She took a breath and stepped forward. They didn't need to speak anymore. Their path had narrowed to a point. This place, this moment, was the eye of everything.

They had taken no more than three steps deeper into the corridor when the shadows moved. A figure detached from the gloom between two broken columns, slow and deliberate, as if rising from the stone itself. His armor caught the dim glow of Ezra's arcane light, a warped reflection of the holy warrior he once was. His white surcoat was stained rust-red, a half-burnt sun symbol barely clinging to his chestplate. And his eyes–gods, his eyes–shining with an unnatural white brilliance, not light but obliteration.

"Adinah," Dolran said, lethal voice smooth as velvet. "You made it." She raised her sword. Ezra stepped closer at her side, hand already crackling with arcane energy.

"Dolran," she said evenly, though her heart hammered. "You look like the hells made flesh."

He smiled, slow and crooked, lips just a little too thin. "I've been given purpose. Something you'd understand, wouldn't you? Funny how it's always the most faithful who stray the farthest."

Ezra raised a hand, magic coiling outward, but Dolran moved. In a blur, he ducked left, vanishing behind a pillar. A bolt of magic sizzled through the air, striking the stone and exploding in a flash of colorless sparks.

Dolran's laughter echoed off the walls. "You'll have to do better than that, *wizard*."

Adinah moved forward, sword up, eyes sweeping the darkness. "Come out and face us."

"Oh, I'm right here." His voice came from the far end of the corridor. "Isn't this what you wanted, Adinah? A clean line to righteousness? An enemy to slay, a sin to purge?"

Something whistled through the air. She spun at the sound, and a bolt ricocheted off her vambrace, skittering across the floor. She'd triggered a trap. She darted forward, closing distance toward the voice, only to see Dolran again, impossibly, down another hallway. Ezra fired a volley of searing missiles that spiraled after him, but they struck a collapsing statue instead, detonating with a thunderclap.

"Coward!" Ezra called, already running after him. "Show yourself!"

"Oh, I'm showing," Dolran's voice called. "Just not to you."

Adinah took off after Ezra, boots pounding the stone, torchlight and arcane glow dancing around them as they chased Dolran deeper into the ruin. The temple became a maze of broken archways, caved ceilings, and rooms eaten away by time and warped magic. Dust choked the air.

Still, Dolran stayed ahead, always just out of reach. Her sword never got within striking distance. Ezra's magic sizzled after him, always a

205

second too late.

There were more traps, peppering them with bolts and fire. She managed to avoid it, never having to move more than a half-step to one side or the other. At Ezra's cursing behind her, she paused, heart racing. That's when she noticed it.

Ezra had burns streaking his robes. There was blood on his sleeve from a cut she hadn't seen before. He had a dozen small wounds, each a sharp distraction. She realized everything Dolran had sent them had gone toward Ezra. Not her.

Not once had he struck at her. No fire or spikes or bolts. Everything was funneled toward holding Ezra back. *He's trying to split us,* she realized.

She pushed harder, navigating the half-collapsed corridors as Dolran's laughter wove around her. It didn't echo naturally. It came from walls, from ceilings, from cracks in the stone. He was everywhere and nowhere.

Suddenly, he was there, right in front of her, at the end of a long, ruined hall beneath the broken remains of what must have once been Varkhal's main altar room. Dolran stood on a shattered dais, arms open wide like a prophet, his white eyes gleaming with a light that no longer belonged to Ptyraxa.

"Come now," he purred as Ezra skidded to a stop beside her, breath ragged. "The Heart awaits." His voice was low and reverent, almost awed.

Before she could move, he raised his hand, two fingers glowing with divine fire. He slashed the air with them, sending a wave of golden energy snapping out in a sharp arc. It struck the floor just in front of the dais. The stone groaned, then cracked, a fine spider web of fissures glowing with soft white light seeping outward like spilled dawn. With a seismic groan, the center of the chamber sank, slabs grinding down into place like teeth locking into a jaw.

The ringed pit that formed beneath the dais exhaled stale, long-buried air. In the hollow space it revealed was the Dawnfire Heart.

At the center of it all, a heart of molten light pulsed within a ring of blackened stone, the faintest glows reaching out toward her through the cracks. It wasn't floating freely, but cradled in a basin of obsidian, as if it had been carefully preserved. It beat, soft and slow, golden fire encased in shifting crystal. The surface appeared layered like glass but with an inner radiance that rippled like the sky before sunrise, awake and alive.

Adinah stared. She took a step forward, and the cracks in the ring widened, the stone's edges shivering like something trying to open to her. It responded to her: when she drew back slightly, the obsidian firmed again, resealing like an eyelid.

Behind her, Dolran's voice deepened, full of some awful wonder. "It recognizes you."

She turned to face him. "What do you mean, Dolran?"

His expression flickered between awe and something more desperate. "Because you're the one who can wield it. Ptyraxa's favored, but Veylan's chosen. The gods have moved their pieces, and you, Adinah, were always meant to stand at the center."

Her voice went cold as she raised her sword towards him. "You want me to become your weapon."

"No," he said softly, almost pleading. "I want you to become something greater. Not just a champion, but a catalyst." The light of the Heart behind him pulsed once, brighter.

Adinah lifted her blade, ready to strike. "I've heard enough."

Dolran exhaled like he was extinguishing a candle. "Then we begin."

The shadows behind him stirred as a fearsome figure came forward.

207

Chapter 44

Ezra

The shadows behind Dolran rippled like disturbed water and then split open. The air turned to ice. From the hollow dark stepped a horrifying specter, neither living nor dead.

Veylan. The truth of recognition rang in him like a bell. Long black robes of dark silk, rotted at the edges, carried the sigil from the amulets, presumably his sigil. A long mantle trailed behind him. His skin was like cracked porcelain, black veins lacing from his exposed cheek into empty sockets. Where his eyes had once been, twin stars now burned in molten gold. He was monstrous, an unholy being tainted with borrowed divinity.

The sight of him choked his breath.

"Ezra."

His name rang inside his head, as it had with the amulet, sharp and silken. The voice was carried by sheer will rather than air, slipping past defenses like a knife through satin. His skull rang with it, his breath catching as if his lungs had seized.

"You've carried it so long," Veylan whispered into his mind. *"That hunger, that terror. You're always afraid you'll lose her, always afraid you'll be too late."* Ezra's hand trembled. He summoned a shield around his thoughts, but Veylan moved through it like silk slipping between his fingers.

"You carved your skin to chase the divine, tore yourself open to hold power never meant for man. And for what? To be cast out, to watch Adinah suffer, to kneel in fear that you might not be strong enough next time. You fear that Ptyraxa won't save her." Veylan advanced—not physically, but psychically. His presence grew like the red dawn over a battlefield.

"You know the truth already. Xernaea feared you. With me, though, you could surpass Her, surpass even Ptyraxa. You could protect Adinah. Save her." A low hum of power began building in Ezra's fingertips, as if

208

his body were answering the temptation before his mind could deny it.

"Convince her to wield the Heart for me. With it, we could unmake this world of pawns and tyrants. You'd never lose her: not to time, not to death, not to any god's whim." Images flickered through his mind. Adinah, crumpled in firelight. Adinah, calling his name, bleeding out. Adinah, gone.

Ezra roared and threw out his palm, arcane sigils exploding into the air around him. "You bastard—!"

Veylan moved, flowing through the air like liquid hate. His hand lashed out, striking Ezra's hastily raised barrier with a clang that sent shock through bone. His mere touch rotted the air. Pain blossomed down Ezra's arm, biting into the place where Xernaea's sigil still burned on his skin.

He dropped to one knee, gasping. "I won't trade her for power." He pushed himself to his feet. For a moment, Veylan's silence was deafening. Then, suddenly, he struck.

Faster than thought, he lunged. Ezra's ward lit up, too slow. An arc of force screamed through the air, crashing into his ribs and slamming him against the wall. Pain burst white behind his eyes. Something cracked.

He held fast, suddenly certain of what needed to happen. He let go of the seal on his soul and reached out. Not for Adinah, and not for Xernaea directly, but for Her divinity. His tattoo flared, the connection opening like a floodgate.

Power surged. Blue-white arcane light roared through him like a second heartbeat. It consumed his lungs, his blood, and even his bones. He barely heard himself scream. The runes around him exploded, glyphs spiralling into the air in wild, erratic patterns. His form blurred, robes whipped and torn by wind that didn't exist.

Ezra struck, sending a wave of raw magic lancing forward to collide with Veylan. The explosion cracked the ceiling. Rock shattered as Veylan staggered back with a snarl, a long gouge ripped through his side, bones exposed beneath withered flesh.

"Enough," he hissed. *"This ends now."* He vanished in a whip of shadow, reappearing beside Dolran, who was locked in a furious clash with Adinah across the chamber.

Ezra dropped to one knee. His vision swam, pulse faltering. The edges of his being blurred, like ink run under water. His mouth tasted like lightning and blood. He had overreached.

He had minutes. Seconds. His whole form was coming apart at the seams, but she was still standing. Still fighting. He turned, pain radiating down his spine, and began to move. Step by step, he dragged the weight of magic and divinity and purpose behind him like a tattered cloak. Every movement peeled something away. Breath. Skin. Memory.

He made it. He reached her, standing at her back, existing more as force of will than man.

Chapter 45

Adinah

They moved like fire and shadow. Steel clashed in brilliant arcs. Dolran's blade met hers again and again, each impact a cry of memory, each parry a fracture in her soul. His white-gold eyes were fixed on her, not with fury but with yearning, as if he could reach through the fight and find the girl she used to be. As if he could drag her backward from everything she'd become.

"Adinah," he said, voice a mix of thunder and desperation, "I loved you before the gods ever noticed you." She struck at his shoulder.

He dodged. "I chose you before Ptyraxa ever did." Her boot connected with his ribs.

He grunted, but spun with the momentum and pressed in close. "You chose them."

The accusation landed sharper than his sword. She shoved him back, breathing hard. Her pauldron was dented, her tabard slashed, but her grip didn't falter.

"You betrayed every oath we made," she spat.

"I wanted freedom!" Dolran's voice cracked. "Freedom from dying and praying and waiting. Freedom from begging for signs that never came!" He advanced again. His strikes were powered now by something more than muscle as warped divinity crackled at the edge of each blow. Gold threaded with black, a bastardized halo of light. It wasn't his power—not truly.

"Veylan's giving you nothing but leashed magic," she growled. "You're a puppet—"

"I'm free!" he roared. "He offers what Ptyraxa denied. Peace. Power enough to protect you, to keep you. Don't you see Adinah? We could leave this all behind. No more wars, no more gods to bow to. Just you and me, eternal."

For a heartbeat, she faltered. She could see herself, unburdened, her

211

hand in Dolran's. She could see a world where the cycle stopped spinning, where none of them were pawns on a divine chessboard. Then she pictured Ezra, broken and bleeding, the man who'd followed her here, helping her on a quest with no reward for himself.

"No." She drove her blade forward. He deflected it, but the force staggered them both.

"You want me to choose you?" she said, low and raw. "Then you should have stayed the man worth choosing."

They circled again. Light flared from her hands, raw and radiant, drawn straight from the Dawn. Dolran's eyes flared as he pulled corrupted power from Veylan, sending his own brutal magic. The clash sparked static and shook the floor. Neither of them could win, Ptyraxa's divine magic split too many ways.

She couldn't end it like this, nor could she let the Heart fall to Veylan. She couldn't let him hurt Ezra, couldn't break her oath. In a moment of blind desperation, she reached, touching the Heart.

The instant her skin met the crystal, she was overcome by blinding pain. Her scream tore free before she could bite it down. It felt like her body had been hollowed out and filled with fire. Bones became light, muscle unspooled into burning threads. Her blood sang with it, a hymn of creation and annihilation.

She couldn't breathe or move. She couldn't withstand it. Just as she nearly faltered, however, he was there. Ezra. She felt his hand touch the back of hers.

Cool, steady magic rushed from his touch, like moonlight pouring into her soul. Not cold, but calm, a balm against the searing heat. Her mind heard him. There were no words, just his presence, gentle and unwavering, his hand around hers.

He was grounding her, bracing her, letting her channel the arcane.

The light from the Heart swelled, uniting with Xernaea's magic. Holy gold met brilliant blue, and the Heart answered. Her eyes ignited, her skin lit like sunrise over water. She rose from the floor, blade still in hand, flame rippling off her body. Dolran stumbled back as Veylan's form coiled near him, unreadable.

The obsidian basin sat empty below.

"You will not break me," she said, the Dawn carried in her voice.

The golden flame that lived within her surged through her limbs, up her throat, and into her mouth and eyes and soul. Her body was a vessel now, holy fire wrapped in flesh, divine wrath channeled into muscle and motion. Her sword caught the light and answered.

Adinah brought her blade down with a cry that was equal parts agony and war hymn. The moment it struck, everything ruptured. A ring of blinding light burst outward from her, golden at the center and rimmed in molten flame. The floor cracked, pillars buckled. Sigils that had lain dormant for centuries shattered like glass.

Dolran raised his hands too late. Veylan screamed, the awful shriek of something cruel being undone. His body tore like smoke caught in a gale. It was consumed in the blast, pulled apart completely. Shadows flared and vanished, leaving no trace. Not even ash remained.

She dropped to the ground, staggering, her lungs seizing on the heat. The light flared again, brighter and higher, the temple refracting it in wild streaks until no wall remained visible, only searing brilliance and roaring sound.

And then–nothing. No enemy, no movement. No sound but the sizzle of molten stone and her own ragged breaths. Veylan was gone; Dolran was nowhere to be seen. Only Adinah remained, kneeling in the silence. She dropped her sword in exhaustion, a halo of scorched stone around her boots. Smoke curled in lazy spirals from the cracked floor.

She looked up slowly, blinking against the afterimage. "Ezra?" she rasped. There was no answer, only silence and the distant hush of light dimming in holy retreat.

She looked in every direction. "Ezra!" The chamber echoed the name back at her, empty.

She saw it, then, what she hadn't before. She remembered the blinding flash of arcane blue, the way she'd felt Ezra rather than heard him. Her memory of him when they'd fought the monsters, how he'd frayed at the edges, crashed over her like a wave.

Her knees hit the stone hard, fingers clenching in his absence. She hadn't seen it happen. She'd been too consumed, too slow. He was gone.

She sobbed. It wasn't the wail of a paladin overcome after battle. She grieved like a woman whose soul had been torn from her chest. Her hands curled against the floor as her heart heaved. The sound of it was raw, primal, as if she'd been consumed by the very concept of loss.

Something inside her answered as she cried out his name. The pain didn't dull; it expanded. Deep in her chest something pulsed. Touched by grief so sharp it could cut through creation, something responded.

Light bled out from her, as if fleeing the aching absence she couldn't bear in soft, unfurling tendrils of radiant gold and cool, arcane blue, like sunrise slipping through mist. Her eyes followed stray sparks as they moved to coalesce a few feet away. They shimmered, gathered, and formed. Skin reknit, breath returned. The pieces of a soul found one another, stitched together not by spell, but by will. Hair spilled over a familiar brow as his breath stuttered back into his lungs. His sigil flickered faintly.

Ezra lay at the base of the dais, eyes closed, but alive. She scrambled to him, her sobs starting again as she bowed her head, offering up desperate faith.

I did it, she thought. *I kept my faith.* Deep in her bones, she saw that this, not the Heart, was her reward. Ptyraxa had given him back.

It was enough.

Chapter 46

Ezra

Ezra awoke to weeping. Not just sound, but sensation. The shape of sorrow hung in the air, the echo of a soul breaking beside him.

Adinah knelt, clutching his robe with white-knuckled hands, her shoulders trembling with each sob. Her face was blotched with ash and tears, hair wild, armor cracked along one gauntlet. Her sword lay forgotten a few feet away.

For a moment, he didn't understand why.

His limbs felt real, solid, but there was a strange hum in his bones, a memory of unraveling. He tried to sit up but he had no strength.

"I…" His voice was raw and distant. "I thought I was–"

"Ezra?" she breathed, eyes widening.

He tried to speak again, but it was too late. She'd already pulled him into her arms. She crashed into him with the force of the tide, kissing his brow, his cheeks, his mouth, anywhere she could reach. He held her through the shaking, the sobs, and the stunned joy. He felt her heartbeat pounding against him, like it tried to beat hard enough for both of them.

"I felt you," she whispered. "When things were over, I realized… You died."

He remembered only fragments. He could recall the burning in her eyes, the glow from the Heart across her face, and the impossible pull of arcane current as he touched her hand. The cool embrace of something old and vast, like being held in the arms of the universe, had taken hold of him. Xernaea had been there somewhere. For the first time, She carried no judgement, just peace. Silence had taken him, and then he'd been nothing at all.

"I can't imagine there was anything left," he whispered.

"You were so willing to sacrifice yourself," she said softly, pressing her forehead to his. "I may be a paladin, but you are the one with a martyr's heart. One I never want to see break."

He closed his eyes, swallowing hard. "Then you'll have to keep it safe for me." She nodded, tears falling anew.

Eventually, the silence softened. They stood, hands still linked, the warmth of her fingers proving again and again that he was real. They surveyed the chamber, and not far from the edge of the dais, was a thick trail of blood. Not Veylan's, surely, and definitely not a forgotten stain in the ruin. This was still wet.

Dolran. Even the thought of his name set his teeth on edge. The blood trail led to the far side of the room, curving toward a ruined wall where, just visible now, a crumbling altar jutted from the shadows. It was old, faintly marked with the symbol of Varkhal.

The trail stopped there. The blood simply vanished, no sign of a body or of passage. Ezra felt Adinah's hand tighten slightly in his.

"He's gone," she said. "Destroyed, or drawn into whatever was left of that god's dominion." He nodded, though something in him twitched with unease. Still, there was no more war to fight here. The chamber was quiet, the divine pressure lifted. The storm had passed.

"Let's go," she whispered. The "together" was unspoken. They left the ruined temple hand in hand, the path behind them fading. The world felt lighter, softer, as if some great weight had been lifted from its spine.

They didn't look back.

216

Chapter 47

Adinah

A few weeks later, they found themselves back in Taranok at Morningstrike Hall. The main hall shimmered with the quiet hush of reverence. Sunlight poured through the high stained glass windows, dousing the floor in fractured light. The scent of oil and incense clung to the air like memory, the familiar cadence of Ptyraxite chant echoing faintly off the walls. It felt different now.

Adinah stood tall before the dais, the dust of distant temples still clinging to her boots, the edge of her slashed crimson tabard darkened by ash and divine fire. She had given her report, truthful and thorough, only sparing pieces about quiet nights in Ezra's arms in temple quarters.

High Archivist Orlan, silver-robed and solemn, studied her in silence. The brazier at his back added to the golden light cast across his lined face, but his eyes remained sharp beneath the glow, appraising.

"And the artifact?" he asked, voice low but clear. "The Dawnfire Heart?" Adinah hesitated. Her hands were steady, but her soul thrummed.

"It vanished when I touched it," she said truthfully. "Consumed by divine fire, maybe? Or transformed somehow? I don't know where it is now."

Orlan's gaze did not waver. "And yet, you returned whole. Or rather, more than whole."

Her skin glowed faintly, even now, as though the sunrise had stitched itself into her flesh. Her armor had taken on a luster no polish could grant, the edges of her sword catching the morning light like it was born to wield it. Even the air around her seemed to bend with warmth and radiance, like the first breath after a long winter. Orlan inclined his head, something unreadable behind his eyes: suspicion, maybe, or awe. Maybe both.

"You've walked through darkness," he said finally, "and returned as a vessel of light. Ptyraxa's halls have not seen such a transformation in generations."

217

He stepped back, raising his hand. "Let it be known," he intoned, his voice ringing through the chamber, "that Adinah Thorne has proven herself true of heart, unwavering in faith, and has been chosen by the Morning Lord as His champion."

The doors opened. A procession of priests entered, bearing a white and gold tabard embroidered with a sunburst. They passed it to Orlan, who unfolded it solemnly.

"Come," he said.

Adinah stepped forward and knelt.

Her crimson tabard, the color of service and sacrifice, was removed with care. In its place, the white and gold was laid upon her shoulders, shimmering like starlight woven with sun. Her sword was returned to her, now blessed anew, the edge kissed with celestial fire.

Orlan took her chin in one hand, lifting her gaze to his. "Rise, High Paladin Thorne, Champion of Ptyraxa."

She stood, tall and sure, and turned to face the gathered witnesses. Ezra sat in the first row. His hands were clasped tightly in his lap, his hair still wild from travel. His eyes shimmered, tears spilling freely down his cheeks as he looked at her, utterly undone, overcome with joy and pride and disbelief.

She smiled, the world narrowing to him, the truth of both her oaths ringing in her soul.

Later, in Orlan's study, the three of them sat with warm tea between them, the last dregs of ceremony fading into silence.

"I'll always carry the Light," she said. "But I'm tired, Orlan. I've seen too much. I want peace."

Orlan regarded her over the rim of his cup. "A High Paladin is never truly released from service," he said gently. "You are the Morning Lord's chosen now. That bond is eternal."

"I'm not asking to be released," she said quietly. "Only to be allowed to choose how I serve." There was a pause, then a smile tugged at the corner of Orlan's mouth.

"It's not unheard of," he said slowly, "for High Paladins to embark on far-flung missions, sometimes personal ones. High Paladin Starcrest once vanished for a full decade, only intermittently working with the temple thereafter. Her final official quest is one you're all too familiar with, but her actual final pursuit was never recorded in the archive." His gaze flicked to Adinah meaningfully.

She recalled the tomb in the hidden temple where she'd found Elidane buried beside Sereth. The trail had ended not in tragedy, but in love.

They let her go. Let her live.

"I understand," she said softly, biting back her own smile.

Orlan bowed his head. "Then may your next journey be full of light, wherever it takes you."

The sun was setting by the time they left Morningstrike Hall. Adinah stepped onto the road with Ezra at her side, his hand entwined with hers. The golden warmth of dusk fell over them like a blessing, and for the first time in what felt like a lifetime, she felt no weight pressing against her chest.

There was only promise and hope.

She turned to him. "It's a long way to Surland," she said. "Let's go home."

He smiled. "Ours?"

She nodded. "Ours."

And together, they walked into the light.

Epilogue

Dolran

Dolran crawled. The stone beneath his fingers was slick with his blood and the taste of ashes clung to his tongue like a curse. Light still roared behind him, holy and pure and blinding, tearing through the ruins of the temple as if the heavens themselves had opened. He did not look back. He couldn't. He had seen what Adinah had become, and what she wielded.

She had chosen the light over him. Again.

The magic inside him shuddered, splintering like glass under pressure. Somewhere behind him, Veylan screamed, his putrid soul unravelling. Dolran reached the far wall of the crumbling sanctum and pressed a bloodied hand against the stone, blindly searching–

There.

A mark, old and mostly faded, scorched into the wall. A sigil of conquest and war. It was the sigil of Varkhal. A whisper stirred at the edge of his thoughts.

"Come."

The world tilted. A great pull yanked him from flesh and bone, from ruin and temple and pain. He fell through meaning rather than space, into shadow, somewhere older, fouler, and forgotten by time.

He landed on shattered obsidian in a throne room of ruin. Blackened spears jutted from the broken ground. The air reeked of dust and molten metal. A shape waited on a throne of skulls, body formed from tattered banners and blood-forged armor. It was a god, or at least what was left of one.

The dead god of conquest leaned forward, hollow sockets burning red.

"You are worthy, Dolran. I offer you a bargain. Return to the world in my name and conquer in my sign. I shall live again through your hand, and you will have power beyond kings."

Dolran laughed: a short, sharp, broken thing. "I have no use for gods," he spat. "Ptyraxa cast me out. Veylan perished. Adinah turned her back.

220

And you are nothing but bone and rot." Varkhal rose in fury, the throne quaking behind him.

"Mortal fool—"

Dolran moved. He turned his focus inward to the last scrap of light he had stolen from the unraveling god of dawn. It was a tiny spark of Ptyraxa, faint and fractured, but divine all the same. By will alone, he forged it into something physical, sharpening it into a blade. Drawing it from himself, he drove it into Varkhal's chest.

The god screamed. Light exploded. Black ichor sprayed across the throne in a blinding arc, spattering the fractured obsidian, seeping into the dirt and decay in the cracks. Dolran did not hesitate. He surged forward with feral desperation, seizing the god's broken body. He tore into it with bare hands, ripping through muscle and sinew that smoked with divine heat, clawing past ribs that cracked like brittle iron. He tore at the god's fading light with a fury born of grief and hate, ripping loose what scraps of essence still clung to Varkhal's withering form.

The taste was fire and blood. It scalded his throat as he drank, choking on radiance gone foul with corruption. Still, he drank deeper, lips pressed to the rent seams of a dying divinity until the torrent broke into him like a flood. The god's power poured down his throat, through his veins, searing him from marrow to skin. He convulsed with it, every nerve alight, every scar searing as if reopened from within. It was agony and rapture in equal measure.

Varkhal's voice split the chamber in a final, wordless cry. His form collapsed completely, bones withering into dust, armor and banners sloughing away like burnt paper. What remained was only a hollow skin of divinity, remnants of a god reduced to refuse.

Dolran, unrelenting, drew the last embers from that husk, wrenching it into himself. It tangled with the remnant of Ptyraxa's broken light still festering within him, twisting and fusing. The Light of Dawn and the Fires of War burned together into a new and terrible alloy.

He fell to his knees, shuddering, choking on smoke. His body buckled, collapsing on the broken ground before reforming. Black steel coiled across his shoulders like molten ore hardening into armor, smothering every gleam of rust and white. His breath steamed, thick with power. When his eyes opened at last, they burned from within, dim and merciless, like the final light of dying stars.

When it was done, silence claimed the chamber. The skull throne had shattered, sending bone fragments skittering like insects across the floor. Varkhal was nothing but carrion, leaving Dolran so much more than he'd ever been. He stood above the ruin, remade and burning with purpose.

He remembered Adinah. Her eyes, her glow, and the pitying look she gave him before delivering judgement. He clenched his fists.

"Enough," he whispered, voice trembling with fury. "No more gods. No more mercy." The power inside him answered. He stepped forward and disappeared, ripping through the veil between realms in a crackle of divine energy.

He landed on soil. The wind carried the smell of grass and smoke in the distance. The towers of Brightmere, capital of Viremor, rose before him, proud and sunlit, crowned in banners bearing the crests of the gods.

Dolran smiled, no longer a priest, no longer a paladin, no longer a servant of anything but his own wrath.

"I will burn your altars," he said, voice soft and full of promise. "One by one, until the heavens are empty."

With the ashes of gods beneath His feet, He began to walk.

About the Author

Torrin Taigh is a high fantasy and romance writer originally from the southern United States. When not daydreaming about Viremor, she writes, travels, and consumes books and caffeine in equal measure. Between it all, when the words aren't flowing, she looks to the horizon as if some hidden love story might be looking back. She currently resides in Wisconsin with her two pets.

www.ingramcontent.com/pod-product-compliance
Lightning Source LLC
Chambersburg PA
CBHW011515100726
47899CB00010BD/3378